PRAISE FOR *PLO*

"*Plot Twist* gave my rom-c⸻⸻⸻ it could hope for: pop-culture refere⸻⸻gh-out-loud lines, an enduring friendship, a de⸻⸻a heroine to root for, and (of course) a love story with plenty of twists and turns. Bethany Turner's voice is fresh and fun, and it's a joy to read about Olivia as she grows and changes over the course of ten years. A sweet, funny read about the many kinds of love in our lives, perfect for anyone who loves love or dreams about meeting George Clooney."

—**Kerry Winfrey, author of** *Waiting for Tom Hanks*

"With a decade-long span of pop-culture fun, playful romantic possibilities, and the soul-deep friendships that push us to be real, *Plot Twist* is everything a reader has come to adore from Bethany Turner . . . plus so much more!"

—**Nicole Deese, award-winning author**
of *Before I Called You Mine*

"Funny, clever, and sweet, *Plot Twist* reminds us that sometimes love doesn't look just like the movies—and that it can be so, so much better than we ever dreamed. Bethany Turner has gifted us all with another winning story with her trademark wit, wisdom, and charm!"

—**Melissa Ferguson, bestselling author of** *The Cul-de-Sac War*

"Bethany Turner just keeps getting better! *Plot Twist* is like experiencing the best parts of all my favorite rom-coms, tied together with Turner's pitch-perfect comedic timing, an achingly sweet 'will they or won't they?' romance, and the BFF relationship most girls dream of. Add in some Gen-X nostalgia, and you have a book you'll want to wrap yourself up in and never leave."

—**Carla Laureano, RITA Award–winning author of** *The*
Saturday Night Supper Club **and** *Provenance*

"With a sassy Hallmark-on-speed hook and a winning leading lady, Turner loans her fresh, inimitable voice to her strongest offering yet: a treatise on how love (and the hope for love) paints across a canvas of fate and happenstance, and how life undercuts our expectations only to give us the biggest romantic adventures. Winsome and wise, Turner draws on beloved romantic tropes and zesty pop-culture references to provide a surprising comedy that is the sweet equivalent of Beth O' Leary and Emily Henry."

—Rachel McMillan, author of the Three-Quarter Time series and *The London Restoration*

ALSO BY BETHANY TURNER

Hadley Beckett's Next Dish

Wooing Cadie McCaffrey

The Secret Life of Sarah Hollenbeck

Plot Twist

Published in Nashville, Tennessee, by Thomas Nelson. Thomas Nelson is a registered trademark of HarperCollins Christian Publishing, Inc.

Published in association with the literary agency of Kirkland Media Management, LLC, P.O. Box 1539, Liberty, TX 77575.

Interior design by Mallory Collins

Thomas Nelson titles may be purchased in bulk for educational, business, fundraising, or sales promotional use. For information, please email SpecialMarkets@ThomasNelson.com.

Publisher's Note: This novel is a work of fiction. Names, characters, places, and incidents are either products of the author's imagination or used fictitiously. All characters are fictional, and any similarity to people living or dead is purely coincidental.

Library of Congress Cataloging-in-Publication Data

Names: Turner, Bethany, 1979- author.
Title: Plot twist / Bethany Turner.
Description: Nashville, Tennessee : Thomas Nelson, [2021] | Summary: "An aspiring screenwriter has a chance encounter with an actor on his way to an audition. Over the next ten years, she'll write the story . . . but will he end up being the star?"-- Provided by publisher.
Identifiers: LCCN 2020056012 (print) | LCCN 2020056013 (ebook) | ISBN 9780785244486 (paperback) | ISBN 9780785244936 (epub) | ISBN 9780785244943
Classification: LCC PS3620.U76 P56 2021 (print) | LCC PS3620.U76 (ebook) | DDC 813/.6--dc23
LC record available at https://lccn.loc.gov/2020056012
LC ebook record available at https://lccn.loc.gov/2020056013

Printed in the United States of America
21 22 23 24 25 LSC 5 4 3 2 1

PLOT TWIST

BETHANY TURNER

THOMAS NELSON
Since 1798

To Gerard Butler, who was with me when this book's journey began. (Metaphorically with me. Not literally with me. Though that would have been cool too.)

You're lovely in the way you dress,

And how you fix your hair.

You're lovely for the way you always

make me feel you care.

And though we're just beginning on this path

To who knows where . . .

I'm glad you smiled.

I'm glad we talked.

I'm glad we met.

Heartlite® Greeting Card Co., Number 03-6293E

FEBRUARY 4, 2003

"Mind if I sit here?"

I looked up, already disgusted. I'd been hit on four times in the three hours I'd been taking up space at Mugs & Shots, my neighborhood coffee place. As a thirty-year-old in a typical java joint in downtown Culver City, just seven miles from UCLA, I didn't usually have to concern myself with such things. The caffeine-fueled flirting and socializing usually skewed a bit younger, freeing me up to write and think and enjoy my latte in peace. I wasn't sure if the typical female demographic had all been detained by sorority pledging or if the management of the coffeehouse had decided to add Old-Timer Tuesdays to the endless list of theme days written on the chalkboard, but I just wasn't interested. And while the man who spoke to me presently was more attractive than the first three had been, I'd had enough.

"You can sit wherever you like, but I'm busy, so if you don't mind . . ."

He set his espresso on the table in front of the couch where we both now sat. He hadn't even waited for me to finish my sentence before he made himself at home.

"Not a problem," he said in some European dialect. Maybe Irish? I'd never been good with accents. Or geography in general. I'd always lived in locations where such things didn't matter much. The first twenty-two years of my life, in Boston, I'd only had to keep track of the water. Near the Harbor. Across the Charles. After eight years in Southern California I knew I could get pretty much anywhere as long as I never lost track of the Pacific and the 405. "I won't bother you. Man, I've never seen this place so busy."

I looked up from my notebook full of hopeless plot ideas and conversation starters, headed nowhere, and felt like a fool. The seat next to me on the couch, where the possibly Irish stranger now sat drinking his coffee, had in fact been the only empty seat in the building. I could have no doubt that my earlier indiscreet declarations to various men that destiny in fact played no role whatsoever in our mutual love of java were all that had kept other earnest would-be sitters at bay.

"Sorry if I was rude. I didn't realize there was nowhere else to sit. I guess I've been kind of lost in my own little world."

He smiled. "And you thought I was hitting on you?"

"No! I mean, maybe. But not because . . . I mean, a few other guys . . ." I sighed, grateful that now I was in my thirties I at least seemed to know when to cut my losses and shut up. I was pretty sure I hadn't possessed that skill even weeks before when I was still twenty-nine. Maybe when I turned forty I would be gifted with the wisdom to never open my mouth in the first place. "Never mind. I am now thoroughly embarrassed, and I believe that's my cue to leave." I closed my notebook and threw it and my pen into my purse, which had been secured between my hip and the end of the couch.

"Hey, hey. No need to be embarrassed. And no need to leave. You appear to be working on something important. I, meanwhile, hope to ingest enough caffeine to make my blood hop. This is a place that can accommodate us both. Stay. I won't bother you."

He smiled at me and guzzled down more of his steaming drink before turning his attention to the *Backstage* magazine rolled up under his arm. An actor. Of course. I'd been in Los Angeles long enough to know that everyone was an actor or a writer despite the fact that our paychecks came from In-N-Out Burger or Trader Joe's. Or, in my case, Heartlite Greeting Card Company. Those of us sitting around with pens and notebooks, boasting normal, nonperfect teeth like most mere mortals possess and shamefully neglected dark hair roots tied up in a messy bun—not of the intentionally messy variety, mind you—and dressed in layers of casual, unflattering clothing that made us look like we'd just gone for a run, though we most assuredly had not? Writers. We were easily set apart from our attractive onscreen counterparts who were tied down by the necessity of putting effort into their appearance.

Take my couch mate, for instance. He had this messy flop of curls alongside perfect sideburns that accentuated his chiseled jawline. Even in that moment the word *chiseled* came to mind, as did the realization that I had never before thought of the word *chiseled*. But he was the very definition and perhaps the reason it had been created. He wore a black leather jacket over his white T-shirt, but not the seventy-five-degree day nor the steaming espresso nor the fire code–violating swarm of patrons caused him to break a sweat. Every style choice was perfect. Every tooth was perfect. Every messy curl? Perfect.

All actors looked like they had rolled out of bed that way while we writers gave off the impression that despite our best efforts nothing more could be done to save us.

"It looks like your drink is running low," a new voice stated from above me.

My eyes rose in disbelief and frustration, but having learned a lesson from my recent hastiness, I took a deep breath. Maybe . he worked there and needed the tips. Maybe he was just proud of his newly acquired observation skills and wanted to take them out for a spin.

"I've got what you might call a gift."

Huh?

"Congratulations," I muttered as I pulled my notebook and pen back out of my handbag. Even if I couldn't get any work done, I needed to at least make a note to remind myself to implore management to offer whatever discounts and incentives necessary to bring back the co-eds.

"No, I'm serious," the gifted one said. He helped himself to a seat next to me on the arm of the couch. "I can name your drink, down to the number of shots and the way you like your dairy."

Ignore him and he'll go away. Ignore him and he'll go away.

"Or . . . maybe not. You're not a dairy girl at all, are you? You're . . ." He drummed his fingers on his chin. "You're all soy."

Well, the guy deserved points for originality. I could honestly say no man had ever before hit on me by referring to me as a legume derivative. "Look, I don't mean to be rude, but I'm just here to get some work done."

"I've got it," he continued. "Soy cappuccino, three shots, extra foam, extra hot."

"Ooh, so close. Hazelnut crème breve, extra whipped cream. Now, if you'll excuse me . . ."

Once again I threw everything back into my purse. But just as I stood to leave, he propped one cowboy boot–clad foot on the corner of the coffee table in front of us and blocked my exit.

"'Extra whipped cream'!" He laughed as if I had just told him that handlebar moustaches *weren't* all the rage among other thirtysomethings in SoCal. "I like your spirit."

"Hey, look, pal." My possibly Irish couch mate leaned forward and addressed the gifted cowboy. "I believe my friend made it clear—"

"Your 'friend'?" I repeated as I turned my head to face him. Even as I said it, I realized the words weren't the problem, and by zeroing in on them I'd lost the impact of whatever empowered, independent-woman vibe I had hoped to give off. *He didn't call you "dollface," Olivia,* I lectured myself. *Just end this and get out.* "I appreciate your help, but I've got everything under control."

"Are you two together?" the Great Drink Detective asked my "friend"—not me. I sneered, affronted.

"Yes" and "no" rang out in unison, resulting in an amused smirk on the face of my interrogator.

"No, we most certainly are not," I declared, looking in shock from one stranger to the other.

"I'm just trying to help," the actor whispered as he sat on the edge of his middle seat cushion.

"I don't need your help," I whispered back through clenched teeth.

7

"We go way back," he said at full volume, ignoring me. "And the fact is you're interrupting an important conversation."

"No, you're not," I assured the other guy, whose Wranglers had now brushed up against my knee one too many times.

The man on my left—much handsomer, much less slimy, but currently no less infuriating—kept on. "Yes, he is. The fact is we're in love—"

"We are not!"

My eyes flew wide in complete disbelief and confusion. His grew equally round, twinkling with mischievous delight. He wagged his eyebrows up and down and nudged me with his elbow, but there was no way I was going to play along with this ludicrous game.

"What's it going to take for me to convince you we belong together, my love?" he implored of me. He turned his attention to the cowboy. "You see, we shared this magical weekend when we were both overseas on assignment. After college. During our time in the Peace Corps. It was while we were in—"

"I don't need your help."

All I'd wanted was to utilize stupid amounts of sugar and caffeine and a soundtrack of alt-folk singer-songwriters while I finally made progress on a screenplay the Coen brothers would want to direct. Was that so much to ask?

He sighed and raised his *Backstage* in surrender. "My apologies. No offense intended, I assure you."

"None taken."

I turned my back to my Peace Corps buddy as he went back to reading. My Wrangler-wearing suitor was waiting. "I appreciate you taking the time to demonstrate your supernatural talent for me—I do—but I'm not looking for conversation right now, or anything else. No offense, but I'm just going to take off."

"So, you aren't together?" he asked, his voice slick and oily and as befitting a cowboy as the pink-flamingoed button-up shirt he was wearing.

"We aren't," I replied with a sigh, confident he hadn't heard anything else I'd said.

I would have stood up and awkwardly stepped over Irish Guy to get away, but Hipster Cowboy was sitting so close there was no way to avoid some incidental contact, and the thought made me icky. I could have asked Irish Guy to get up and let me out—I instinctively knew he would acquiesce—but we had a silent couch partner reclined on the other end with his feet up on his corner of the table. Well, he was silent apart from the occasional snores and slurping back in of drool.

"Good." Hipster Cowboy's expression morphed into the one Sylvester always has when he wraps a napkin around his neck after he finally catches Tweety Bird. "So how about that second cappuccino?"

"Or hazelnut crème breve, extra whipped cream. Same difference." Irish Guy murmured it under his breath, but I heard every syllable. More important, I heard the disgust behind every syllable. In an instant I realized my obstinate independence had, for the second time since making his acquaintance, caused me to withhold the benefit of doubt that the other conscious third of the couch deserved.

"Sri Lanka!" I exclaimed, causing many a random passerby to glance at me—and that smarmy confidence to temporarily drop off of Hipster Cowboy's face. "I've been madly in love with him since our time in Sri Lanka."

What? Sri Lanka? Why had I said Sri Lanka? Where *was* Sri Lanka, anyway? Not good at geography. Also not good at making it up on the fly.

Hipster Cowboy looked at me as if I were insane—and not just in the Southern-California-girl-in-her-thirties-who-believes-in-whipped-cream-and-whole-milk sort of way.

"'Madly in love' . . . What are you talking about?"

I cleared my throat and dove in, finally convinced this guy would never succumb to traditional rejection. "Yes. It's true. I've been too scared to confess my feelings, but he's right."

"Who's right? Did I miss something?"

Oh goodness. Where to begin . . .

I felt the cushions shift as Irish Guy eased up to the edge again. "Finally!" He grabbed my hand in his. "Tell me, my love. When did you first know we were destined to be together?"

I flashed my eyes toward him and was met by his playful gaze. "Um . . . like I said . . . I've known since Sri Lanka."

"Yes, but *when* in Sri Lanka? I want to know the exact moment. The exact intake of breath when your heart began beating in time with mine."

A laugh began rumbling its way up from my chest, but I refused to unleash it. He thought he was pretty funny, and I was inclined to agree. But by taking the long, dramatic way out of my uncomfortable situation, he'd forfeited his right to receive that confirmation.

"I think it was at that tribal ceremony—"

Dear people of Sri Lanka,

  Please don't take it personally if I'm completely butchering

the authenticity of your culture. I promise it's not personal. I'd
be just as clueless about Boise.

Love,

Olivia

"With the fish! I'd forgotten all about that!" He chuckled
and squeezed my hand, and I swallowed the laughter once
again.

"'Fish'?" Hipster Cowboy lowered his boot to the ground.
Finally. He was still too close, and there was bound to be some
incidental contact, but at least I could make a quick run for it
and not have to step over him.

If only my hand weren't still being held.

"We should go . . . my love." I was so far out of my comfort zone. And though I was amused, I wanted nothing more
than for it all to be over. I wanted to go home. I wanted to
take a shower and clean the smarm off of me. I wanted to start
searching for a new coffeehouse that wasn't the Generation X
equivalent of Studio 54.

"Yes, darling, but our friend wants to know about the fish.
Oh, blimey, this is a good story."

I rolled my eyes at him. "Yes, *darling*, but . . . I mean,
I want to . . ." *Oh, good grief. Think, think, think.* It was
no wonder I couldn't finish a screenplay. Even basic sentences
seemed to be just out of reach.

His smile was bewitching. Stunning. And not just because
he was an undeniably beautiful actor sort of man. But there,
in that moment, as the corner of his lips lifted and trembled
slightly in his amusement at what was being said and what

wasn't, I think I got lost in that smile just a split second too long. Before I knew it, he was off and running.

"So, we're in Sri Lanka and this tribal elder starts telling us this legend about a mystical fish that is only seen once every four hundred years. But when it is . . . Well, you tell him, sweetness." He winked as he looked at me with a sly grin. "You tell it so much better than I do."

"Oh, I'd love to," I replied, smiling back at him in spite of myself. "But I really am so very desperate to be alone with you, after all this time."

A laugh burst out of him, ruining the façade. With the hand that wasn't holding mine, he grabbed his cup and swallowed the rest of his espresso in one gulp, then stood and pulled me up with him. He faced Hipster Cowboy. "I'm sure you understand—"

"Oh, yeah." The guy stood and moved out of our way so we could pass. "Enjoy yourselves. Love is a beautiful thing."

Irish Guy stopped in his tracks. "It really is," he agreed. "And it's right around the corner for you."

"Thanks, man," Hipster Cowboy replied as he settled into my abandoned cushion on the couch, looking as moved and introspective as I'd ever seen any man look.

"No, I mean it," I said through my laughter fifteen minutes later as we continued standing and chatting by his car—some little convertible thing that seemed perfect for him. It wasn't showy at all. Not super fancy or expensive and far from new, but very cool. Like, legitimately cool. Not midlife-crisis cool. "I'm sure your big break is just around the corner."

"See, you keep saying that, but you also keep giggling when you say it. Forgive me for not being convinced that your faith in me is absolute." He smiled as he shifted his weight from one foot to the other. "I do actually get work occasionally."

"Good for you."

The heartiness of his laughter overshadowed mine. "'Good for you' means 'Bless your poor hopeless heart,' right? Kind of a 'Yeah, good luck with that.'"

"No, not at all," I insisted, though of course that was exactly what I meant. "I mean 'Good for you, following your dreams!'" I punched him on the arm in a way I knew conveyed all of the emotional depth of "Go get 'em, Sparky!"

This guy was cute. And he was charming. And funny. In life, he was unquestionably a leading man. Becoming a leading man in Hollywood was a completely different thing, though. But maybe he would make it. Maybe I'd be sitting in front of my television one day, writing condolences for bereaved pet owners, and he would pop up on my screen as a comatose body in a soap opera. Or in a Rogaine commercial. The guy had nice hair. Lots of men would buy Rogaine if they thought it would give them hair like his.

I sighed. "Sorry. I'm not trying to be patronizing. It's just that I know how hard it is to make it in this business. In this town. But if you're getting any work at all, that is fantastic. I mean it."

"You sound like you know that of which you speak. You're an actress?"

I guffawed at the thought. "No. In fact you were just witness to my entire acting reel."

"Well, you were a modern-day Ingrid Bergman."

"I was impressive, it's true."

We were quiet for just a moment, and it was far more comfortable than stillness and silence with a stranger should ever be. I found myself hoping I could actually become friends with this guy. He was gorgeous, I realized more and more with each passing moment, but that wasn't it. I liked him. I didn't necessarily even want to date him. He was too handsome. Too rugged. Too charming. Too perfect, perhaps? He wasn't my type at all. I had long ago accepted the fact that I was a supporting character, and supporting characters don't fall in love with leading men. But it's perfectly acceptable for them to be friends. In fact, that's the whole reason supporting characters are there.

"So not an actress," he finally said. "Though I would hold 'I really am so very desperate to be alone with you' right up there with the great performances of our time. Brando in *Streetcar*, Welles in *Citizen Kane . . .*"

"And at least one or two of the award-winning performances from *Saved by the Bell: The College Years*," I added with a grimace, which made him laugh again.

"Then what is *your* Hollywood dream? We've all got one, right?"

I was hesitant to give the predictable West Coast answer, true though it might be. "I'm working on a screenplay."

"Wow! You're a screenwriter? Have I seen anything you've written?"

"Not unless you read a lot of Heartlite greeting cards. I write for Heartlite. The screenplay is just a dream."

He leaned up against his car and crossed his arms. "As a matter of fact, I think I've read everything Heartlite has ever done. I'm a bit of a fan boy, actually."

He wasn't belittling what I did for a living any more than I had meant to showcase my skepticism about his impending big break. He couldn't help but ooze charm and sincerity from every pore.

"Try me. I think I'm all caught up through the Fall Collection."

"Okay, let's see." I grinned and played along. "Oh, I know. Here's one of my biggest hits. 'You're lovely in the way you dress, and how you fix your hair. You're lovely for the way you always make me feel you care.'"

"Ooh! I know this one!" he shouted, standing up straight. "But I know, you no-good loser, that you're having an affair . . ."

"And if you don't stop seeing her, I'll have you killed, I swear."

"Happy anniversary!" we exclaimed in unison through our mirth.

"Maybe I should start a line of cards like that," I said as I swiped at the moisture in the corner of my eyes. "The 'Real Life Collection,' you know? My job would be much more interesting. Husband having an affair? There's a card. My kid beat up your kid on the playground? There's a card. Can't pay this month's rent but you want to let your landlord know that you at least thought about it? Well, we've got a card for that."

He nodded. "I like it. That would have been so handy when I accidentally ran my grocery cart into that BMW last week."

I was still chuckling as my imagination ran on. "Just think of all the possibilities in LA alone. When you have to fire your agent. When your agent has to fire you. For your friends when they have a horrible audition. The 'Break a Leg' line alone will be a game changer."

His eyes widened, and he looked down at his watch. "Is that the time?" The panic and urgency suddenly invading the relaxed air between us was nearly tangible. "I am so sorry, but I've got to run. I'm about to be late for an audition. I completely lost track of time. I hate to cut this short," he insisted.

"Oh no. Don't think anything of it. Just get going." I stepped away from his car so he could open the door. "I'd send you a card if I could, but, you know, break a leg."

"Thank you." He climbed into the driver's seat, but his eyes didn't leave mine.

"And thanks for getting me out of that situation back there," I called out as he shifted the convertible into gear and adjusted his rearview mirror slightly. I didn't want him to go. Not yet. It felt like there was more to say, but this guy—of all guys—deserved every shot at his big break, and I wasn't going to be the reason he missed it.

"You wouldn't have had any trouble at all getting yourself out." He grinned. "But I do think my way was more fun."

He backed out of the parking spot. I waved and smiled and began making my way to my own car. I'd only walked about ten feet, however, when I heard running footsteps approaching. I glanced over my shoulder and laughed as I turned around. "Do I need to come up with a 'Sorry you missed your audition, but it's your own dang fault' card?"

"Let's make your movie."

Amusement turned into bafflement. "What movie? What are you talking about?"

"Your screenplay. Let's take a big leap for no other reason than maybe we can believe in each other's dreams when it gets tough to believe in our own."

Tears began to pool in my eyes, and I didn't even know why. "I've barely even begun my screenplay—"

"That's okay. I'm pretty sure I'm not worth casting at this point anyway. But you keep writing and I keep auditioning . . . and then we meet back here in, what? Five years?"

I laughed as I thought of the meaningless doodles in my notebook. "You definitely have more faith in yourself than I have in myself."

"Okay, then. Ten."

I shook my head in dismay. "I'm pretty sure you're a crazy man."

"So what if I am? Worst-case scenario, I get to spend the next ten years knowing there's a screenwriter out there writing a role for me, and you get to spend the next ten years knowing there's an actor whose greatest ambition is to be in your film."

"I think right now your greatest ambition should be to be in *any* film! You've got to go, before you miss—"

"I know. I'm going. But ten years from today—" He looked at his watch. "February 4, 2013, I'm going to be sitting in there on our couch."

"I may not even recognize you. Once you hit the big time and have fake teeth and a fake tan," I said in the sincerest tone I could muster.

"I'll be the one with an armful of Academy Awards." He began walking backward toward his car, parked a few spaces away with the door still open and the engine running. "So, are you in?"

"Sure. Why not? February 4, 2013. I'll be here, completed screenplay in hand."

He reversed his backward trek and hurried over to me one

more time, cupping my shoulders and drawing me in for a gentle embrace. As he pulled away, he brushed his lips against my cheek and whispered, "It's a date."

My skin tingled from his unexpected touch, and my heart pounded with adrenaline and illogical hope.

"This is insane! A lot can happen in ten years!" I called out once I regained use of my voice.

"I'm counting on it." He climbed in his car and smiled at me as if there was nothing else to say. But as he drove past, he shouted, "Regardless, we'll always have Sri Lanka!"

I shook my head and laughed as he disappeared from view. And then I realized there had, in fact, been one more thing we should have said. But maybe there was something about feeling like you'd known someone your entire life that made you forget to ask their name.

I want you to know I thought of you today.

It's the little things—a scent or a song...

Those are the things that make me think of you.

And each time, I'm thankful for the scent or the song.

And I'm thankful for you.

Although we're not together, we're never apart.

Thinking of you.

Heartlite® Greeting Card Co., Number 04-5Y87U4

FEBRUARY 4, 2004

I had entered February 4 on my online calendar, just in case I decided to follow through with my date with destiny in 2013, and then I hadn't given it much thought. Oh, I thought of him occasionally when I got coffee. When I walked into a room and a soap opera was on television, I wondered if he would appear as Cop #2 or Man on Pier, perhaps. But I hadn't given any serious thought to our 2013 plan. Not until the moment when I sat on the floor of my West Hollywood apartment and heard the ding of my computer, indicating I had a reminder. I started laughing, which led to Fiona, my roommate, asking what was so funny.

I still didn't know his name, and it didn't matter. In the telling of my story he became Sexy Irish Guy, and that was good enough. It was a good story—a story that was probably made great because we didn't know each other's names. I felt nostalgic as I shared it, and each detail made me smile. As I sat there on the floor, I thought of the progression that had occurred in my mind. With the benefit of sentimentality and the distance of time, he had transitioned from cute to handsome to undeniably sexy. And unquestionably Irish.

"Maybe we should go tonight, just in case."

"Go where?" I asked, opening my eyes and brushing away the memories.

Fiona threw her hands up in the air. "To get coffee, of course!"

"Oh. Well, I'm meeting Liam for dinner, but we should be done by the time you get off work. I could meet you after. Or I could bring him along?"

"No, ding-dong. You can't bring Liam! What if Sexy Irish Guy is there?"

I should have known. Of *course* Fiona's romantic-comedy instincts had kicked in with a vengeance.

"What? No! Why would we go tonight? I've still got nine years." I chuckled at the thought. It was all so absurd. What were the odds that he and I would both still be living in Los Angeles in nine years? That we'd both remember? Maybe he wasn't as nerdy as I was and hadn't thought to put a reminder on his calendar.

No, Olivia. The chivalrous, strapping, acting Irishman is most assuredly not as nerdy as you are.

Maybe the coffeehouse would close down. Maybe he'd be too embarrassed to show up and reveal he'd gained fifty pounds, gone gray, and given up on his dreams altogether. Or maybe that would be *my* excuse.

"What if he's there waiting, just in case? What if he's spent the last year thinking of you, wishing he'd gotten your number—"

"Or at least my name?" I closed my laptop and stood to go into the kitchen, grabbing a snack to tide me over until dinner.

"Maybe he's just hoping he's not too late. It's been a year of regret, and he's worried he missed his chance. Livi, listen to me. What if he has decided to go to that coffeehouse every single February 4 until he dies, just in case you're thinking of him too?" Her eyes and mouth flew open. "It's like *The Notebook!*"

For months Fiona had been a bundle of nerves and anticipation since learning that her favorite Nicholas Sparks novel was being made into a movie, and I'd been subjected to her endless cycle of sighs and tears as she continually reread it cover to cover. She seemed bound and determined to make sure her intimate knowledge of the source material allowed her to track every out-of-place rainstorm and abandoned plantation by the time the film released.

I peeled my banana and snorted. "It's nothing like *The Notebook.*"

"It's a little like *The Notebook.*"

"Yesterday you thought going to the store was like *The Notebook.*"

"No, that's not true. All I said was it was weird that we couldn't find the grocery list, and maybe someone had hidden it from us, like Allie's mom hid the letters Noah wrote."

Fiona Mitchell. Roommate, hopeless romantic, best friend, and my favorite human on planet Earth since the first day of kindergarten when we both peed our pants and had to sit in the office together waiting for our parents to bring us dry clothes. We had been inseparable for the twenty-five years since.

"It's not like *The Notebook*—thank goodness—and he's not going to be there tonight. Or next February 4. He's probably not even going to be there in 2013. It doesn't work that way, Fi. As much as you want to believe life is a Tom Hanks rom-com, it's really not."

She took a noisy bite of raw carrot. "No one in a rom-com ever thinks they're in a rom-com."

"There wasn't even anything romantic about it!" I protested. "Seriously. He was a nice guy with a nice sense of humor and a nice head of hair, and we had a nice conversation and we clicked in a nice, platonic way. And then he got in his nice little convertible and drove away to his nice little audition for his nice little acting job. That's it. The end."

"But that doesn't mean it couldn't become something more!" Fiona trilled as she walked into her bedroom to change clothes for work.

After high school Fiona and I had attended Boston University together. I earned my degree in mass communications while Fiona was the recipient of BU's first, and to my knowledge only, degree in undecided. Seriously. Just because she's magical like that. She studied hard, never partied, and passed even her most difficult classes with flying colors. At the end of four years, she still hadn't declared a major. She had taken classes ranging from Film Scores of Ennio Morricone to Advanced Evolutionary Biophysics, temporarily convinced each time that she had found her calling. But another calling always came along. When I decided to move to LA to try to make it as a writer in Hollywood, she decided to go with me, confident it was finally time to put her BA in Undecided to good use.

While I plugged away as a writer of bad poetry for Heartlite, my best friend landed awesome job after awesome job. In 2004, she was handling public relations for Grauman's

Chinese Theatre. That meant she arranged media coverage for movie premieres and was quite often called upon to work with celebrities to make sure they weren't seen entering with whichever scandalous date they weren't supposed to be seen with. More than one Hollywood heartthrob had entered Grauman's with Fiona on their arm, just because she was doing her job, and then left with her on their arm, just because they'd realized how fabulous she is.

"I don't want it to be more, Fi. I would gouge out my eyes before I'd start a relationship with an actor, and I certainly don't need some ruggedly handsome, funny, charming stud of a man in my life. Who needs that pressure? Besides, I've got Liam."

Liam Howard could not be accused of being any of those things—apart from charming, though his charm was more of the dorky variety. He was totally brilliant and kind and pretty sexy himself in a hot nerd sort of way. But he couldn't have been more different from my coffeehouse stud. There was nothing rugged about him, that was for sure. He was more like Clark Kent at his best—not in the beginning when Lois is annoyed by him, but later, after they've had a few heart-to-hearts and she's beginning to subconsciously see in him what she sees in Superman. That was Liam. Minus the Superman stuff. Liam would need much more than contact lenses and a change of clothes to become The Man of Steel, but that was okay. We aren't all meant to be superheroes, and we aren't all meant to date Superman.

"Liam?" she asked, peeking her head out from her bedroom. "Really, Liv?"

"Really, what?"

"I just wish you wouldn't settle on Liam."

"I'm not settling. I like Liam."

"I like Liam too. I do. But he's so dull."

"He is not dull!" I exclaimed, doing my best to disregard all the thoughts that began flooding my mind. Unrelated thoughts that weren't worth dwelling on. Primarily, if I had to classify them, thoughts about how dull Liam was.

Liam was a supporting character, just like me. Why anyone would ever want to be anything else was a mystery. I'd spent my life with Fiona by my side—a leading lady if ever there was one. And that meant she was always on, because everyone was always watching. She never got a break from the spotlight, and for her that worked. She had never known anything else or even thought about the fact she was the star, I suspected. It was just her lot in life—like it was my lot in life to stay in the background, provide support, be a little bit quirky, not worry about my dress size quite as much, and date the Clark Kents of the world. Like all supporting characters, I might have had fewer lines, but I had the best lines. A tough gig to beat.

The only problem with dating Liam was that he didn't always appreciate the brilliance of my lines. He had no sense of humor. None. The man could explain the breakdown of chemical particles and recite the names of all the presidents— along with their date of inauguration, their vice president, and the Supreme Court justices named during their term—but he didn't know funny if it fell on him. That was a problem, but not a deal breaker. If things worked out between us, I would always have the Fionas and Sexy Irish Guys of the world to acknowledge my humor.

Fi came out of her bedroom, transformed into a significant Hollywood player with the simple addition of a short skirt, high heels, and a lot of eyeliner. It didn't take much for her. I had always been blown away by her effortless beauty, and even more blown away by the fact that it didn't matter to her. It was a tool and often a valuable resource, but she was never defined by her perfect cheekbones and her sultry eyes and her deep, rich, auburn tresses for which most of us would, if not sell our soul, at least lease it out for the weekend.

"You know, your home life wasn't bad. You have parents who love and accept you, a good job, decent friends . . ." She smirked at me as she tilted her head and put in her earring. "Someday I hope we can get to the bottom of these issues of yours."

Issues. I didn't have issues. "He's a sweet, smart guy who treats me well. Is there something wrong with that?"

"Nope. Nothing wrong with that. What there *is* something wrong with is the fact that one year ago, months before you started dating Liam, you met another sweet, smart guy—"

"We don't know that he's smart," I protested.

"He's heard of Sri Lanka."

"Well, even I've *heard* of it."

She held up her finger to silence me. "But . . . but not only is he sweet and smart, he's also gorgeous. Spontaneous. Ambitious."

"Liam just got promoted—"

"And, oh yeah, Sexy Irish Guy made you laugh. When was the last time Liam made you laugh?" I opened my mouth to answer but was rendered speechless when she added, "And I do mean intentionally."

The expression she saw on my face resulted in a fair amount of smugness on hers. She threw her Burberry handbag over her shoulder, completing her look, as she continued. "But if you choose to stay with Liam and completely ignore the perfect Irishman, that's up to you. It is kind of you, I must say, to be so self-sacrificial. Every woman in Los Angeles is grateful that you've left him on the market. In fact, right now, at some little 'ladies who lunch' thing on Rodeo Drive, you're probably being toasted. You're a saint for letting him be, Olivia Ross. A saint!"

"I'll see you later." I smiled, ignoring her jabs. "Have fun being fabulous, doing fabulous things."

"Now, I'm serious, Livi. Say the word, and I'll call in sick tonight, and we'll spend the evening waiting for Sexy Irish Guy."

"Nope. Thanks, but no thanks. As much fun as I'm sure that would be, I choose to live in reality rather than a Nora Ephron film."

As soon as Fiona walked out the door, I reopened my laptop and read the little bit of plotting drivel I had worked through that day. *Landing's Edge*, I think I was calling it at this point.

A small, fictional ~~midwestern~~ New England town called Landing's Edge is sent into a tailspin when it is revealed that their ~~most prominent citizen~~ mayor is involved in ~~a money laundering and bribery scheme~~ corrupt dealings. Of some sort.

That was about all I had.

I sighed in disgust and closed the laptop, once again convinced I would never get a movie made. How did I have even less of my screenplay on the page than I'd had a year ago? At least I'd upgraded from my notebook of handwritten scribbles to an actual word-processing program. I figured that should count for something. Hopefully things were going better for Sexy Irish Guy. I did wonder what he was up to. I hoped he was getting work, and I wondered if he made a habit of creating joint histories and unrequited love stories with random women or if it had been a one-time thing.

I also wondered, very much in spite of myself, if he might have been good for me if he had stayed in my life. I'd completely meant what I told Fi about there being no romantic feelings there whatsoever. I did admire his confidence, though. I admired the comfort he seemed to have in his own skin—skin, which, admittedly, was probably more comfortable to live in than most. If we'd had each other to lean on, might we have been a good support system for each other? All of that stuff about knowing there was someone out there who believed in our dreams was great, but what if we'd been able to remind each other of that from time to time? Might he have pushed me? Inspired me?

"Might he have met me at the top of the Empire State Building on Valentine's Day?" I whispered with a laugh, rolling my eyes at myself. "Oh, shut up, Olivia!"

I stood to go into the bathroom to wipe the banana off of my hands and freshen up—Liam would be here in a few minutes to pick me up for our customary Wednesday-evening dinner-and-a-movie date—but the phone rang before I got there.

"Hello?"

"Hi. It's Liam."

We had been dating for eight months and he still identified himself each and every time he called. "Liam? I'm sorry. Liam who?"

"Liam Howard. Your boyfriend."

I stifled a groan and smiled. "Yes, Liam. I know. I was kidding."

"Oh, sorry. I guess I thought you might not recognize my voice. I've had a bit of a raspy throat today."

"No need to explain." *You aren't funny. I get it.* "So, what's up? Shouldn't you be on your way here by now?"

"Well, I thought I would be done with work for the day, but the best-laid plans . . ." I could hear the exhaustion in his voice. "I can get away for a little while, but then I'll have to head back. Do you mind if we just grab some coffee?"

Liam was one of the lowest lawyers on the totem pole at the legal firm of Kubrick & Coppola, Attorneys-at-Law. I'd told him that law firm was much too edgy for him, and with a name like Howard he would fit in better across town at Spielberg, Reiner & Marshall.

He didn't get it.

"Sure, babe. Coffee will be fine."

"I'm sorry. I owe you."

"I'm just glad I'll get to see you at all. Should I meet you at the usual place?"

Well, the usual place was too far away from his office, so we ended up at a location I used to know well, though I didn't recognize the address when he gave it to me. I parked about three blocks away, and the setting grew more familiar as I walked from my car. I examined every entrance I passed, but none of the numbers on the glass doors matched up with the address scrawled on the note in my hands.

"Surely not," I muttered as I slowed my approach in response to the aroma of coffee and the gaggle of patrons clustered on the sidewalk with biodegradable cups in their hands. I looked down at the paper and then held it up against the light of the setting sun and squinted to verify the location one more time, but doubt was replaced by incredulity when I spotted Liam waiting for me at a bistro table just outside the entrance.

"You okay?" he asked as he stood. He greeted me with a quick kiss and then held the door open for me and ushered me inside.

"Yeah, fine." I looked around and marveled as we walked in. "It's just strange. This used to be my regular coffeehouse when Fi and I lived in the apartment on Venice Boulevard. Back when I used to go into the Heartlite offices every day." I chuckled at the coincidence. "I was actually here last February 4 too."

Fi and I had moved from Culver City to West Hollywood shortly after she got the job at Grauman's. The move took me farther away from Heartlite, but by then I'd been promoted from an assistant writer to writer/associate editor. That meant I not only got to write my own cards, I also got to oversee a small group of assistant writers and tell them when their Grandparent's Day cards were a little too hip and their First Communion cards were a little too peppy. I also had enough clout to be able to work from home most days.

"Do you always remember specific dates on which you went to particular restaurants? That's an impressive, if somewhat useless, skill to have."

"No, not usually."

As Liam placed his coffee order at the counter, I glanced around the wide-open space and felt a flutter in my stomach. I hadn't been in there since that day—not because the memories were too raw, though I was sure that would be Fiona's assumption, but because when I needed a coffeehouse, I needed a place to work. Not a place to have conversations with a wide range of men from disgusting to delightful. The Mugs & Shots on Venice Boulevard had failed me spectacularly in that department.

I glanced over at the couch—"our couch," he had called it—and smiled at the memory.

"Olivia?" Liam's voice snapped me out of my nostalgia. "Do you know what you'd like?"

I was going to order a hazelnut crème breve for old times' sake, but they were out of hazelnut. Thank goodness. It was time to snap out of the Sexy Irish Guy daze and focus on the Handsome Uptight Lawyer I wanted to be there with. A caramel macchiato and a cranberry scone it was. No sentimentality, no dreaming of "what if," and still plenty of sugar.

Liam paid, and we grabbed a small table in the back. As we sat he asked, "So how do you remember that you were here last February 4?"

"Oh, you know. I told you about that actor I met here." His expression was blank, so I prodded. "You know, the other guy was hitting on me . . . We talked about Sri Lanka . . ."

Still nothing, so while we waited for our coffee, I told him all about Sexy Irish Guy. And as I did, I couldn't help but look up each time the door opened.

"Are you in love with this guy?" Liam asked minutes later as he sipped his Americano.

"No! Of course not. What I just told you—that is literally the extent of the story. That's it. In its entirety."

He smiled. "And yet, here we are, having coffee. Here. Today. Exactly one year later."

"Yes! And I told *you* how weird that was. But this was your pick—"

"I know. I wasn't saying you orchestrated it." He placed his hand on top of mine. "I'm just saying it's pretty ironic. Don't you think so?"

"It's like—" No. I stifled my inner Alanis Morissette, knowing he wouldn't get it.

But then he surprised me by continuing. "It's maybe even a little bit *too* ironic, Olivia. Yeah, the more I think about it, I really do think . . ."

I looked up at him, and he was smiling a provocative smile. He knew what he was saying. He knew he was treading on sacred Alanis ground. I even suspected Liam Howard knew he was being funny.

I stared at him in wonderment, in awe of the way his eyes twinkled when they were full of humor. I'd never seen that before, and I knew that was probably a good thing. I wasn't accustomed to the strange little flutters and convulsions that were occurring in my chest, and I didn't know if I liked them or not.

An Olivia Ross romantic relationship tended to fit within some unstated but undisputed guidelines. Fiona led with her heart while I led with my head. That had probably always been the case, but as I got older the desire for sensible and practical was cemented. I'd never drooled over wedding dresses or practiced signing my name as Mrs. Imaginary Husband. It wasn't that I didn't want love and not that I didn't appreciate romance. I did. But I wanted—no, I *needed*—love and romance to fit into the life I had chosen to live. Like the way a great scarf can make an outfit you love even better. But you can't go out dressed in just the scarf.

So, though I may not have understood the way I felt as I looked at Liam in that moment, and I absolutely could not understand why my heart was beating faster than it had been a few seconds prior, there was one thing I understood perfectly.

Something had shifted.

I leaned over and kissed him a little more passionately than I normally would in public, simply because I couldn't stand not to.

"What was that for?" he asked, not at all displeased.

"Oh, don't you know? A well-timed, properly used Alanis Morissette reference is the equivalent of a love potion for all Gen X-ers."

He blushed. "Is that right?"

"Absolutely." I nodded in earnest.

"Well, in that case . . ." He set down his coffee and jumped up. Then, in the middle of a coffeehouse in Culver City, California, dressed in his pinstripe suit, Liam Howard, Esq., began belting out the ironies of it raining on your wedding day, paying and then being offered something for free, and refusing to take good advice.

I giggled uncontrollably as he made his way through the entire chorus of "Ironic." I was also tempted to bury my head as we—well, *he*—drew the attention of every single customer and employee, but I couldn't take my eyes off of him. When he was finally done, ending with a very Alanis-like "It fig-gers," everyone in the coffeehouse applauded. Liam took a bow before sitting back down and calmly taking another sip of his coffee as if none of it had happened. As if he hadn't just changed the rules. As if he hadn't just changed . . . everything.

"That," I gasped, still trying to regain my breath as delighted laughter coursed through my body, "was fantastic."

He smiled at me, but even more notably, he watched me. He didn't superficially look at me or glance my way as he continued ingesting his caffeine. No, he watched me. Studied me, even. I don't know what he saw, but there seemed to have been a shift in him like there'd been in me. An invisible border had been breached, and we'd somehow stepped into undiscovered territory.

With that delicious twinkle in his eyes still having its effect, rendering me defenseless, he whispered—regretfully, I think—"I need to get back to work."

I stood from my chair and moved over to sit on his lap. I kissed him again, but this time the passion took a different form. It was no longer an impetuous impulse finding its life. This time our lips chose to be united in a soft, intimate partnership.

"Must you?" I asked as I rested my head on his shoulder and inhaled his scent, needing rations to help me survive this new, unfamiliar emotional domain.

"Unfortunately." He sighed as he wrapped his arms around my waist. "But thanks for meeting me. Sorry I can't make it to see *Schindler's List*. I was looking forward to this third viewing with you."

"Hey! It was my turn to pick!"

"I know. But exactly how long is that awful retro theater you love so much going to be showing that one? I don't know if I can take much more, Olivia. Can't we please move on to something more upbeat, like *Sophie's Choice* or *Kramer vs. Kramer*?"

I sat up straight so that I could once again get a glimpse of the twinkle I instinctively knew was going to be brightening his eyes again. "I didn't complain last week about going to that awful thing you wanted to see—"

"Oh, you mean *The Lord of the Rings: The Return of the King*?" He laughed. "That awful thing that has made a gazillion dollars and that you and I were actually the last two people in North America to see? That one?"

"That's the one." I grinned. "It was so long!"

"Oh, yes. And it's clear from your film choice that you have no interest in long films . . ."

"That's different. *Schindler's List* is important, Liam."

"Middle Earth is important, Olivia."

The teasing was new as well. How had everything shifted so dramatically, so quickly? Who was this amazing, perfect man, and where had he come from? And how was I ever going to bring myself to rise from his lap so that he could go back to his stupid job, away from me?

"There was just so much manufactured suspense," I continued with a groan, determined to prolong the conversation as long as I possibly could. "So much sweeping background music telling us exactly how we should feel, as if we weren't capable of figuring it out on our own. So much running. So much—"

"Color," he deadpanned.

"Exactly." I nodded. "Far too much color."

I made the mistake of pausing, which allowed him the opportunity to continue on with his mature, adult life where careers were something that mattered. "Thanks for meeting me. Even if just for a little while. See you tomorrow?"

"See you tomorrow."

He brushed his lips against mine one final time, then he held my hand as he stood. When he let go, I watched him and his dashing pinstripe suit make their way to the door, and I took in every single detail of him. His masculine walk and his perfectly pressed slacks. The way he smiled at every person who walked past him—and the way each of them smiled at him in return, no matter what their countenance had been prior to the brief interaction. I watched women turn to look at him as he walked past and then turn back to their friends with flushed faces or self-conscious giggles. I watched him step out of the way so an elderly man could exit before him, and I saw him get caught holding the door for a mother with three children under the age of five, though nothing in his demeanor communicated that he was inconvenienced in the least.

They were all things I hadn't noticed before, though I couldn't imagine why. Each of those things had always been there. Each of them was unmistakably Liam Howard.

As he finally moved to exit, I called out to him, across the coffeehouse, "Hey, Liam!"

When he turned around, his smile was quizzical. Bewilderment, which I suspected had been caused by the evening's strange chain of events, was as evident on his face as I guessed it was on mine.

"That whole 'Ironic' thing? That was funny, you know."

He winked. "I know." And then he walked through the door and went to work.

I sighed and picked up my things to go, trying to reconcile

the happiness Liam had made me feel with the sadness that had sprung up from nowhere. Somehow, right before my eyes, Clark Kent had transformed into Superman without so much as the necessity of a phone booth. Faster than a speeding bullet, everything had changed.

Each time you doubted you could do it,

I knew you could.

Each time you didn't believe in yourself,

I knew you should.

And now you've found the success that

I always knew you would.

Congratulations!

Heartlite® Greeting Card Co., Number 05-X672C4

FEBRUARY 4, 2005

I went to see *Magnum Opus Phantasm*, the movie version, on February 3, 2005. Fi made me go. I hated musicals, but she loved them. I mean, I suppose I didn't hate *all* musicals, but the ones I liked were a little more obscure, and usually off-Broadway. They usually didn't get big-screen adaptations. Fi, on the other hand, was a mainstream Broadway purist. Everything from *West Side Story* to *Miss Saigon* to *Wicked* . . . the bigger, the better. *Magnum Opus Phantasm* was right up her alley.

I just could never get into the randomness of the singing and dancing. I didn't mind *A Chorus Line*. Yes, there was a ton of singing and dancing, but they were singers and dancers auditioning for a musical. The singing and dancing made sense. *Les Misérables*? Not so much. "It's the eve of our first battle in the French Revolution! Sing and dance with me, won't you?" Huh? No, thanks.

When Fi was a little girl, her family would fly from Boston to New York to see Broadway shows all the time. Just for the day, or the weekend. They took me with them on a few occasions, and usually I was miserable the entire time. At least while the show was going. I did, however, love New York. I loved the food, the skyscrapers, the people. I had a fascination with the subway, despite the fact that the Mitchells were not subway people. I would stare longingly each time we passed a station entrance, and I would watch the people going down the steps and coming up. I loved watching the people. You saw every type of person when you spent a weekend in New York. And there were a few places—probably lots of places, but I only knew of a few—where you could hear the subway beneath you as you walked. There, near Central Park, people could hear, if only they would listen. I thought that was magical.

But the shows? Not my thing. I thought *Cats* was the worst. I'd thought the title was a metaphor—for what, I didn't know—so when I saw the show was actually made up of a bunch of cats singing, dancing, and playing in garbage, I was disappointed beyond measure. Fiona's mother thought I was an ingrate for liking the prostitute cat, Grizabella, while Mr. Mitchell insisted I was mistaken. She couldn't have been a prostitute, he believed. They wouldn't have put that in a family-friendly musical. Fi and I giggled about it when they weren't around and wondered what show they had been watching. For years after that, whenever Mr. and Mrs. Mitchell were oblivious to whatever scheme or machinations Fiona and I were concocting right under their noses, we would call it Grizabellaing.

Anyway, all of that is to say Fi dragged me to *Magnum Opus Phantasm* kicking and screaming. I knew I would hate it. Yes, it was based on a classic piece of French literature, and yes, in some ways the singing made sense, seeing as it took place in the context of an opera house and all. Still, I remained convinced that whatever virtue it possessed would be beaten out of it in its Hollywood adaptation, brought to you by the same team who produced *Coyote Ugly*.

"But the Phantasm is just your type of guy, Liv," Fi declared, continuing our argument as we took our seats, popcorn in hand. "He's melodramatic and brooding, and oh so serious. He'll never go for the easy laugh or the appealing turn of phrase, that one. You may be in for a treat. I have a sneaking suspicion you're really going to love this one."

I didn't. As expected, I hated it. I actually dozed off a couple of times. But whenever the Phantasm himself was onscreen, I was somewhat mesmerized. Not in an attraction sort of way, and certainly not in an I'm-enjoying-this-movie sort of way, but in a "Where have I seen that guy?" sort of way. Also, perhaps, in a the-people-who-made-this-movie-should-be-exiled-to-a-leper-colony sort of way.

"Who plays the Phantasm?" I leaned over and whispered as a scene at a masquerade ball droned on and on.

"Hamish MacDougal. He's super cute without the mask."

Never heard of him. "What's he been in, besides this?"

Fi turned to me and whispered through gritted teeth, "Shut up. You're ruining the magic!"

For me, the magic was that it finally ended.

"Liv, come on. Let's go." She nudged me awake, and after I wiped the slobber off of my chin, we stood to make our merciful exit. "Enjoy the movie?" she asked, her voice dripping with snark.

For more than twenty years, Fiona and I had disagreed on movies. It all began in 1983 when we got to go to a movie by ourselves for the first time. We weren't *totally* by ourselves—my older brother, Brandon, had just gotten his driver's license, and Mom said he could only go to the movies with his friends if he took Fi and me along. Brandon and his buddies were supposed to see *Return of the Jedi* but snuck into *Octopussy* instead. Fi and I, meanwhile, were supposed to watch *E.T.*, and Fi did. I snuck into *Gandhi* and cried when I had to leave early.

From that day on, she and I only went to movies together if we had time to see two, back-to-back. She would pick one, I would pick the other.

We left *Magnum Opus Phantasm* and headed directly to *Hotel Rwanda*.

"What else has that Phantasm guy been in?" I asked again as we waited for the underappreciated Don Cheadle instant classic to begin.

"Hamish MacDougal? Umm . . . he was in that *Crypt Scavenger* movie with Angelina Jolie."

"I saw that," I said, munching on popcorn. "I didn't like it, but I saw it."

"Yes, I know. I'm the one who took you to see it. But he wasn't in that one." Fi smiled and pulled her legs in as a studly stud of a man scooted past us to his seat, making googly eyes at my best friend. "He was in the sequel. I didn't bother taking you to the sequel."

"And for that I thank you."

I didn't think of Hamish MacDougal again until the next morning, when he popped up on *Good Morning America*. In an instant, I knew.

"Fi! Fi! Come here!"

But I'd forgotten she wasn't there. She had just started her new job as Vera Wang's office manager. And don't think for a moment that this office manager position meant she sent faxes or got coffee or ordered paperclips. Oh no. This is Fiona we're talking about. Her job duties included sitting down with rich (often celebrity) brides and finding out what dreams they had for their wedding dress. She would then take her notes to Vera, who would decide if she was willing to create a dress for them or not.

I picked up the phone and called the only other person who would understand.

"Kubrick & Coppola, this is Liam. Can I help you?"

"Liam, it's me. Do you remember me telling you about Sexy Irish Guy? Remember? The guy I met in the coffee shop?"

"Um, yeah, I remember. I think. But I'm actually working right now."

"I know, but I had to tell someone. So, this guy, who I was sure would never be anyone—it was Hamish MacDougal!" I was still staring at him on my television, absolutely certain it was him. I wasn't listening to a word he said, though I had heard enough to recognize the accent. All I saw was the kindness and humor in his eyes and that wonderful, curly hair. It was definitely him.

"Seriously?" Liam squealed. "Hamish MacDougal? *The* Hamish MacDougal?"

"Yes! Can you believe that?"

He sighed. "I assure you, Olivia, I have no idea who Hamish MacDougal is."

Would I ever quit reaping the benefits of Liam's unearthed sense of humor?

"However . . ." I heard keyboard clacking in the background. "The results of a quick internet search inform me that he is not Irish. He's Scottish. I will say, however, no matter how much it threatens my masculinity to do so, he is pretty doggone sexy. And most assuredly a guy. A guy who doesn't appear to own a shirt . . ."

"What?" I yelled, running to my computer. "He's on the internet?"

Liam laughed. "It's 2005, my friend. Everyone is on the internet."

Wow. "Okay. Scottish. So I wasn't *too* far off, right?" I searched for "Hamish MacDougal," spelling it as well as I could. Only a few seconds passed before I discovered, much to my embarrassment, that he'd already been a fairly successful working actor before I ever implied he was destined to achieve heights no higher than Angus & Marie's Detective Diner Murder Mystery Dinner Theater on the corner of Sunset and Van Ness.

"I'm fairly certain all of Scotland and Ireland would beg to differ, but whatever makes you happy. Can I go now?"

Dear people of Scotland and Ireland,
>You know the drill. Sorry.
>>Love,
>>Olivia

"Of course," I said as I continued scanning my screen. "Thanks, Liam."

"Do we call him Sexy Scottish Guy now?" he asked, no doubt teasing me.

"Well, I suppose we call him Hamish MacDougal."

"Actually, according to IMDb, his friends call him Mac. And it appears his mother calls him Mish. Should we start calling him Mish?"

"Goodbye, Liam." I smiled and got ready to hang up, but he caught me.

"It is ironic, though, don't you think?"

"What is? Please don't sing again."

"Well, that would make it doubly ironic. Last year you ended up in the coffeehouse where you met him, and this year, on the same date, you found out who he is. That's pretty ironic."

I looked up at the calendar in surprise. He was totally right. After last year I had removed my computer notification, knowing instinctively that Fiona would never allow me to forget the date. But I hadn't counted on Fiona being too busy with Vera Wang to bombard me with her hopeless romanticism.

Apparently I had a backup.

"I can't believe you remembered that."

He cleared his throat. "Well, believe it or not, I don't get dumped often. I am somewhat of a catch, you know."

Ahhh! The guilt!

I'd paced the hallways of his apartment building for hours until he finally showed up after getting off work at 11:00 p.m. Then, in fairness, I hadn't so much dumped him as simply pointed out all of the reasons he and I would never work out, all of which had been cemented in my mind while I waited. For the most part, they had been true, actual reasons. I needed to focus on my career; he needed to focus on his career; more and more dates were being canceled as his schedule became more and more unpredictable. Nothing but truth in any of that.

Of course, I hadn't bothered to tell him that the moment he started making me laugh, hours earlier in that coffeehouse, he had morphed into a package of perfection I felt ill equipped to handle.

He hadn't fought me too hard on any of it. He'd apologized that his work schedule had become so hectic and assured me he completely understood. He was so sensible and matter-of-fact about it all that I immediately began to wonder if I was making a huge mistake. Maybe he wasn't the spontaneous, unpredictable leading-man type I feared he was. After all, the leading man would never go down without a fight.

On the phone, a year removed from all of that, there was a moment of silence I attempted to overanalyze into submission before I asked, "We're okay, right?"

"Oh goodness, yes!" He laughed. "Sorry. Didn't mean to imply otherwise. It's just ironic."

Liam and I were better as friends. I was sure of that. It hadn't been a seamless transition from romance to friendship, but when you get stuck in an earthquake shelter with your ex-boyfriend four months after you break up, and everyone else seeking protection alongside you looks like they wandered out of a particularly rough tribal council on *Survivor*, it's difficult not to strike up a conversation. That claustrophobic first post-breakup conversation had continued over lunch, and then it had pretty much continued for the eight months since.

"Hey, look," my good friend said, interrupting my reverie. "He was in a Bond movie!"

Embarrassment washed over me anew. *Don't hit on me. Good luck with your career. Don't give up on your dreams!* Sheesh.

I hung up the phone, then spent a few more minutes obsessing over every little Hamish MacDougal detail I could find on the internet. The internet on which he was, indeed, quite prevalent. As I obsessed, I kept trying to convince myself that it wasn't a good idea to bother Fiona at work in only her second week on the job. Ultimately, of course, I just had to. Liam had been such a glaring disappointment in the share-my-enthusiasm department.

I hurried to the refrigerator, pulled Fi's new business card from its magnetic home, and quickly dialed the number.

"Fiona Mitchell," she answered.

That took me off guard. "Seriously?" I asked, as impressed with her as ever. "You get to answer your phone with your name, when you work at a company that is completely built on someone else's name?"

She chuckled. "What's up, Livi?"

"I'm sorry to bother you at work, but I have to tell you something. And I'm prepared for the possibility that you might not believe me. This is the biggest thing that has ever happened in my life."

I may have overshot a little, but more than anything that was probably an accurate reflection on the lack of big things in my life to that point.

"I'm nervous," she replied softly.

"Hamish MacDougal, Fi. Hamish MacDougal!"

She paused, understandably confused. "Um, okay. Am I . . . am I supposed to name someone else, or—"

"No, listen. Hamish MacDougal is Sexy Irish Guy."

"But he's Scottish."

I groaned. "Yes, I know that now. Considering how horrible

I am at dialects and geography and everything, I think I was actually pretty close."

"You do know they are completely separate countries, right?"

"You're missing the point, Fiona! It was Hamish MacDougal. I had the most real, most genuine encounter with a stranger that I've ever had in my entire life, and it was with Hamish MacDougal, who just happens to be the biggest star on the planet!"

She laughed. A little too much. "He's not."

He wasn't? No, I didn't follow celebrity news like Fiona did, but I thought *Magnum Opus Phantasm* had taken over the world. I sure hadn't been able to escape the billboards. "But that movie is huge, right?"

"Eh," she replied, underwhelmed. "It's done okay, but not as well as anyone thought it would. Better internationally, I'm guessing. He certainly got some good press from it, and I think he'll blow up here pretty soon. But so far . . . eh. It doesn't help that you can only see half of his face, but—"

"Fiona!" I shouted into the phone a little more emphatically than I had intended, but I was without regret. "Forget it. I'll talk to you later."

I heard her exhale, and then she sweetly said, "I'm sorry. You tell me what you want me to say, and I'll say it. What's more, I'll sell it."

I smiled, having no doubt that was true. "No, it's fine. Thanks. I think I just got excited, and I thought you would be excited too."

"Yeah, sorry." She sighed. "I don't know. I think for me it's probably a little bit sad that the mystery is over. Does that make sense?"

That made total sense, though it hadn't occurred to me. But it only made sense that Fi felt that way. I certainly didn't. The mystery had been an annoyance that caused me to slap my forehead on occasion to chastise myself for not asking his name—a simple thing that would have helped me avoid all mystery from the onset. But I knew Fiona, and I knew that to her the mystery represented romance. And romance was her lifeblood. As all of that dawned on me, I started to apologize. I felt horrible that I had ruined it for her. But I didn't get the chance.

"Hang on a minute," she blurted out as new energy coursed through her romance veins. "You know who he is now. You can track him down. We can find his agent, at least."

"And then what?"

"Well, now that you know who he is, you know who he *was* when you met him. You know that he was already working and somewhat successful by the time he met you. And he was still crazy about you, Liv!"

"He wasn't crazy about me."

She ignored the reality I had attempted to infuse into the conversation. "I think the key is to get to him before he blows up and gets too big to socialize with the little people."

Fiona was, without a doubt, the most important person in the world to me, and she pretty much always had been. Nevertheless, I did, on occasion, fantasize about dropping her off in the middle of a hayfield or something, just for a few hours.

"Have we met? Do you know me at all? Seriously, after nearly thirty years together, how can you possibly think that I want to be with a big movie star? That I would want to squeeze in there before he becomes too important to mess with me? If you recall, two years ago I knew I wasn't interested in him because he was too handsome. Too charming. Too . . . whatever. So now that I know he's famous, you think that will win me over? Quite the opposite, I assure you. You know me, Fiona. You know I'm more likely to be interested in a romantic relationship with the guy who counts the votes. The accountant guy who gets to rent a tux and go to the Oscars so he can be introduced and stand there looking uncomfortable for thirty seconds while the host assures us for the millionth time that no one has seen the list of winners except for *that guy*. *That's* the guy I'm more likely to date."

I made a mental note to do a little more research once I got off the phone and make sure Hamish hadn't already won an Oscar by the time he told me he'd be back with an armful of them in ten years. That would confirm he'd just been messing with me, and that would be disappointing. One likes to believe one can trust a stranger one spends thirty chaotic minutes with. "I could not be less interested in a romantic relationship with Hamish MacDougal. There's no love story there, Fi. Sorry to disappoint you."

"Okay." But it was not an "okay" of resignation. She was just preparing to step up to the bench as an advocate on behalf of her plaintiff, the devil. "Then why do you care? Why are you so excited? Why, may I ask, is this the biggest thing ever to happen to you in your entire life?"

Those were all good questions. I had never been impressed by celebrity, after all. As a fifteen-year-old girl I'd gone with my dad to game four of the Stanley Cup finals, and I'd had the good fortune to be seated next to Scott Baio during the infamous Boston Garden power outage. Not once in the forty-five minutes we spent seated next to each other in total darkness did I gush about how I wanted Charles in charge of me. I hadn't begged for a *Joanie Loves Chachi* reunion. But I did walk away with his mother's recipe for pork chops and fried apples, which I then proceeded to de-celebritize as much as possible through the years, passing it off as my own on the odd occasion that I cooked and never once giving Chachi's mom the credit she deserved.

"I don't know," I grumbled, thoroughly disgusted by how quickly my balloon of excitement had been completely deflated. "I just thought it was cool."

"I'm sorry, Livi." I heard the smile in her voice and knew she was probably picturing me pouting with crossed arms, like we were eleven again and she was refusing to join the Model UN Club I'd started at school. "It *is* cool. And it certainly should go a long way toward getting your screenplay made into a movie."

I was sprawled out on the couch and therefore producing no tracks, but if I had been, I would have stopped dead in them. "Say that again."

"Hey, sorry, I've got to go. A client just got here. We'll talk tonight, okay?"

"No, wait, wait, wait!" I pleaded. "What did you just say? Say that again."

"What? You mean about how the fact that the guy you are meeting up with in 2013 is already starring in big movies can only mean good things for you?"

"Yes," I whispered. "That."

"I'll talk to you later. Love you."

I was left alone with that singular thought. One which, shockingly, had not occurred to me as I'd watched the artist formerly known as Irish on television and vividly remembered that day. Suddenly I wasn't working toward an impossible dream or even a far-fetched aspiration. I was writing a film for Hamish MacDougal. And perhaps *Magnum Opus Phantasm* hadn't been the box-office smash that its marketing campaign wanted us to believe it was, but it was a major Hollywood film. And he was the title character. The lead role. *The star.* I was writing a screenplay for a star.

Supporting characters might not have happily-ever-afters with stars, but I had no doubt they wrote screenplays for them all the time.

I walked over to my laptop and disconnected it from its charger, then took it with me as I plopped back down on the couch. I opened my word processor and pulled up my work in progress—a list of characters, a poorly set scene, and a brilliant monologue or two made up of lines such as, "This isn't New York, Mr. Mayor. We don't have [INSERT SOMETHING NEW YORK HAS AND VERMONT DOES NOT] on every street corner, and that goes for our principles as well."

I read a few of the plotting notes I had written for my story's hero.

NAME: Nigel Patton

ROLE: As the chief prosecutor in Landing's Edge, Nigel is faced with the unexpected fight of his life when he unearths a path of corruption that affects almost everyone in town, all the way to the top. Possibly including Nigel's estranged wife . . . the coroner? (The DA? A successful businesswoman? Nail this down later.)

PHYSICAL DESCRIPTION: Slender and refined. Late 40s/early 50s. The toll of a failing marriage (and maybe the loss of a teenage son, and that's what drove Nigel and his wife apart?) is evident in every line on his face. A Geoffrey Rush or Gary Oldman type.

Despite the fact that I'd hated the one movie I'd seen him in, I had no reason to doubt Hamish was a competent actor. I didn't have any difficulty believing he was more than just a pretty face. I mean, all I had to do was look at how he had sold the Peace Corps and Sri Lanka to Hipster Cowboy. But a Geoffrey Rush or Gary Oldman type he was not. A Geoffrey Rush or Gary Oldman type he would never be.

"Alright, Hamish MacDougal," I muttered aloud as I crossed my legs under me and adjusted the windows on my screen so my character description document was on one side and a photo of Hamish in some movie without a shirt—Liam wasn't kidding—was on the other. "I'll play your game. What would this thing look like with you in it?"

NAME: ~~Nigel Patton~~ Jack Mackinnon

ROLE: As the ~~chief prosecutor~~ newly appointed sheriff of Landing's Edge, ~~Nigel~~ Jack is faced with the unexpected fight of his life when he unearths a path of corruption that affects almost everyone in town, all the way to the top. Possibly including ~~Nigel's~~ Jack's estranged wife . . . ~~the coroner? (The D.A.? A successful businesswoman? Nail this down later.)~~ the deputy mayor.

PHYSICAL DESCRIPTION: ~~Slender and refined. Late 40s/early 50s. The toll of a failing marriage (and maybe the loss of a teenage son, and that's what drove Nigel and his wife apart?) is evident with every line on his face. A Geoffrey Rush or Gary Oldman type.~~ Hamish MacDougal

I spent the rest of the day working on *Landing's Edge*, disregarding the virtual stack of Hanukkah cards that currently sat in my inbox waiting to be edited. By the time Fiona got home, I'd fleshed out enough of the story to know it was definitely not the right vehicle for Gary Oldman. And it was that thought that remained dominant as I made sure my changes had saved and closed the document.

I right-clicked on the file on my desktop, clicked on Rename, and then hit Backspace fourteen times before typing out my new working title: *Untitled Hamish MacDougal Project.*

A hug from one you love...

Warm shelter on a cold night...

A meal when you're hungry, and a

drink when you thirst...

All of these things you wouldn't dare refuse.

And so it should be with opportunity.

Bon Voyage!

Heartlite® Greeting Card Co., Number 06-89DOoW

FEBRUARY 4, 2006

"Does Fiona know?"

I sniffed, determined to put an end to my tears long enough to enjoy the waffles that had just appeared before me as if courtesy of a wish granted by a Belgian genie. Liam thanked the waiter and asked for more orange juice, and that gave me a moment to think about his question.

Would Fiona even care?

She had gone with Vera Wang to fashion week in Paris and had fallen in love—with Paris, which didn't surprise or disappoint me, and with some forty-nine-year-old designer she hardly knew named Luc Pierre, which did both. It was doomed to fail, and throwing away her life in Los Angeles for some guy she had just met was the most irresponsible thing she could possibly do. But it was awfully difficult to convince her of that when Vera Wang was offering her a dream job running her Parisian office. She'd packed up her things, accused me of being so miserable in my own life that I couldn't cope with her getting everything she could ever want, and left for France. That had been four months ago, and we hadn't spoken since.

"No," I finally replied after the waiter walked away. "She doesn't know. You know I haven't talked to her."

He nodded. "Yes. I know. That's why I asked."

"Oh, Liam. Don't start that again."

In her absence, I'd moved from West Hollywood to Los Feliz, where I found a great deal on a studio apartment and began living by myself for the first time in my life. In her absence, I took on some freelance writing jobs to bring in more income—and to keep me busy. In her absence, I took a trip to Napa Valley and discovered I possessed a covetable nose and palate for fine wine—which was a complete waste since, in her absence, I discovered I didn't like wine much at all. And, in her absence, I met, fell in love with, and had my heart broken by Malcolm Larcraft.

In her absence, Liam was the person I talked to about all of it.

"I just think it will be a shame if you don't get in touch with her while you're in the area." He had run out of juice again, so he reached over and grabbed my coffee and took a sip.

"Liam, I've never been the best at geography—that's no secret—but I do know that Italy to France isn't quite like here to Burbank." I quickly visualized the boot of Italy on a globe and tried to picture where France was, just to be sure. Yep. Definitely farther than Burbank.

"But compared to France from California? You'll be in the area, Olivia."

I smiled at him. It was the first time I had smiled in a few days.

"Why do you always call me Olivia?"

He took another sip of my coffee as he looked around impatiently for the waiter. "Do you mind?"

"No," I answered truthfully, though I wasn't sure if he meant did I mind that he called me Olivia or did I mind that he was stealing all my coffee. With Liam, I didn't mind any of it. "But I think you and Fiona's mother are the only people who have ever called me that on a regular basis. It's usually Liv." Fiona called me Livi. That was my favorite.

He finally got the waiter's attention and arranged for more juice for him and more coffee for me, since he had finished it off.

"I'm just curious," I continued. "Is it because you want to be different from everyone else? Do you want it to be a special connection shared only between the two of us?" I'd been teasing as I first began proposing that theory, but I'd accidentally gotten caught up in the appeal of it. "That would be a nice reason."

"That *would* be a nice reason." He smiled. "But sadly, no. The truth is nothing quite that charming or dashing, I'm afraid. When we met, you told me your name was Olivia. You never asked me to call you anything different. So I haven't."

Ah, Liam. Pragmatic, sensible Liam, who never got caught up in romantic fantasies or unrealistic expectations. With Liam, hidden layers were only waiting to be discovered—not disguised in order to create an aura of mystery. I suspected that any mystery that remained was every bit as mysterious to him as it was to me. What I saw was what I got. After years of Fiona's romance and rose-colored glasses, I told myself it was nice to spend most of my time with someone who saw the world as I did.

We finished breakfast, and Liam paid the bill. With his generous tip he left a polite note explaining that he would have tipped more, but he did have to wait quite awhile for his orange juice. Then I bundled up in my jacket, scarf, and hat, and we left.

"It's sixty-eight degrees. You can't be that cold."

I sighed. "Sadness makes me cold."

Despite the fact that I couldn't allow myself to spend more than five unprotected minutes in the sun without burning and freckling, I loved the heat. Yes, I had moved to California to make it as a screenwriter, and I had grown to love LA for its laid-back vibe and general "chill" mentality, but deep down it was all about the heat. I loved the salty sea air on my skin, and I loved the boost that a few minutes under the sky's natural heat lamp always gave me. Boston was great—and would always be home—but Boston got cold in the winter. Sometimes, unfairly, Boston got cold when it wasn't even winter at all. The chill of the air off of the Harbor compared to the warm breeze off of the Pacific? No contest.

Misery and cold go hand in hand, and each results in the other.

We walked in silence for a few minutes, and then Liam said softly, "I'm so sorry about Malcolm. I feel responsible."

I'd be lying if I said I hadn't once thought, *If Liam had never introduced me to him, my heart wouldn't be crumbling into the million little pieces that it is now.* But I didn't blame him. Of course I didn't blame him.

"You can't blame yourself. I should have known better. How could it have ever worked out?"

Boynes & Madison, Attorneys-at-Law, had become

Boynes, Madison & Larcraft a year earlier when, at age thirty-five, Malcolm became a senior partner. In August of 2005 the new partner made his first hire, stealing Liam Howard away from Kubrick & Coppola—thereby taking away the many opportunities for humor I'd always managed to discover each time Liam's employer was mentioned.

Liam and Malcolm had attended Harvard Law together and were part of the same graduating class. After graduation, Liam moved to California, passed the bar, and began working his way up the ladder from one small firm to the next. Malcolm, meanwhile, moved to DC and clerked for a Supreme Court justice before being hired by Boynes & Madison. In addition to all of his legal brilliance, he had this gorgeous blond hair that reminded me of the end of *The Way We Were* when Barbra Streisand brushed Robert Redford's bangs out of his eyes and he grabbed her hand and pulled her into his arms. On more than one occasion I had called Malcolm "Hubbell" and told him his girl was lovely while doing my best Streisand impression. The fact that he kept letting me do that should have been my biggest indication that it was all too good to last.

"Well, I'm glad you've decided to go through with Italy. It will be good for you." Liam made a gallant attempt to divert the conversation away from Malcolm as we reached the stoop of my apartment. My sad, lonely apartment. "I could go with you if you want."

Tears welled up in my eyes, and I hugged him. "Thank you. That's very sweet. Unfortunately, I'm not sure that's a good career move for you."

Malcolm had given the tickets to me at Christmas, but we'd put the trip off because he was in the middle of an important case. We were scheduled to leave February 7, but now, of course, I was going alone. When we broke up, he'd insisted I keep both tickets. "Take a friend and have the time of your life on me," he'd said. As it turned out, my only friend was his employee, who just happened to be another ex of mine.

"How long are you going to stay?" Liam put his arm around me and ushered me into my apartment after he used his emergency key to unlock the door.

I shrugged. "I don't know. A couple weeks, I guess."

"I think that's a mistake."

"It should be okay. That's one good thing about my job. I can work from anywhere."

"No. I don't think that's long enough."

I thought about that as I took off my Southern California winter wear and replaced it with a blanket. I'd just said it myself—I could work from anywhere. I knew Liam would check on my apartment for me and water my plants. Now that I lived in Los Feliz, I was only about two miles from his East Hollywood apartment. Why *not* stay longer? Apart from the fact that it was just too depressing, of course. I had no way to know for sure, but I had strongly suspected Malcolm was going to propose in Italy. We had only dated for three months, but we'd both fallen hard and fast.

I had. *I'd* fallen hard and fast. Who knew what Malcolm had felt?

"I was in love with him, Liam."

"I know." He sat next to me on the couch and let me cry on his shoulder, as he had countless times over the course of the last week since Malcolm had ruined everything.

I had been completely blindsided. We were together all the

time, and when we weren't, we were calling each other or texting. E-mailing. Writing each other long letters that spanned days. I hadn't been able to work out how he'd even found the time to cheat on me.

"And I thought he loved me. How stupid am I?"

"You're not stupid."

"No, seriously, I am. I let it get away from me."

He leaned his head against mine. "You let *what* get away from you?"

"All of it. I think I just wanted . . ."

"What?"

I sniffed. "I don't know. Maybe all of that stuff Fiona said. I think I wanted to maybe not think so much. Just for a while. To see if she was right. To see if I was keeping myself from being happy by insisting that relationships checked off all my boxes." I shuddered at the memory of her words and, more painfully, the distance in her eyes as she said them. "I knew he wasn't my type. I knew I was not meant to spend my life with a guy like Malcolm Larcraft."

But, hey, what harm could come from spending time with him? From having some fun? From seeing, just for a little while, how the leading men of the world spoil their girlfriends? From being whisked here, there, and everywhere in the name of romance? From not thinking so much for one blasted time in my life?

Turns out a lot of harm could come from it. I should have paid more attention to the lessons being taught in *The Way We Were* rather than focusing so much on how pretty Robert Redford was in his prime.

"I wish I knew how to explain how it feels, Liam. Can you

even imagine? Knowing that this is the person you will be with forever. Knowing—I mean *knowing*—that this person prizes you above all others. And then finding out that you had it completely wrong. Finding out it was one-sided? It's humiliating."

I exhaled as I patted him on the knee and stood to go to the kitchen to make coffee.

"You're right," he called after me. "That *is* humiliating. But that's not the case here."

As I mindlessly made coffee, I thought that through. I'd known Malcolm and I could never work—I'd known it from the beginning—but somewhere along the way he'd convinced me otherwise. It hadn't been easy for me to accept that he loved me in the first place. Or, going back a bit further, that he was even interested in going out with me. I'd seen him, that night we met, surrounded by women who fit with him. The Fionas of the world who sought after the epic love story and seemed right at home within its pages. But he was also surrounded by supporting characters, like me. Unlike me, those other kooky best-friend types didn't seem to know they didn't get to ride off into the sunset with a Redford. They clamored for his attention while I watched from a safe distance, offering humorous commentary for Liam's benefit. If only I had managed to keep my guard up. If only Malcolm hadn't convinced me, for one glorious season of my life, that a Redford wouldn't always choose a Michelle Pfeiffer or a Demi Moore or a Meryl Streep. At some point along the way I'd allowed myself to believe that sometimes a Redford chooses . . .

"Joan Cusack." A bitter laugh escaped as I walked back in and stood by the window.

"I'm sorry?" Liam asked.

"Nothing," I said, shaking my head.

"He loves you, Olivia. He didn't want it to end . . ."

His voice trailed off, and I turned to him. His eyes darted away from mine, and I stared at him in desperate shock.

"He talked to you?"

"I shouldn't have said any—"

"Did he tell you that?" It didn't matter. He'd cheated on me. I'd gotten it wrong. I was better off. *All true.* And how nice it would have been if all of that truth had been enough. My voice trembled as I whispered, "Liam, what did he tell you?"

He groaned, then stood and walked toward me. "Okay, listen to me. And I mean listen carefully. If we're going to have this conversation, it's not going to be without some ground rules. You know my loyalty is to you, and I will tell you whatever you want to know. Yes, he talked to me. Unfortunately. He talks to me about, well . . . far too much."

"Do you know who she was?"

He raised his hand to silence me. "I will tell you whatever you want to know. But anything you learn you can't unlearn, Olivia. Do you understand what I'm saying? All I'm asking is that before you ask me any questions, you make sure you want to know the answers."

Of course I wanted to know. Of *course* I did. Why wouldn't I? The bigger consideration in my mind was *what* did I want to know? I wanted to know how he could do that to me. I wanted to know who she was. I wanted to know if he loved her. I wanted to know why he'd wasted his time on me in the first place.

Tears sprang to my eyes.

No. Liam was right. Whatever I found out, I would always know. What good would any of that newfound—yet eternal—knowledge do me, apart from breaking my heart anew? Yet to have answers—there was tremendous appeal in the possibility. Each night, as I inevitably tossed and turned and made feeble attempts to count sheep, my brain only ever found distraction by compiling an ever-growing list. So many questions. The desire to receive even one answer for a change felt irresistible. But which answers could I handle? Which ones were better left unknown?

I stared into Liam's eyes for the longest time, trying to decide how much I could handle.

Finally, I laughed through my tears. "I don't know what I want to know!"

"Okay, then," he said quietly. "How about I tell you what I think you *need* to know?"

Tears rolled down my cheeks as I silently nodded.

"He loves you. I know you're doubting that, but don't. He's fully aware you were the best thing that ever happened to him. He screwed up. It was a one-time thing that didn't mean anything. And yes, I know how trite and predictable that sounds, but I don't think they're just empty words in this case. I'm pretty sure he would give anything for it not to have happened. And probably the most important thing you need to know is that he still doesn't realize that you and I used to date, so he has no idea how awkward it is for me when he tells me all this stuff." He smiled and winked.

I grinned at him and felt a swell of pride and appreciation, as I always did when he was funny. And, as always, that swell of pride led to resurfacing guilt—and questions about my own sanity. How much longer would Liam and I have stayed together if I hadn't seen the writing on the wall? Fiona had always questioned my sanity, I was pretty sure. She had never understood why I couldn't go along for the ride in relationships and see where they took me. She'd never been the biggest Liam fan, but she'd also never understood why I chose to walk away from him just when, in her mind, he was beginning to get interesting. With the end of that relationship, she had finally granted me full-blown admittance to the Fiona Mitchell Dating Disaster Sanitarium.

Just imagine if she had been around through the Malcolm era.

Liam was a good guy. A *great* guy, even. And the thing was, he always had been. Though obviously a cliché that sends shivers down the spines of all single adults, our breakup had been a textbook case of "It's not you, it's me." Fiona had been wrong, and so had I. Liam had *always* been interesting, with or without an unleashed sense of humor and the ability to make my heart question my brain. I was so glad he was my friend, and without a doubt, ending our romantic relationship had been the best thing that ever could have happened for our friendship. So why, when the guilt came to light and I was forced to consider how different life might have been if we had stayed together, did I always end up wondering if I had made a horrible mistake?

What would have happened if I had paid attention to Fiona's criticisms earlier, when they were still loving pieces of advice—before they became parting shots meant to inflict pain? What would have happened if I had allowed myself to get caught up in the romance rather than the checkboxes with Liam rather than Malcolm?

I shook it off, as I always did when those thoughts came

to mind. It wasn't that I had those thoughts often. I didn't. It was usually just in moments when Liam's goodness came shining through in full force. Moments when he was there for me and no one else was. Moments when his button-up shirt was unbuttoned just low enough that I could see enough of his chest to realize what a good body he had . . . and remember what a good kisser he was . . .

"So, how's the screenplay coming?" he asked, oblivious to the new direction my thoughts had taken me, thank goodness. I was taken aback by his abrupt change of topic, but I welcomed it.

I rolled my eyes and removed my top-layer shirt—feeling warmer all of a sudden. "What screenplay?"

"That's what I thought." He grabbed my hands in his. "Look, why not take some time? *Lots* of time. Go to Italy on Malcolm's dime and get inspired. Pour all of your emotions about Malcolm and Fiona and whomever or whatever else into creating something you're proud of. And then, when you're ready, come home."

"'When I'm ready,'" I muttered. "Ready for what?"

"I don't know. *Ready.* For whatever comes next."

"I'm thirty-three years old, Liam." I sniffed and attempted to focus on the warmth and security radiating from his hands into mine. "If I'm not ready by now—"

"I don't think we should ever stop getting ready. If we're ready for the thing that's two, three steps down the road, what's the point of the thing that's supposed to come first? Just think of how many things we might end up skipping."

The sun reflected through the window and off of his dark hair, which perfectly matched his eyes, and I noticed how the natural light brought out the hidden shades that at first glance could so naively be interpreted simply as "brown." How many other things about him had I diminished in a similar way? Just like giving hair color a one-word name, I guess it had been easier that way.

"Should I give Malcolm another chance?"

I think the question surprised Liam nearly as much as it surprised me.

He pulled away gently, grabbed me a tissue, then turned and faced the window. "It's not for me to say."

"I'm asking for your opinion." The confusion bubbling up inside of me threatened to boil over if the pressure didn't release somewhere. "I trust you, Liam. And if you say it was a one-time thing, I believe you. If you say he still loves me, I believe you."

Without the warmth of his hands and his eyes, my misery took on the form of a chill once again. I forced myself to disassociate the coldness and misery from Liam and instead remember the life I thought I was going to have with Malcolm. I forced myself to remember that Malcolm was the man I loved. *Malcolm* was the reason my heart was in shambles.

"Will you please tell me what you think?" I pleaded.

He turned and walked back to me again, and I saw that the warmth in his eyes had grown into a fire. "No, Olivia. You shouldn't give him another chance. I don't care if it was one night or if he had a wife and a houseful of kids you never knew about. If he's able to let his thoughts drift away from you and to another woman for even one moment, then he doesn't love you enough." A touch of anger permeated every word he spoke. I understood that I was neither the source nor the recipient. "Yes, I believe he loves you, but he doesn't love you *enough*. Plain and simple. You deserve someone whose love for you causes them to be a person worthy of you."

The fire intensified as his fingers touched my cheek and he gently wiped my tears. "And then the tricky thing is going to be convincing *you* that you're worthy of *them*," he said so quietly that I couldn't help but wonder if he had meant to say it aloud at all.

He seemed to be wondering the same thing. He cleared his throat and broke our eye contact. "When you find someone who loves you enough to be good enough for you . . . I think that's the one you shouldn't let go."

I'd never made a habit of allowing my heart to stand in the way of my brain—the Malcolm Larcraft months aside—but in that moment, Liam captured them both. That was a difficult combo to dismiss.

"Hey, Liam," I whispered hoarsely. "Maybe it's time we talk about things."

His shoulders fell and his eyes darted away from me again. "'Things'?"

"Yeah. Things. *Us* things. I know we've avoided it like the plague for two years, but—"

He silenced me by gently grabbing my face in his hands. Our eyes locked, and he whispered, "Olivia," as he slowly leaned his face toward mine. I closed my eyes, not realizing until that moment just how much I had missed the feel of his lips, or how desperate I was to experience the sensation again.

But he only kissed my cheek before pulling me into a gentle, platonic hug. The tears began to fall again, and I felt a shiver of disappointment and desire run down my spine even as I jumped at the opportunity to seek refuge in his comforting embrace.

"Let's not do that," he whispered in my ear. "I can't be your rebound. And I know you don't mean it that way, but . . ."

He pulled away but kept his hands on my face as he pressed his forehead against mine, looked into my eyes, and sighed. "The thing is, I *do* know how that feels. To know that this is the person you will be with forever. To know, I mean *know*, that this person prizes you above all others. And I understand what it's like to find out you had it completely wrong. I can't go back there, Olivia. In the past two years, somehow, against my better judgment at times, you have become my best friend. Let me hold on to that, please. I . . ." He took a deep breath and released it slowly. "I don't think I'm strong enough to go through that again. Especially now, if I had to go through it without my best friend by my side."

I sobbed into his shirt with my head still against his chest, and he held me. How had I ever let a little thing like him not being funny convince me that Liam Howard was not a leading man? And how had I ever let a little thing like realizing he was perfect for me compel me to do anything other than hold on to him for dear life and never let go?

I wanted to say something. I wanted to say a *million* things. But there were no words that could capture the confusion and the chaos of my heart.

"I need to get back to the office," he said, and he pulled away from me just as abruptly. "Call me if you need help packing."

"Liam . . ."

As he headed to the door, he looked back at me—so briefly—and I saw the despair in his eyes. And for the first time I realized the despair hadn't just suddenly appeared. It had been there for two years, while I had been perfectly content seeing things as nothing more than brown.

He stopped with one foot out the door and whispered, without turning to face me, "I did tell you not to ask anything you weren't sure you wanted to know."

He was gone, and I was left gasping for breath, having no doubts about what I had just learned. Liam never would have cheated on me. Liam had loved me enough to be good enough for me. And, perhaps even still, Liam never let his thoughts drift away from me to another woman. Not even for a moment.

I could never unlearn that.

Sometimes the words just aren't

there when we need them.

We know how our heart feels,

And we know what we need to say,

But when we try . . .

Nothing.

It's not enough, but let me start with "I'm sorry."

Please don't give up on me while I work through the rest.

Heartlite® Greeting Card Co., Number 07-FC8oN2

FEBRUARY 4, 2007

"Hey, Liv! We're running just a few minutes late, but we should be there before you even get through customs. Can't wait to see you!"

"Okay. We're here now. The arrivals board says you've landed, so we'll wait for you at baggage claim. I'll grab your luggage if it gets here before you do. I'm assuming you're still using the Samsonite set your parents bought you in college? Seriously, Livi... can't wait to see you."

"Did you go to the right baggage claim? We have all your bags, I think. I like what you did with the spruced-up duct tape. I was telling Liam I'll probably never get you to throw these suitcases away, now that they've proven they can survive internationally. Where are you? Hurry up! I keep looking at all of the people standing around, and none of them are you. At least, I don't think they are! Is it possible that we haven't seen each other in so long that I don't even recognize you? No telling what a year in Italy does to a Boston girl. Have you started wearing designer? Oh, please say you've started wearing designer! Oh! There you are! Nope. Not you. Unless you're a lesbian now. Are you a lesbian now?"

"I'm starting to worry. Liam is scaring me with all sorts of legal horror stories. What if you are being detained for smuggling something into the country illegally? Ooh! What if it's a Fendi bag? If it's a Fendi bag, all you have to do is somehow get a message to me, and I'll find a way to break you out. I just happen to have a lawyer here with me. We've got this. In the name of Fendi!"

I was not, in fact, being detained. I was also not dressing in designer. Or a lesbian. What I was, if I were to be completely honest, was tipsier by the minute from mango margaritas. I'd almost made it out. I'd gotten off of the plane and through customs pretty quickly, but I'd gotten hung up at Señorita Taqueria, just past Gate C36 in the international terminal.

I listened to the four messages Fiona had left me, and I felt guilty. I did. But not guilty enough to make my way to baggage claim, and certainly not guilty enough to keep from ordering the third margarita before I had finished the second. I knew I should have been honest with her when she asked if it was okay if Liam came along, but what could I possibly say?

Making up with Fi had been easy, but I knew that reclaiming my friendship with Liam would present a different set of challenges. I felt lucky that he was even willing to lay eyes on me again, much less give me a ride home from the airport. So I'd decided I could just keep my mouth shut—apart from occasional well-timed apologies—and my head down, and maybe eventually he'd get used to me being there. Like when they put a new stop sign in your neighborhood. But now, knowing he was just thirty-six gates, a security checkpoint, an escalator, two moving sidewalks, and another escalator away, I didn't know if I could go through with it.

After I had been in Venice for about six months, I'd decided it was time to move on to Rome. Why? Because I could. I had decided that if I was going to live the vagabond life, I was going to do it right. I made no real plans, and I had no real structure in my life. For the first time ever, I didn't set an alarm each night before I went to bed. That was something I had always done, even as a writer of maudlin greeting cards—a job for which I had only to meet quotas and deadlines without the confines of structured work hours. I don't know why I did that, but I did. But not in Italy. No, sir. I awoke when the sun peeked through the window of my little apartment, and even then I didn't always get out of bed. I would stay there until I was forced to address my body's needs, either for bladder relief or cappuccino, whichever came first. And then I would spend the day writing—meeting my Heartlite quota, of course, but always being struck by so much creativity and inspiration that there was plenty of time to focus on my screenplay.

And one day I'd decided it was time to go to Rome. But when I got online to make travel arrangements, I discovered that a local airline was having a weekend special on flights to Paris. I didn't think twice. I just booked a flight. It wasn't until I stepped off the plane at Charles de Gaulle that I remembered Fi was there, and I decided it was time to let bygones be bygones. So I casually walked into Vera Wang's studio and interrupted Eva Longoria's bridal-gown fitting.

Okay, that was a lie, of course. All of it. I had found myself, on more than one occasion, desperately trying to convince myself it had actually happened that way, but none of it was true—apart from the Eva Longoria part. The truth was just far too depressing.

The reality was that in Venice I'd still set an alarm each and every day, and when it went off, I would get up, take care of my body's needs, do a little work—for Heartlite and as many freelance assignments as I could round up, but rarely the screenplay—and then quite often take a nap. The sun probably would have been peeking through the window of my apartment if I hadn't covered it with a scarf to keep it as dark as possible. While on sabbatical in one of the most beautiful cities in the world, I went through the darkest period of my life.

I am not a person who requires many people in my life, but there in Venice I discovered that I did require Fiona Mitchell. I didn't have her number in Paris, so I called Vera Wang's studio. They told me they had no one by Fiona's name working there. I knew what that meant. Fi was so desperate to avoid me that she'd told her staff if some woman with a slightly Bostonian but mostly nondescript American accent ever called, they were to tell her there was no one there by that name. That was the only explanation.

Well, I wasn't going to put up with that. Fi and I had the bond that never fades—that of pee in our pants. She couldn't get away from me that easily.

It was true that I was getting ready to go to Rome for

a while, but only because my lease agreement in Venice was expiring and I'd found a much less expensive studio apartment in Rome. I got moved to Rome and then hopped on a flight to Paris. I certainly did not casually walk into Vera Wang's studio. In actuality, I sat at a café across the street and spied for four hours, waiting for Fi to enter or exit. When she did neither but Eva Longoria entered through a side door, I realized she was no doubt there to meet with Fiona.

It was then that I decided the moment had come. After checking my hair and makeup (because that's all that's needed to make me look like I belong at Vera Wang), I crossed the street, and then I tried to casually stroll in. I got to the door and attempted to pull it open, but it wouldn't budge. I pulled harder, determined that would do the trick. Then it turned into a scene from a Garry Marshall movie as Eva Longoria herself came to the door to assist me and pulled the door open from the inside. (Apparently I'd just needed to push, though I certainly wasn't familiar with all the French customs.) The force of the door opening threw me smack-dab onto the floor in the showroom, where I found myself surrounded by Eva Longoria, Vera Wang, and several other confused and amused women.

None of whom were Fiona.

See, here's the funny part: she actually didn't work there anymore. According to Vera, Shonda Rhimes had stolen her away to work on the set of her new medical drama, *Grey's Anatomy*. In Los Angeles, of all places.

"That doesn't make any sense!" I voiced my frustration to Vera and Eva once I'd gotten up off the floor and convinced them I wasn't a crazy lady.

"That's what I told her," Vera said. "It's a much more difficult job for a lot less pay."

"Hey, isn't that the McDreamy show?" Eva asked. Vera and I nodded and sighed. "Well then, I don't know anything about your friend, but I'd say it makes all the sense in the world."

After we spent a few minutes McDaydreaming about Patrick Dempsey, Vera spoke once more. "You know, I suspected at the time that it was more about wanting to go back to LA, and now that I've met you, I'm pretty sure I was right."

"Vera Wang, you are so wise," I marveled.

I went back to Rome and called my Los Feliz apartment to check my messages—just in case Fiona had reached out. And Liam answered.

I hung up.

What was he doing there? Ridiculous scenarios flooded my mind. Had Malcolm found out about Liam's past with me and fired him, leading to Liam losing his apartment because he couldn't afford it and moving into my empty place because he had a key? Or did he miss me so much that he spent all of his free time there, smelling my sweaters and listening to Alanis? Was it possible that after all that had happened and the way I had fled to Italy without another word, he was still considerate enough to water my plants?

When my phone rang minutes later, I jumped as if the device were about to attack me.

Stupid caller ID!

I had not received a single phone call the entire time I was in Italy, and I only occasionally chatted with my parents and my brother, Brandon, on Skype. I'd made sure to leave my parents' number at the apartment for Liam in case of an emergency, and Brandon would always know how to get in touch with me. Needless to say, Liam had not reached out—for emergency or any other types of reasons.

"Hello?" I answered nervously after the third ring.

"Livi . . . It is so good to hear your voice."

I burst into tears, and for a moment all of the wondering went away. I didn't think about how Fiona got my number, and for a little while I didn't think about Liam at all. We laughed, we cried, we apologized, we lamented the lost time, and we got all caught up. Fiona had, in fact, taken the *Grey's Anatomy* job, at least in large part, in order to return to LA and make amends with me. She had left behind Paris, Luc Pierre, and Vera Wang. For me. She had chosen our friendship. (Also, Luc Pierre was sort of a jerk, it turned out. But still. It was for me.) There were new tenants living at the West Hollywood apartment, so she'd called Brandon to track me down. When she learned I had gone to Italy, she decided not to contact me because she knew I would choose her, just like she had chosen me. She was right. I would have. I would have run home, and she didn't want that. She was happy that I had gone to Europe to focus on my screenplay, and she thought it was something I needed. And she would be there waiting, whenever I got home.

Considering I had made no progress whatsoever on the screenplay, I'd decided to make the most of the four months left on the lease of my apartment in Rome and then make it back to the States in time for Christmas. But in early December, another phone call from Fi led to another change of plans. Actually, it led to a change of everything.

Greetings. Small talk. Comfortable rhythms. A lifetime of inside jokes.

It was all wonderfully normal for a few minutes, and then she said, "Hey, can I ask you something?"

"Of course."

"What do you think of Liam?"

The question seemed so absurd and impossible to answer at long-distance rates that at first I didn't know what to do except make jokes. "Liam who? Gallagher? Yeah, I don't know . . . Oasis is okay, but I honestly don't know which one is Liam and which one is Noel."

She chuckled. "I'm serious, Liv."

Our first transcontinental phone call had run so long that we'd both vowed to give up coffee for a month to help pay for it. (I failed spectacularly, but I was in Italy and I'm only human.) We had spoken on Skype a few times since then, but never about Liam, apart from the initial confirmation that he was, indeed, still checking on my apartment. When he saw the international number on the caller ID, he'd picked it up. When I hung up, he'd taken a chance that Fiona still had the same cell phone number I'd once given to him as an emergency contact. Within about three minutes, he had gotten in touch with Fi, she had gotten in touch with Brandon, and my phone had rung in Italy for the first time. Apart from that explanation, there had been no other mention of Liam—and for that, my still confused heart was grateful.

"You know what I think about Liam." Who was I kidding? Even *I* didn't know what I thought about Liam. "He's a fantastic guy. Brilliant, kind, funny . . ." My voice trailed off, but the echo of regret filled the silence.

"He *is* funny, isn't he?" Fi asked. "I sure didn't think so when I first met him."

I swallowed down the bitter taste forming in the back of my throat. "Oh, so . . . you've talked to him? Recently, I mean? I mean, since you've been back or . . ."

"Well, you know he called me when you called your apartment . . ."

"Yeah . . ."

"Obviously we only talked for a few seconds then. But, well, he'd asked me to call him after I talked to you. He just wanted to make sure you were okay, I think. So I did. And then, yeah . . . We've talked some since then."

I had no idea what I was feeling. It was sort of like I was experiencing *all* the emotions. Every last one of them. I was worried about what either one of them might have revealed about me to the other; I was jealous that Fi had gotten to talk to Liam, and jealous that Liam had gotten to talk to Fiona without having to even *pretend* to drink less cappuccino for a month; I was tickled pink that they'd managed to carry on a conversation with each other, as they never had when Liam and I were dating; I missed them both so much.

"That's great, Fi. I'm glad you two were able to connect a little. The truth is I didn't exactly leave in the best way. With Liam, I mean. I think it's good that—"

"Yeah, Livi, he told me." I heard her take a deep breath.

I hadn't called him before I left. I hadn't taken him up on his offer to help me pack. I hadn't asked him if he would give me a ride to the airport. I hadn't even met him for dinner on Monday evening the night before I was supposed to leave, despite the fact that I hadn't missed a Monday dinner with Liam in months. By Monday I was already gone, having given in to my desire to be a complete coward. I left a day early, just because I couldn't bear the thought of seeing that despair in his eyes again. Especially once I understood what caused it.

I didn't think about what came next. I couldn't allow myself to, I guess. I just left. I figured he'd still water my plants for a while out of a sense of responsibility and obligation, and then after a few weeks, he'd stop. I figured he'd try to call my parents to get in touch with me, but they were under strict orders to (1) not give Liam my contact information, and (2) get in touch with me the instant he called. Then I would decide what to do. By then, maybe I would be ready to stop being a coward.

Liam never called. But why would he? Apparently he'd had Fiona to talk to.

"Oh. He did?" The sunlight reflecting off of the white walls of my little apartment was blinding all of a sudden. I closed the shutters and welcomed the return of the darkness. "Look, I'm not proud of the way I handled any of that, but I was in a bad place. I'm sure he told you all about the breakup with Malcolm—"

"No, he didn't," she interjected. "Not much, anyway. Just that the two of you were planning to go to Italy together, and then he let you keep the trip when you broke up—but you told me that much the first time we talked."

"Look, it's fine if he told you what a mess I was. I get it. I'm going to tell you the whole story eventually anyway. I just kind of lost control—because of Malcolm, I mean."

"He didn't tell me anything about that, Liv. Honestly. He said it wasn't his story to tell."

"But the way I left . . ."

She sighed. "Yeah. Your story overlapped with his there, I guess."

I lay back on my bed and rested my arm over my eyes to further block out the little bit of sunlight slipping through the wooden slats of the shutters. "Well, I'm glad he was able to talk to you about it. Are you . . . I mean . . . Are you friends now?"

"We are."

My breath caught in my throat. Her confirmation was so instant. So absolute.

"That's great."

"And, well . . . the thing is, Livi . . . I think I really like him."

Fiona and I had never been interested in the same man. Not once. Well, with the possible exception of Matt Damon. But even then, Fiona loved *The Bourne Identity* while I was more of a *Talented Mr. Ripley* kinda gal. Those two Matt Damons do not count as the same man.

"You . . . you like Liam? As a friend, you mean? Or, like . . . as *more* than a friend?"

Having never been interested in the same man, or even the same boy, I suppose we had been able to skip over this sort of conversation in junior high and ever since. It felt awfully out of place in our thirties.

For the first time I noticed the slight tremble in her rambling voice. "I think as more than a friend. But that's why I called. I mean, nothing's happened. *Nothing.* We've just become friends, and that's all it ever has to be. I just . . . I guess I just wanted to see what you think. And, obviously, nothing has to happen, Livi. I know this is weird, even thinking about going out with your ex. But, I mean, you guys broke up, what? Like, four years ago? But I also know you got closer while I was gone. If you hadn't said that you were better as friends . . . I mean, that's what you said, right? But if it's just too weird, I completely understand. Seriously. Just say the word, and I won't give it another thought."

Fiona and Liam?

Nothing about that idea made sense to me. Nothing at all. Apart from the fact that they were my two favorite people in the whole wide world, and no other woman I had ever met was good enough for Liam, and no other man on the planet could probably ever be good enough for Fiona. He was exactly the type of man I'd always hoped she'd find. She was precisely the amazing kind of woman he deserved. They were both geniuses—though very different brands of geniuses. She would help him relax. He could help keep her grounded. They'd look amazing together—that was undeniable. Their children would be beautiful, perfect little brainiacs with a lot of ambition and a keen fashion sense.

But I was getting ahead of myself. There was one major flaw in the eternal bliss I was mapping out for them—and the Miserable & Heartbroken Spinsters Hall of Fame induction ceremony I was preparing for myself.

"No, of course I wouldn't mind, Fi. Except I'm not sure if he's interested in dating right now."

I hadn't spoken to him in ten months, so I hoped she didn't press my authority on that opinion. Especially since the only authority I could claim was the realization, the last time we talked, that he was still in love with me—and, nearly a year since in Italy, hoping and fearing equally that he loved me still.

Her nervous laughter seemed out of place. But then, didn't everything? "I think he's interested. He's been asking me for weeks, and I've been putting him off. I knew I had to talk to you first, but it seemed so complicated, and I didn't even think it was worth it. But then . . . I just got off the phone with him, Livi. Right before I called you. And . . ."

My arm over my eyes wasn't enough of a dam to keep the tears contained. "And what, Fi?"

I heard the smile in her voice as she said, "As soon as I hung up, I missed him."

Now here I was, two months later—tipsy and afraid. Placing the blame on an unexpected rush of productive creativity, I'd extended my return flight one last time. But now they were just thirty-six gates, a security checkpoint, an escalator, two moving sidewalks, and another escalator away. And I couldn't handle it.

I looked down at my phone as it rang again, and this time I had consumed enough tequila to forget I wasn't supposed to answer it.

"Hello?" I answered innocently, having lost track of the fact that I was in hiding.

"Liv, where are you? Are you okay?"

"Hey, Fi Fi. No worries!" I slurred. "I just stopped for a refreshment."

"Did you just call me Fi Fi?" She paused, and then I heard her take a deep breath before she whispered, "Are you drunk?"

"Yes!" I laughed. "I most certainly am. Are you?"

"Livi, where are you?"

I told her, the best I could, comforted by the knowledge that I was in a sanctuary reserved only for ticketed passengers with their passports. And then we talked for quite a while. She didn't plead with me to make my way to baggage claim, and she didn't even ask me what was wrong. In retrospect, I should have known that was weird. But I had just enough alcohol in me to make me think, *This is nice.*

"Olivia."

I heard my name from a couple of feet behind me, and I turned around, still not suspecting a thing. And there he was.

"Oh, Liam. Hello," I said with a calm that could only be attributable to tequila and denial. "Fi, you'll never guess who's here."

"I'll see you soon, Livi. I love you." She hung up, and I was left with him. And the calm and the denial—and the tequila—faded a bit too quickly for my taste.

"May I sit down?" he asked as he gestured to the chair across the table from me.

"Hang on. How are you here?"

"Just on my way to—" He paused as he glanced down at the boarding pass in his hands. "Bandaranaike International Airport, apparently." I didn't say a word, but I looked at him with questions in my eyes, and he answered my unspoken inquiries. "It was the least expensive international flight of the day."

"Sorry," I said softly. "I'll pay you back."

"Don't worry about that."

"What are the odds you had your passport on you?"

"It was in my briefcase in the car. Fiona made me go get it about forty minutes ago, just in case. I think she was genuinely convinced you were being detained by the Fendi police."

"Can I get you another one? Or something for you, sir?" Josh, my margarita dealer, appeared beside the table.

"How many have you had?" Liam asked as he sat across from me, having given up on me ever giving him permission.

"Um . . . this next one would be . . . what, Josh? My second?" There had been a brief moment not all that long ago that I'd been convinced Josh and I were going to get married someday. I'm not sure which one of us broke it off.

"The next one would be your fourth," Josh answered, and I remembered why we ended things. We were never on the same page about anything.

Liam's eyes flew open but he recovered quickly. He pulled his wallet out of his back pocket and handed a credit card to Josh. "I think we're good. Thanks."

"Thanks, Josh!" I called out as he walked out of my life for possibly the last time.

A twitch overtook the corners of Liam's mouth. "His name tag said 'Kenny.'"

I shrugged. "I don't know what to tell you. He lets me call him Josh. It's fine."

It was quiet for a long time, and when I finally got up the nerve to look up at him to see why, I wished I hadn't. The corners of his mouth were still upturned, but his eyes—those breathtakingly complex eyes that seemed to have locked with mine from the moment I raised my head—were sad. I suddenly felt frighteningly and uncomfortably sober. Sadly, sadly sober. (But not so sober as to avoid a brief mental diversion as I convinced myself that if I were ever to form a rock band, I would name it Sadly Sober.)

"I'm sorry I left like that, Liam. Without saying goodbye or anything. I am. I just . . . I just couldn't deal with it. I didn't know how to deal with it. And it seemed like the easiest thing to just . . . not deal with it. Sorry."

"I'm not going to act like I wasn't hurt. I was. And then I was angry—for quite a while, actually. And then I just got, well, sad. It made me so sad to think that you didn't have enough faith in our friendship to know that it could withstand you telling me you didn't feel the same way about me that I felt about you."

I was so confused, but if he was saying what I thought he was saying, I knew it was time to set the record straight. "Liam—"

"No, let me finish." He placed his hand on mine, and I felt a shiver down my spine as I realized it was the first time I'd had anything more than incidental physical contact with another human being in a year. Liam had served as the bookends of those cold, desolate twelve months. "You see, one day I got out of bed, and I had this new sense of clarity about it all. If the roles were reversed, what would I have done? I had put you in such an awkward position. There you were, days from the end of a serious relationship, and I made it about us. About *me*. I wasn't much of a friend to you in that moment. Everything I said was true—I couldn't stand the thought of being your rebound, and I couldn't stand the thought of losing you again. I don't regret that. But you needed a friend, and instead I added my unresolved feelings for you to the pile you were sorting through. That wasn't fair to you. If I were you, I might have done the same thing you did."

"Run away to Italy without so much as a goodbye? Hide for a year? Completely discard one of the most important relationships, one of the most important people—" No. I refused to cry. I choked it all down and wished for a do-over. Somehow I just needed a do-over. "You never would have done what I did," I said softly. "You're better than that."

"No, I'm not better than that. I'm probably just not spontaneous enough for that." He laughed sadly. "I did let your plants die, though. During the angry period."

Everything in me wanted to tell him how wonderful he was. How sorry I was—not just for going to Italy the way I did or for letting a year pass without a peep, but for *everything*. For not being a better friend. For not being a better girlfriend. For not seeing how much he loved me when I was his. For not realizing how lucky I was when he was mine. And I almost—*almost*—had enough tequila in me to say it all. But he wasn't mine anymore. He was Fiona's.

We sat there in silence for several seconds. His hand had broken away from mine, and my eyes had broken away from his—it was too painful—and now I stared only at the melting ice of my mango margarita.

"I'm glad you have Fiona."

"Olivia," he began. "When Fiona came back, we bonded over—"

"Over me, and your mutual sense of abandonment," I said with a bitter laugh, adding only slight embellishment to the truth, I figured. "I get it, Liam. Really. I'm happy for you both."

Alcohol still coursing through my veins, I began weighing my options. As if I hadn't obsessed over every single ounce of option since December. I'd even weighed it all in milligrams while in Rome, just to make sure the metric system didn't reveal a better solution. I could either pretend I was over him, pretend I hadn't spent the last year thinking of nothing but him and what an idiot I'd been, and maybe—just maybe—I could keep him in my life. Or I could lay it all on the line right now and tell him how I felt. Tell him that letting him get away was the biggest mistake I'd ever made. And then I could see if he would choose me. If he didn't, I'd never be comfortable in his presence again, of course. And whether he chose me or not, I'd undoubtedly lose Fi, once and for all.

Unless, of course, she was so impressed with me for acting like a leading lady for the first time in my life that her pride outweighed the betrayal. I'd been watching *Grey's Anatomy*, if for no other reason than to spot Fiona's name in the end credits each week, and the show had taught me a thing or two about great dramatic "Pick me!" monologues. I mean, if I pulled it off, that would have to earn me *some* forgiveness points, right?

Except he wouldn't pick you. And you'll have lost them both for no reason whatsoever.

That was the problem. There was absolutely no precedence for a Joan Cusack begging a man to choose her and him responding by sweeping her into his arms and declaring his eternal devotion to her.

"Olivia, I can't believe . . . I mean, you know I'm not usually the type to get caught up . . ."

I looked up at him and saw that he was fidgeting nervously—running his hands through his hair, squirming in his seat, biting his lip.

Hang on! Was *he* going to deliver the speech?

"What? Caught up in *what*?"

He scooted his chair closer to mine and grabbed my hands again, and then he began laughing. The laugh was slightly unhinged and extremely frantic. It seemed to originate from his toes and increase in intensity all the way up. I'd never heard anything like it from him before, and it was the sexiest sound imaginable.

"I'm not the impetuous, spontaneous type, you know?"

I smiled so widely I worried my face might crack. "Yes, Liam, I know." How well I knew. How well I knew *him*.

"But do you know what day it is?"

I didn't. Not a clue. "Wednesday?"

The laughter ceased as he stared at me, amused, and then it—*everything*—was replaced by warmth. "No, it's Sunday. But I meant the date."

"Um . . . February 3?"

"It's the fourth."

"It was the third when I left Rome, I think. Or maybe it was the fifth—"

"Olivia!" He silenced me as he scooted his chair closer and placed his hand on my knee. "Don't you realize? It's Ironic Day!"

It was a miracle that my jetlagged margarita brain didn't seem to dampen his enthusiasm. And it was a miracle that I didn't spontaneously combust beneath the feel of his fingers on my leg.

"It's the day you met Hamish MacDougal," he continued. "It's the day we broke up. It's the day you realized who he was. It's the day . . ." He faltered for just a moment. "It's the last day I saw you, before you left. And now here we are."

Fiona would understand. She would have to understand. She'd been dating him for a few weeks, but what Liam and I shared was a *history*.

He didn't wait for me to speak, and that was a relief. I would have failed spectacularly.

"When you have a moment—a moment like this, years in the making—if you don't just go for it, you might regret it for the rest of your life. It can't just be a coincidence that you sat here inhaling margaritas until this moment, and it can't be a coincidence that I bought a ticket to Bandaranaike International Airport, of all places! It can't be a coincidence that we're sitting here together now, Olivia. It can't be, can it?"

I shook my head and struggled to breathe, and I watched his lips and tried to make sense of everything that was being spoken by them. But the more I watched, the more I wished they would stop making noise and instead find other ways to engage themselves.

"That's crazy!" The manic laughter returned. "Bandaranaike! This is the moment, and it needs to be seized."

Okay, so I didn't grasp the details of much of what he was saying, but I knew it meant he loved me. I knew it meant he was about to kiss me. He was going to kiss me good. And I knew it meant we were about to fly away together to . . . to . . .

"I'm sorry. Where is Bandana, Bananarama, whatever International Airport?" *Not that it matters*, I thought as I realized that wherever this place was, it was the new romance capitol of the world as far as I was concerned.

He erupted in delight. "Good to see your geography knowledge wasn't corrupted by a year in Europe. It's in Sri Lanka, Olivia. Sri Lanka!"

Sri Lanka. Hmm. Sure. I could work with that.

"It's warm there, right? As long as it's warm." What was

I saying? I'd have Liam to keep me warm. "Never mind. It doesn't matter."

Except he suddenly looked disgusted with me. "Have you forgotten?" I suppose the clueless expression on my face was the first indication that I had indeed forgotten whatever it was I was supposed to remember. "'We'll always have Sri Lanka,' right? Isn't that what Hamish MacDougal yelled at you as he drove away?"

Oh! Yeah, okay. *That's* what he was talking about. Though, actually, I still had no clue what he was talking about. *Just shut up and kiss me already, Liam!*

But he kept talking. "I'm just saying, it's more than a little ironic. Don't you think?" He winked and then began glancing behind me nervously. Was he afraid Fiona was going to buy a ticket to Iceland or somewhere and sneak up on us? Did *I* need to be afraid of that?

No, she'll understand.

"I just want to make sure we're on the same page here. You agree, don't you, that when a once-in-a-lifetime moment comes along, you need to go for it?"

"Of course!" I practically squealed. This was it. He wasn't making a lot of sense, but that didn't matter. I was ready to go for the once-in-a-lifetime moment. With Liam. Finally.

"Okay, then." He beamed. "It's February 4, I'm holding a ticket to Sri Lanka, of all places, you've just spent a year in Italy working on your screenplay . . . and Hamish MacDougal is in that men's room right behind you."

I opened my mouth to speak, but then it closed again. I didn't turn around or jump up or feel a rush of excitement. My mind was utter pandemonium. "I'm sorry . . . What?"

"Go for it, Olivia. When he comes out, go tell him who you are. So you're six years early. So what? What are the odds of this? Oh, man . . . Fiona is going to be so upset she missed this. You have to jump at this opportunity. It's your day. It's *his* day!"

Opportunity?

I didn't have a screenplay. Instead, I'd spent a year in Italy pining for Liam and writing as many greeting cards and freelance articles as I could so I could afford to keep running away from him. February 4 wasn't my day or Hamish MacDougal Day. It was Liam Howard Day. I didn't care about a connection with a Scottish stranger or the potential career breakthrough awaiting me in 2013. I only cared about Liam—and every February 4 seemed to pull me further and further away from him. I had allowed myself to believe that being with me was the opportunity he couldn't allow to pass by, but no. It was all about grabbing Hamish's attention as soon as he finished relieving himself.

"Oh, Liam, I don't know," I said as I let out a shaky breath, willing myself not to cry.

"Hey, hey," he whispered. "There he is. Go say something to him."

I couldn't make myself care enough to even turn around. "I don't have a screenplay, Liam. I have nothing. Italy was miserable and lonely and not at all inspiring. This was . . ." The sobs bubbled from my chest and throat and threatened to break free. "This was the worst year of my life, and I am nowhere closer to having a completed screenplay than I was a year ago. What could I even say to him? 'Congrats on the superstardom. Oh, me? Yep, still at Heartlite.'"

"Just say hello, Olivia. You have to."

That made me huffy. "No. I don't *have* to. There is

absolutely no point in it. He won't remember me anyway. Why would he? To him, it was probably just—"

There he was, walking past us with his carry-on over his shoulder, coffee in one hand, newspaper in the other. His hair was a lot shorter than it had been the day we met, but that wasn't the most noticeable difference.

"Holy muscles, Batman!" I exclaimed.

"That is possibly the lamest thing you have ever said," Liam accurately observed. "And there is quite the selection to choose from."

"Well, just look at him! What the crap? He looks like he could bench press me!" And that was after a year of tiramisu every night for dessert.

Liam stood and gathered my things for me. "He has that new movie coming out soon. He's a Greek god or something."

"No, Scottish," I muttered as I mentally warned myself not to drool.

I was flooded with memories of his arm around my shoulders. His laugh. His warmth. And whereas before each of those memories had been strictly platonic—a gentle reminder of a pleasant encounter with a pleasant man—my thoughts of Hamish MacDougal were now heading in a decidedly different direction. Perhaps somewhere between friendship and love there existed a February 4 consolation prize for my troubles. Liam was right. It was ironic beyond belief—and I'm not talking about needing a knife and being presented with ten thousand spoons or something. This was irony at its best.

Hamish MacDougal could be the greatest consolation prize in the history of all mankind.

"Make sure to tip Josh, alright?" I made a mental note to

pay Liam back for my bar tab, which was probably only slightly less than a flight to Bandaranaike International Airport, and then I wandered off in pursuit of my destiny.

He had a pretty good lead on me, but people kept stopping him to ask for autographs, so I figured I might have a chance. I knew I didn't look my best—after nearly twenty-four hours on planes and in airports and, at the risk of sounding repetitive, massive amounts of tequila—but if destiny had control of the wheel, it wouldn't matter.

"Hamish!" I called out when I thought I was close enough for him to hear. But there were ten other women and a few photographers calling out his name at the same time.

"Thanks, everyone," I heard him say over the crowd. "I must run now, or I'll miss my flight."

"Hamish! It's me! Olivia Ross." *Oh, wait, he doesn't know my name.* "We'll always have Sri Lanka!"

It only took a moment before I realized that with that statement, I had captured the attention of the wrong ears. Many, *many* wrong ears.

"You know him?"

"She *is* an actress! I knew I'd seen her in something."

"What happened in Sri Lanka?"

"It's so hard to recognize them when they're dressed like normal people."

About twenty women were surrounding me, pressing me for information, happy to at least talk to someone who knew the object of their affection if they couldn't talk to the man himself. I stood on my toes and tried to look over their heads, determined not to lose track of him before I could break free. But as they swirled around me and heat rose to the top of my head and I quickly surveyed the distance to the ground—preparing myself to pass out in spectacular fashion—I realized that romance movies do us a disservice by always treating someone's destiny as a good thing.

My destiny was that February 4 was always going to suck.

Peanut butter and marshmallows?

Peanut butter and bananas?

Peanut butter and mayonnaise?

Peanut butter and jelly?

Some pairings are a matter of preference.

But the two of you together?

That's a pairing everyone can agree on.

Congratulations to the perfect pair!

Heartlite® Greeting Card Co., Number 08-9V54D2

FEBRUARY 4, 2008

"I'm sure Fiona will be here any minute, Mr. and Mrs. Mitchell," I said as I glanced nervously at Liam, who was glancing at me the exact same way.

"Darling Liv," Mr. Mitchell began with a smile as he sipped his coffee. "You've known us your entire life. Why do you still insist upon calling us Mr. and Mrs. Mitchell?"

"Oh, I don't know." I laughed and smoothed out the cushion beside me on the couch. "Probably because I've known you since I was six. It would have felt pretentious to call you Landon and Jocelyn when you were helping us earn our Brownie badges."

"Well, I think it's time. Fiona doesn't still call your parents Mr. and Mrs. Ross, does she?"

"No." I stood and began gathering the empty saucers and cups in front of everyone except Mr. Mitchell, who was still working on his coffee. "But in all fairness, Fi has called my parents Henry and Susannah since well before it was appropriate to do so."

There were stark differences to be found in being reared by Henry and Susannah Ross as opposed to Landon and Jocelyn Mitchell. Though my family was not nearly as well-to-do as the Mitchells, I did grow up as part of the comfortable middle class. But the differences were more philosophical than that. Fiona's parents are kind, but not overly warm. Mine, on the other hand, are affectionate to a fault. At least I thought so as a child. As an adult, I found their devotion to one another comforting. But when I was young? Not so much. They've always been madly in love with each other, and my brother and I were in a near-constant state of "Eww!" and "Yuck!" throughout our childhood.

Fiona, meanwhile, thought my parents were wonderful and romantic, and while I ewwed and yucked, she oohed and aahed. "You're lucky, Livi," she would say. "It's a good thing that your parents love each other so much."

Many years removed from my embarrassment, I knew just how true that was—and I couldn't help but be impressed by the wisdom shown so early by young Fiona Mitchell.

"Here, let me help you." Liam grabbed half of the dishes from my hands and followed me into the kitchen.

"Where is she?" I whispered as soon as we were alone.

"I don't know." He pulled his phone out of his pocket and glanced at it as he had countless times during the hour we had been sitting with the Mitchells. "With traffic, we're going to be pushing it as it is, and after what I had to go through to get this reservation . . ." He stuffed his phone back into his pocket with an exasperated sigh.

"If she doesn't get here soon, we might have to go without her."

"That *does* sound like a fun evening," he replied

sardonically. "What can make an evening with your girlfriend's parents even *more* fun? Why, your girlfriend not being there, of course." He unbuttoned the cuffs of his dress shirt and rolled up his sleeves as he filled the sink with water to wash the dishes. I'd never seen him wash dishes before that day—also, we had a dishwasher—so it was pretty obvious he was just attempting to delay his return to the living room. "Do you think she's doing it on purpose?"

"Not a chance. You know how much she has been looking forward to finally going to Matisse." I grabbed the dish towel, preparing to dry—stalling every bit as much as he was. "Why would she do it on purpose?"

He sighed. "I don't know. She said something this morning about how she thought I could stand to make a little more effort with her dad."

"More effort than an overpriced dinner in Santa Monica?"

"Yes. What is wrong with people these days? When did we as a society decide it wasn't enough to *buy* people's affection?" He handed me a wet plate and washed another one before he spoke again. "I thought I was putting forth a pretty decent effort, actually. I can't help it that we don't have anything in common. What am I supposed to talk about with him?"

My eyebrows rose. "You're kidding, right?"

He shrugged, clueless.

"Sheesh, Liam." I stopped drying and looked at him. "He has a law background, he went to Yale—"

"I went to Brown and Harvard."

"Ivy League. Same thing. He reads big, boring books and watches Ken Burns documentaries, he loves the Red Sox—"

"See! I'm a Dodgers fan."

"It's baseball! You have *baseball*." I got back to drying. "I can confidently say you have more in common with him than all the other men Fiona has ever introduced to them combined."

"They make me nervous."

"Every guy is nervous around his girlfriend's parents."

"I wasn't nervous around *your* parents."

My breath caught in my throat, but I quickly released it. He'd been doing that more often lately. Nonchalantly referencing our past relationship. Liam had completely moved on and had no reason not to believe that I had as well. As far as he was concerned, I'd moved on years ago. The landmines had been carefully avoided for years, but in the past few months he had begun romping through the field with absolute certainty that everything had been defused.

How nice that must have been for him—to possess the freedom that comes with knowing the threat is gone.

"Well, my parents make you forget they're parents."

He laughed. "That's true."

"I love the Mitchells, but the authority-figure air never quite goes away with them." I lowered my voice even though at our new apartment in Studio City Fiona and I had walls thicker than matzo crackers for the first time in our adult lives. "I used to think they had a superiority complex, but they don't. They just legitimately are the coolest, most accomplished, most brilliant people in the room. *Every* room. In case you ever wonder where Fiona gets it . . . there you go."

The volume of his voice matched mine. "I feel like I do okay with Landon. I mean, nothing in common—apart from *everything*, according to you—but he doesn't put me on edge like Jocelyn does."

"For the first ten or fifteen years Fi and I were friends, Jocelyn called me Penny." I replied to his baffled expression with a shrug. "Yeah, I don't know why."

"I don't think that woman and I have said more than three words to each other in the last year, and yet with each of those three words she somehow stole a piece of my soul."

I laughed much louder than I meant to, which led to us both silently approaching the kitchen door and listening intently to make sure we hadn't been overheard. He hid behind the door while I poked my head out.

"You guys doing okay? Can I get you anything?"

Landon was flipping through television channels, and Jocelyn was thumbing through Fiona's newest *Harper's Bazaar*, and they looked about as relaxed as I had ever seen them. California agreed with them. There was something about going out without a jacket in February that people rarely got to experience in Stoneham, Massachusetts.

"Don't worry about us, sweetheart," Jocelyn replied with a smile.

"Any word from Fiona, Liam?" Landon asked, and Liam accidentally hit his forehead against the door he'd been eavesdropping against.

I swallowed down the threatening giggle as he awkwardly made his way around the door in a way that I knew he hoped made it appear as if he'd been across the kitchen. "No, sir. Not yet."

They both returned to their distractions without another word, and Liam and I returned to the four or five dishes left in the sink.

"You're so smooth," I whispered, and he laughed softly.

We washed and dried side by side in silence, until he nudged me with his elbow and said, "So, how've you been?"

I tilted my head and smiled at him quizzically. "You mean since we last spoke ten seconds ago?"

"Nah, it's never just you and me much anymore. We don't get to talk about things. So . . . how *are* things? How's work? Are you seeing anyone? How's the screenplay?" He offered me a saucer, but when I went to grab it, he didn't let go. "Hey! It's Hamish MacDougal Day, isn't it?"

I rolled my eyes. "I thought we were calling it Ironic Day."

"What you choose to call it is between you and destiny. Makes no difference to me."

He smiled and released the saucer into my hands, and I groaned. After the last few rounds of February 4, I'd contemplated petitioning Congress or the United Nations or the Calendar Council or whoever was responsible for such things to strike the date from the records—sort of like how sometimes buildings didn't have a thirteenth floor. A year prior I hadn't become fully coherent until Liam and I were already through security and sitting at baggage claim, Liam on one side of me, Fiona on the other. He'd managed to convince the TSA officers that I was just jetlagged, but I for one was pretty convinced that I had just experienced a complete mental and emotional break. A whole lot of sleep and water improved that part of the outlook somewhat, but I was so embarrassed. Even still, a year later. Of what had happened, sure. But even more about what I'd *thought* was going to happen.

And that wasn't even my worst February 4.

"It's just a day, Liam. Admittedly, it's a day that has seen a string of dramatic coincidences. But it's just a day, and we shall not speak of it again this year."

He smirked. "We shall not?"

"We shall not."

He turned off the water, dried his hands, and turned to me. "Okay, then. Let's talk about all those other things. How are you?"

"How's work? How's the screenplay?" I echoed his earlier questions. "Fine. Work's fine. Nothing new. Graduation-card demand seems to be up, so I suppose that says good things about the state of the American education system." I shrugged and he smiled. "The screenplay . . . not bad, actually. But that's all I'm going to say about that right now—"

"Because we shall not speak of your muse?"

"Correct."

Over the course of the past year, I had dropped some of the freelance jobs—since I once again had a roommate and wasn't maintaining an eleven-hundred-square-foot glorified storage unit in Los Feliz while attempting to escape all my problems abroad. And with all that free time—while Fiona and Liam were usually preoccupied with each other—I wrote. Some of it was decent, though the combination of pining for my best friend's boyfriend and seeing the buffer-than-ever Hamish in person (and recognizing the appealing physical attributes he could bring to the role) had resulted in more of a romantic spin to the plot than I had ever intended.

NAME: Jack Mackinnon

ROLE: As the ~~newly appointed sheriff~~ recently elected district attorney of Landing's Edge, Jack is faced with the unexpected fight of his life when he unearths a path of corruption and deceit that affects almost everyone in town, all the way to the top. Possibly including ~~Jack's estranged wife . . . the deputy mayor.~~ Alicia Moran, the first woman Jack ever loved, and the last person he ever wanted to see again after she broke his heart. As Jack races against the clock to save Landing's Edge, he realizes that Alicia may be the one person he can trust . . . even if he isn't ready to trust her with his heart.

PHYSICAL DESCRIPTION: ~~Hamish MacDougal~~ Greek-movie-god Hamish MacDougal. Not *Phantasm* Hamish MacDougal.

"And what about the other question?" Liam asked.

"What other question?"

"Are you seeing anyone?"

The question felt too personal, and I hated that. My unrequited feelings for him aside, he had, for a time, been the person I talked to about everything. While he was still in love with me, he had listened to me prattle on about how amazing Malcolm was. He had held me and let me cry on his shoulder when Malcolm broke my heart. And now . . . Now I didn't even want to talk about the fact that there was absolutely nothing to talk about.

I cleared my throat. "No. I'm not."

My pulse began to quicken, and I felt like I was forgetting how to swallow. I saw a sudden flash of a conversation from more than two years earlier when he had asked me the exact same question, and I had answered in the exact same way. I had thought nothing of it then. Then, he had just been seeking confirmation of what he already knew. If I had been dating someone, he would have known about it. But with my confirmation then that I was unattached, he had begun talking about wanting me to meet his boss.

I knew I wouldn't be able to stand it if, once again, he was asking because he had in mind to set me up with some guy he knew.

"Hmm," was all he said in reply this time. But it wasn't a casual "Hmm." It was the "Hmm" of an attorney.

"We need to get back out there, I guess." I sighed, offering a half smile, as if I hated to end our conversation. As if I would much rather discuss my nonexistent social life with my ex-boyfriend than anything else in the world.

I set down the dish towel and took a deep breath of preparation for dramatic effect and headed toward the kitchen door. But I didn't quite make it.

"Olivia, wait." He grabbed my wrist as I passed. I didn't turn around to face him. I couldn't. "There's something I have to ask you."

I knew I had to get away. I just didn't know if I could maintain my façade through more questions about my love life or another booby-trapped conversation about the past. I once again took a deep breath of preparation—and this time it wasn't for effect.

"Liam," I began with false fortitude as I turned to face him, but I couldn't continue. I wasn't prepared for him to be looking at me like that. Like his continued existence was dependent upon the answer I would give to the question he was preparing to ask.

I stopped breathing as I stupidly allowed myself to create scenarios in my head. Scenarios that made my senses tingle. But I wasn't without breath for long. This time there was no cheating ex or mango margarita clouding my vision. *He isn't going to kiss you, you idiot.* Someday, when I no longer had any lingering romantic feelings for him, Liam and I would have to talk about how misleading it was when he locked eyes with women and made us feel like nothing else in the world mattered. How many poor witnesses on the stand had been sure he was thinking about their lips as he cross-examined them?

"Sure," I finally consented. "You can ask me anything."

"Do you have feelings for me?"

I should have been uncomfortable. Actually, I should have been mortified. But I wasn't. I was surprised, but not shocked. Nervous, but not filled with dread. Certain I couldn't tell him the truth, but even more certain I didn't have the strength to lie.

He released my wrist but not my gaze. "I'm sorry. I didn't mean to blurt it out like that. I just . . . It's important that I know. If you do, I mean."

His tone as he finished that sentence filled me with the dread that had previously been missing in action. It became clear. I knew *exactly* why he was asking.

"You're going to propose to Fiona," I managed to say in a voice that was something between a whimper and a bull-frog. He said nothing, so I rephrased my despair in the form of a question. "Liam, are you going to ask my best friend to marry you?"

He stepped closer as he took a deep breath, and then he began moving his arms as if he didn't know what to do with them. Because he wanted to touch me? *Shut up!* I screamed at myself inside my head. *He doesn't want to touch you! He doesn't want to kiss you! He . . . he . . . Wow . . . He sure looks like he wants to kiss you.*

Objection, Your Honor. Council is ensnaring the witness with his eyes.

"I don't know," he whispered. "It's time . . . Don't you think?"

"'Time'?"

He shrugged and stuffed his hands into his pockets. "We've been dating for more than a year."

"I didn't know there was a specific timeline for this sort of thing."

I guess I'd always imagined them dating until they didn't. They were a nice idea, Fiona and Liam, and in so many ways they were great together—so many ways that had made total sense to me even when Fi ran the idea of dating him past me while I was in Italy. But the reality? The two of them *forever*? Was I going to have to watch him lift her veil and kiss his bride? Watch him hold her hand and stroke her hair while he helped her breathe in rhythm and encouraged her to push? Would I be awesome Aunt Livi who had no life of her own and no greater joy than spending time with her godchildren and therefore babysat on Friday nights so the Howards could keep the romance alive?

No. No, no, no. Don't get ahead of yourself, Liv. He's just thinking. I began to breathe a little easier. He was not spontaneous. This was one of the biggest decisions he would ever make, and there was no earthly way Liam Howard would make that decision on a whim. There was still time for him to decide that as much as he and Fi were a nice idea, they just weren't endgame. He would prepare. He would calculate. He would make sure the evening was planned to within an inch of its life—

He would make sure the people she loved most were present to surround her with love and attention. He would stress about the traffic and do strange things like wash the dishes to try to calm his nerves. He would pull strings and call in favors in order to get a reservation at the restaurant she had been obsessed with since Vera Wang had invited her to join her for dinner with some friends but Fiona's car had broken down on the 101 (causing her to miss her chance to be the only other person at the table with Vera Wang, Donna Karan, Diane von Fürstenberg, and Calvin Klein).

I gasped softly. "You've already decided. You're doing it tonight?"

"I don't know, Olivia," he whispered, and he stepped closer still. "I have a ring in my pocket, but I really don't know."

He seemed to realize he was standing too close, and I knew that meant the spell had been broken—if there had ever been a spell at all. He took a step back and I prepared to make my getaway, though truthfully, I wasn't certain if my feet would remember how to move. They were glued in place as I tried to interpret the look in his eyes and then convince myself I was interpreting everything incorrectly.

I held on to the counter and tried to make myself think. *Think, Liv. Don't speak. Think.*

Of course it would be today. Somehow even Landon Mitchell's work schedule—which had caused them to move their trip back from their planned visit at Christmas—had gotten involved in the February 4 conspiracy against me. Why shouldn't today be the day?

"Olivia, I'm sorry. I don't know what I was thinking, just blurting that out, asking if you have feelings for me, after all this time."

Oh my gosh, I'd forgotten he asked that!

"There are probably a million ways I could have handled this better. It's just that I'm about to make the biggest decision of my life—"

"What decision?" I was filled with anger all of a sudden. I'd like to believe that the anger was on behalf of my best friend, whose soon-to-be fiancé was appearing to be a bit of a flake, but truthfully, I think I felt it only for myself. "You have a ring in your pocket, Liam. We have reservations at Matisse. It sounds as if the decision has been made."

Would I be able to handle a Mitchell-Howard wedding at which I would undoubtedly be the maid of honor? Could I handle the conflicting emotions? How could I possibly swallow down the despair I would feel each time I looked at Liam and instead focus on the joy that would come from seeing Fiona so happy?

He was as still as stone as he said, "Except I don't think it has. I mean . . . It's time . . ."

"So you've said."

"Why *wouldn't* I propose tonight?"

Be a friend, Liv. You are about to see the two most important people in your life happier than they have ever been. Focus on that.

"I can't think of any good reason," I replied honestly, though the awful, selfish reasons were abundant.

I didn't have time to congratulate myself on keeping it together and being a good friend to them both before his hands were on my face and his lips were joined with mine.

Yes, I was taken completely off guard, but that didn't stop my lips from responding to his desperation, and it didn't stop my arms from wrapping around his waist and pulling him against me. His hands moved from my face and his fingers tangled themselves in my hair as we finally came up for air. But just as his lips returned to mine—this time gently and with unmistakable deliberation—reality came crashing down upon us.

"Livi! Where are you? You won't believe what just happened!" Fiona squealed from the next room. "Hey, guys!" she greeted her parents with exuberance, though she scaled back the squeal. "I thought we were picking you up at your hotel."

Liam and I pulled apart and put as much space between us as the tiny kitchen would allow. The horror was evident in his eyes, as I'm certain it was in mine. But I couldn't help but notice that at least in his eyes the horror was tinged with just a touch of what I interpreted as disappointment—not in himself but in the interruption.

"What do we do?" I whispered as I ran my fingers through my hair and searched for a mirror. "Here," I said as I threw him a paper towel. "You have a little lipstick on your . . . on your . . ." I got lost and couldn't continue. I couldn't look at his lips, or apparently even say the word, without feeling the heat that was still surging through my own.

He took the paper towel and he wiped off the lipstick, but there was no urgency. Unlike me, he did not proceed like a panic-stricken first-time criminal fleeing a crime scene. "Olivia—"

"Liam, we have to get out there! Come on, let's go." I heard Landon ask Fiona about the traffic. "Actually, you go first. Make it casual." Jocelyn complimented her on her outfit. "Or should I go first? Would that make more sense?" I felt horrible. I absolutely hated myself. Fiona and I had been through a lot, and there had been times when neither of us was the model friend, but neither one of us had ever crossed this line before.

Tears flooded my eyes. "No, no, no!" I seethed at myself. "There's no time for that right now!" Even the Mitchell ladies wouldn't be distracted by talk of a Zac Posen skirt forever. I grabbed a magazine from the counter and began fanning my eyes in a fruitless attempt to dry them.

"I love you, Olivia Ross. I have always loved you. And I guess I love Fiona, but—"

"Of course you love Fiona!" I blubbered. "How could you *not* love Fiona?" She was the best, most wonderful, most loyal person on the entire planet, and I was an absolute lowlife.

"I do. She's amazing, but—" He walked toward me again, and I felt my heart break into a million pieces. "She's not you, Olivia. It's always been you, and I'm sorry it's taken me so long to figure that out. I mean, I've always known. I just didn't think you felt the same way. I thought it was just something I had to come to terms with."

For two years I had wondered if I'd made a horrible mistake by ending my relationship with him, and then for two years I had *known* that I had. For two years I had thought of him during the day and dreamt of him at night. For two years I had known that maybe someday I would meet a guy who made me happy, and maybe I would even fall in love with someone who wanted to be with me forever, but for two years I had known that no other guy would ever compare to Liam Howard.

Two years. Compared to almost my entire life that I'd known no one on earth could ever compare to Fiona Mitchell.

"I shouldn't have kissed you, Liam. I'm sorry to have misled you."

I couldn't focus on the way his face momentarily fell but quickly rebounded with determination. I couldn't focus on the fact that I was being handed my heart's strongest desire and what I knew was probably my greatest chance at happiness. I couldn't focus on the strange anomaly happening right before my eyes. Superman wanted to cast aside Lois Lane and instead devote his life to Lois's quirky best friend who made copies and passed around the muffin basket at the *Daily Planet*. I couldn't focus on that. If I did, I wouldn't be able to go through with it. And if I didn't go through with it, my best friend's heart would be broken.

"Didn't you hear me? I love you." His hands enveloped mine, but it was as if that wasn't enough. His fingers moved back to my hair and then onto my face, then brushed up and down my arms, needing to feel me, uncertain where he should land. He was offering me everything he had, and he was desperate for me to take hold. "You are the love of my life. And look, I know I seem like a creep right now, but I'm not approaching this lightly. You know I wouldn't be doing this if I wasn't absolutely sure this was the right thing to do. I love you and you love me, and—"

"I never said that." *Oh, Liam . . . I'm so sorry.*

That took him off guard and his hands, which had been so eagerly searching a moment prior, dropped to his side, lifelessly. "But I know you do."

"Liam, I never said that. Ever. In the eight months we dated, or in the years since, I never once said that." I felt like the scum of the earth, knowing that the words I was saying were true, no matter how misleading they were.

"Livi! Get in here!" Fi called from the living room before poking her head through the kitchen door. "I have to talk to you. This is huge!" She walked all the way through the door and was surprised to see Liam. "Oh, hey, babe! I thought we were meeting you at the restaurant. Apparently I got the details *all* confused."

She ran over to him and threw her arms around him. He wrapped his arms around her gently, but he didn't take his eyes off of me. I didn't know if I could bear another moment of the sting that I felt in my soul.

"So, um, what's this huge news, Fi?" I turned away from them and went back into the living room, knowing Fiona would follow. Hoping Liam wouldn't.

"Okay, are you ready for this? Today Shonda had me make some calls to coordinate Katherine Heigl's shooting schedule for this film she'll be starring in."

Her voice was positively giddy, though of course I didn't understand why. She came home from the *Grey's Anatomy* set every day, and almost every single day she was in possession of some juicy Hollywood gossip. News regarding an upcoming film, which I probably could have learned just as easily by picking up a copy of *Variety*, if I felt so inclined, just didn't seem up to her normal standard. Of course even the celebrity bombshell of the millennium wouldn't have been juicy enough to pull my focus from the way Liam was looking at me as he stepped out of the kitchen. His eyes were an amalgamation of betrayal, confusion, and withering hope.

"That's great," I effused with every ounce of energy I could muster. "Hey, look, I think I'm going to bow out of dinner tonight—"

"No, listen, Liv! This film that she's shooting—it's a romantic comedy. Costarring Hamish MacDougal!"

"Oh, Fi—"

"I already talked to Katherine, and you and I are going to the set! Next Tuesday, you get to talk to Hamish again!"

"I . . . I don't know what to say."

She frowned. "You don't seem very excited. I thought you'd be happy." Her eyes darted toward Liam and back to me, and if I wasn't mistaken, Jocelyn's eyes were doing the same. And then Fi looked around the entire room as if the realization that things were not normal had just hit. "What's wrong?"

Only Landon, whose attention was directed toward a muted baseball game on TV, wasn't looking at me. The walls were closing in.

"I am happy. Of course I am. Thanks for arranging that." I wanted to close my eyes and breathe through the waves of nausea, but it was more important to act normal for a few more moments. "It just makes me nervous. Because I don't have a screenplay, I mean."

She seemed to accept that as the source of my uneasiness, and she was once again smiling as her eyes concentrated solely on me. Whether Jocelyn accepted everything as copacetic or not, I didn't know. But she'd seemingly lost interest in the dynamic of the room in favor of the *Marie Claire* she was flipping through.

"I know you aren't done with the screenplay. I thought about that, but I don't think it matters. Just touch base with him. Who knows? You might hit it off! He is single, I hear . . ."

I took a deep breath. I had to get out of there. And then I could cry. And Liam could move on with his life. And Fiona could be happy. "We'll talk all about it later. You have to hurry if you're going to make it to Matisse."

"Hang on. You're seriously not coming?" Fi asked me with disappointment and concern in her voice. She looked at her boyfriend. I guess in that moment it made sense to her that he was looking at me instead of her. Not that making sense seemed to be his top priority. "Liam, didn't you make the reservation for the five of us? Should I call the restaurant and see if we can add—"

"No, no, it was for five. I have a couple errands to run, and I'm behind on work. But I want the four of you to have a wonderful evening together. You hear that?" I choked out a chuckle as I looked at Liam, who was leaning against the kitchen doorway, still never taking his eyes off of me. If only I could have been as oblivious as everyone else.

Any remaining warmth and hope in his eyes faded as he realized I was giving him my blessing. He understood that I wanted him to go ahead and propose to my best friend. He understood that I didn't love him.

He understood nothing.

It has been said that old friends are like ...

... gold.

... the stars.

... fine wine.

... a comfortable pair of shoes.

If you ask me, old friends aren't like any of those things.

If anything, old friends are like the beating of your heart.

You don't always count each beat,

and you often take it for granted,

But without it ...

Heartlite® Greeting Card Co., Number 09-G655X23

FEBRUARY 4, 2009

"I don't care what you say, Liv. You're coming tonight."

"Fi, I can't. I just can't!" I glanced up from my computer screen briefly to look at her, but even as I did, I felt myself getting behind. "This story is just flowing out of me like . . . butter? No, that's stupid. Like water from a pitcher, gently rushing down toward—"

"Are you writing right now? I mean, seriously?" She shook her head in disbelief. "Are you actually revising the first draft of our conversation, right here in real time?"

I took my eyes off of her and focused them on the screen once more. "I can't help it! That's what I mean. I am so filled with words and ideas I can't even keep up. I've been waiting years for a creative burst like this, and if you think I am going to interrupt it to go to some fundraiser for some charity, you're insane. Besides, it's Ironic Day."

This year I'd decided to give in to the existence of the curse. For whatever reason, the universe or the calendar or Alanis

Morissette was out to get me, and I figured the best thing I could do was get out of their way. *Just try to screw up my life when I'm home alone in track pants and a Boston College T-shirt, Alanis. Just try!*

Fiona walked over to my laptop and closed it on my fingers before quickly apologizing as I began to panic that my work would be lost. In spite of my panic, she didn't stop what she was doing, and soon the computer was behind her back.

"Olivia Ross, you listen to me. I'm taking you *because* it's February 4! Your ticket was free, but we're going to pretend it wasn't. This is a fifty-thousand-dollar end to the irony. You're going to have the time of your life, you're going to flirt a little, you're going to eat a lot, and before you know it, it's going to be February 5, and the world will still be spinning. You'll see. Besides, this isn't just 'some fundraiser' for 'some charity.' This is a fundraiser I am in charge of, for a charity I work for. Every single late night and early morning over the last five months, every boring meeting and high-pressure call from New York . . . It's all been for this night. Walking away from Shondaland and saying goodbye to that magical moment each morning when Patrick Dempsey said hello and got my name wrong—*this* is what it was all for, Livi! And I need you there with me tonight." Her tone and her face softened. "Please."

Well, how could I possibly resist that?

"Of course I'll go."

"Of course you will!" she trilled, validated in her certainty that I couldn't say no to her. "Great! Okay, I'll be back in an hour to get ready, and we leave in two hours."

It was a miracle we were still friends at all, I knew. The fact that she loved me enough to want me to accompany her on such an important night humbled me, and the exuberance on her face made me regret my selfish February 4 preoccupation.

"What?" she asked, an amused grin on her face as she handed my laptop back to me. "Why are you looking at me like that?"

"You're just the best. That's all."

There had been plenty of highs and lows over the course of the last year. The first few weeks after Liam and I kissed hadn't been pretty, and the recovery had taken some work. Truthfully, a whole lot of work—and careful, nonstop consideration of what should be discussed and what shouldn't, what could be lived with and what couldn't. By both of us. And that was just to salvage the friendship. I think what we each went through individually was even worse.

I had broken the heart of the man I was pretty sure was the love of my life, and Fiona Mitchell had been dumped for the very first time.

"You're weird," she responded to my affectionate declaration before hurrying over to me, giving me a quick hug and repeating, "We leave in two hours."

"What should I wear?"

She groaned as she pulled away and headed back toward the door. "Are you actually asking me that question when you have a breathtaking dress perfect for the occasion just wasting away?"

"Oh, seriously? I have to dress up that much?"

"Liv! I wasn't kidding. Tickets to this thing are fifty grand. Yes, you have to dress up!"

In that case, my breathtaking, sleek, ivory-silk gown with an intricate black-lace overlay, courtesy of Vera Wang, would be put to use. I'd had my eye on it that day in Vera's Paris shop, and it had shown up, hand delivered to my door in Rome by a courier, about three months later. Ever since, it had been hanging in a closet. I'd not attended a single formal event in all that time. Actually, I'd attended few events of any nature.

"Next you're going to tell me I have to wash my hair."

"At least brush it!" Her words echoed as she left and closed the door behind her.

The moment she was out the door, I was tempted to open up my laptop and get a little more writing in. But I knew that once I started, there would be no chance of being ready in two hours, much less any chance of my hair getting brushed, as Fiona had insisted. Instead, I set my laptop on the couch and walked to the calendar on the wall, where I had pinned the invitation to the event, in an effort to remind myself what cause I was bothering to surrender my messiest of messy buns for.

"Well, that doesn't help," I mused as I read the name of the charity.

The Lakeside Society.

Was it for environmental preservation? A hospital? A country club in need of a new eighteenth hole? I had no idea. How could I have no idea? Surely Fi had discussed her job in some detail in the five months since the mysterious Lakeside Society had stolen her away from Shonda Rhimes, right?

I pinned the invitation back in its place, and as I did, the date on the invitation stood out, taunting me with its mystical cruelty.

"And a happy Hamish MacDougal slash Liam Howard slash I'm Going to Die Alone and Have to Write My Own Bereavement Heartlite Card Day to you, as well," I murmured to myself.

That had been probably the worst thing to come out of 2008's Ironic Day. I had started caring about things like dying alone. Not that I thought about dying. And not that I was all that bothered by the thought of being alone. What *did* bother me was knowing that if not for one choice on one night after one amazing kiss, I would be with Liam. Again. Still. Forever.

One year ago, after I'd fled the scene, Liam had driven to Santa Monica with all three Mitchells and acted as if everything was okay long enough to make sure Fiona had the fabulous evening at Matisse with her parents that she had been promised. And then her parents took a cab to their hotel, and Liam and Fi took a walk on the beach and ended their fourteen-month relationship. And I was at the center of the end, just as I had been at the center of the beginning.

He told her that he was still in love with me and that he had kissed me, but that it had been all his fault. By the time Fiona got home—where I was waiting after hours of torment, preparing to answer for myself if Liam had told her what happened or congratulate them if he'd gone through with proposing—the stage was set for me to step into my role as Guiltless Bystander #1, who had been taken off guard by his kiss and soon chastised him, refusing to be party to any further betrayal. Technically that was all true. My role in what had happened looked pretty innocent on paper.

And Liam had certainly portrayed it that way—probably for reasons that went so much deeper than simply a noble attempt to salvage the friendship of two women he loved. That was the single biggest reason my heart still ached. By the time all was said and done, he had no reason to believe I loved him. No reason to believe I had *ever* loved him. And if that was the case, it was primarily a one-sided betrayal. I could be accused of nothing more than getting caught up in a moment.

What made it possible for him to walk away from me was also what made it possible for Fiona and me to move forward together.

And that was where the constant dance of figuring out how much to say began. I didn't want to lie to her, so I told her that the kiss had not been as one-sided as Liam had indicated to her. Though I'd given in to my attraction to him and some lingering, unresolved feelings, I hadn't realized that he loved me. I instantly regretted kissing him—and when he began speaking as if he and I should be together, I shut it down.

It was all true. True enough that Liam did not shoulder all of the responsibility, but not so true that Fiona and I could never recover.

I couldn't tell her that I was still in love with him, and I certainly couldn't tell her that I had been in love with him every single day that he had been her boyfriend. If I told her that, she would know how many lies I had told. How many emotions I had faked. How could I tell her any of that without also letting her know what a struggle it had been? Without telling her how desperately I had wanted to kiss him again? Without confessing that I had weighed her heartbreak against my own and for a moment considered letting her suffer? It was, in my mind, the ultimate betrayal. So much worse than a kiss, and so much more impactful than a single evening.

I had refused him—in spite of my love for him, because of my love for her—and it was the most difficult thing I had ever done. That was the truth I had to live with. There was no point in making Fi live with it too.

As for Liam, neither one of us had heard from him since. I'd called his office on his birthday, but it was no longer his office.

And a returned Christmas card told me that his home was no longer his either.

Okay . . . a few more writing minutes. I grabbed my laptop from the couch.

I couldn't talk to Fi every time I thought about Liam, of course, so all those pent-up conversations and emotions had to go somewhere.

> **NAME:** Jack Mackinnon
>
> **ROLE:** As the ~~recently elected~~ single and alone district attorney of Landing's Edge, Jack is ~~faced with the unexpected fight of his life~~ single and alone when he unearths a path of corruption and deceit that affects almost everyone in town, ~~all the way to the top.~~ but especially the people who are single and alone. Possibly including Alicia Moran, ~~the first woman Jack ever loved, and the last person he ever wanted to see again, after she broke his heart.~~ the woman who left Jack single and alone. As Jack races against the clock to save ~~Landing's Edge~~ who cares . . . he's alone . . . he realizes that Alicia may be the one person he can trust . . . even if he ~~isn't ready to trust her with his heart.~~ is destined to die alone.
>
> **PHYSICAL DESCRIPTION:** ~~Greek-movie-god Hamish MacDougal. Not *Phantasm* Hamish MacDougal.~~ To Be Determined

Though progress had been made on the screenplay, I'd made the decision that, regardless of its status in 2013, I would not be presenting my work to Hamish MacDougal. I would not be returning to the coffeehouse "just in case." What was the point? The nice, cute guy who had made the nice, cute comment about making a movie with me had become a superstar who no longer had to rush away to auditions and who would probably never again be able to sit in a crowded coffeehouse unrecognized by the masses. As I thought back over the past few years, I knew that even I, in all my plebeian splendor, would have forgotten about that day were it not for the people in my life who constantly forced me to remember. I could have no doubt there were no such desperately-seeking-excitement influences in his life.

And on top of all that, missing our on-set visit to meet him as arranged by Katherine Heigl—because both Fiona and I had been so emotionally wrecked we forgot all about it—had been just the wake-up call I needed. There were real people and real emotions and real choices and real consequences in my life, all around me. The time for daydreaming had passed.

Two hours later I was ready and actually looking pretty fabulous, though I do say so myself. I was surprised by how much I liked the way I felt in Vera Wang. I made a mental note to pull the dress out at least once a month or so, even if just to go to the post office or whip up an omelet.

"So where is this thing?" I asked as Fiona continued to drive us farther and farther up into the hills. I'd been so preoccupied trying to figure out what cause I was supporting that I'd given no thought at all to where I would be supporting it.

Within a second her answer was redundant. "The Getty,"

she said nonchalantly as she made one final turn of the steering wheel of her Audi and the breathtaking stone and glass of the Getty Center appeared before us, along with its unrivaled views of Los Angeles.

I couldn't take it any longer.

"I'm sorry, Fi, but what is the Lakeside Society? I feel as if I should know, and I'm sorry to have to ask, but . . ."

I had to dress in my best (and only) formal Vera Wang gown, they had stolen Fiona away from the hottest show on television, and this little fifty-thousand-dollars-per-person fundraiser that I'd tried to get out of was taking place at one of the most exclusive venues on the West Coast. I couldn't help feeling as if I had missed some information somewhere along the line.

Fi laughed. "Water. The Lakeside Society exists to bring attention and awareness to the plight of the many countries of the world where there is not enough water to sustain life."

I brushed away the snide and insensitive remarks that were threatening to burst out of me—not in response to the work of the organization but to Fiona's well-rehearsed, straight-from-the-pamphlet pitch. Instead, I focused on the unfortunate irony all around me, courtesy of the beautiful, bountiful water-flowing fountains of the Getty.

"You ready?" she asked with a smile as she shifted into Park and waved flirtatiously to the man working valet parking.

We got out and walked in, and the adrenaline of victory surged through my veins when I made it all the way without tripping on my heels or snagging my lace on anything. Not only that, I felt quite a few appreciative male eyes on me as we entered. Yes, Fiona was with me, and usually I would assume the eyes were on her and I was just catching a few leftover peripherals, as if I were her accessory. But on this particular night I looked the best I had ever looked. I knew it, and they knew it.

"So, don't you have to get to work or something?" I asked her as I grabbed a glass of champagne from a passing waiter and took a look around at the oyster that was my world—at least for that one evening.

"No. I've put in all the work already. We're just here to enjoy ourselves. We deserve it!" She clinked my glass with her own.

"Wow!" I breathed as we stepped into the ballroom and I took in all the surrounding splendor. "You did this, Fi? Wow!"

I was as close to speechless as I figured I ever could be, silenced by the perfect lighting and the subtle opulence and grandeur of it all. It was breathtaking. But what was even more formidable and impressive than the majestic chandeliers and the ideally placed string quartet was the sense that everyone was enjoying themselves. Designer gowns and tuxes could so easily lend themselves to stuffiness, but Fi had created a luxurious atmosphere of warmth and comfort.

The room was Fiona.

"You really think it's okay?" she asked, her voice trembling slightly.

"'Okay'? Fi, it is so much more than 'okay'! This is the most beautiful room I have ever seen in my entire life. This is amazing!"

She took a deep breath. "Thanks."

"Are you okay?" I whispered. I'd rarely seen her so vulnerable and uncertain—especially when her genius was as glaring and irrefutable as it was that night.

"Hmm?" she asked, her distraction evident. "Oh, yeah. I'm fine. Hey, so I probably need to go schmooze some people—"

"And that's not work?"

"Technically I suppose it is. But when the people I have to schmooze include this many rich, handsome men . . ."

Schmoozing had sounded like work. Schmoozing rich, handsome men sounded like torture. "Better you than me."

"I'll be back in a few. You have fun and be your delightful, fabulous self!" She squeezed my hand and then flitted off to join a cluster of Los Angeles elite, seemingly back to *her* delightful, fabulous self.

I surveyed the room and sighed. Who was I kidding? Yes, I looked good that evening, but I didn't look like the kind of woman any of those gorgeous men would be interested in. Not that guy in the Armani tux, or that other guy in that other Armani tux that looked exactly like the first Armani tux. And most assuredly not that guy who looked like Hamish MacDougal, also in an Armani tux. Or was it Hugo Boss? Or—

Holy crap!

It *was* Hamish MacDougal in an almost-certainly-Armani tux!

I looked around for Fiona, certain she would direct me and, most likely, refuse to back down until I built up the nerve to go over and talk to him. At a minimum she would scare me to the point that I would become violently ill, and then I'd get to spend the rest of the evening hiding in a ladies'-room stall. But she was nowhere to be found. Where she had stood only seconds prior was instead a guy who sure looked a lot like George Clooney. But, no . . . it couldn't be George Clooney. This guy, whoever he was, was looking at me. In fact, he had locked in, and it was as if he were drawing me in with his tractor beam.

Me? I mean, I was certain he wasn't actually George Clooney, but *still*. He sure *looked* like George Clooney. And it is a truth universally acknowledged that a guy who looks like George Clooney must be in want of a woman to talk to.

He smiled a sly little half smile as he walked toward me, and I tried to return the sly expression, but I just ended up feeling self-conscious. The miraculous thing was I think it actually came across as sort of a Princess Di shy-and-self-aware upward-glance thing, and the Clooney lookalike picked up his pace. It *was* me that he was coming to talk to. *Alright, Liv, you've got this.* He was actually wanting to talk to *me*. He would not ask me if I knew where the restroom was or where he could get his parking validated. I was pretty sure he wouldn't even begin with the opening line I had heard more than any other throughout my life: "So, tell me about that friend of yours." Nope. Not this time. This time I was about to get hit on—by a gorgeous, salt-and-pepper silver fox of a man in an Armani tux.

"Excuse me, George," Fiona said as she swooped in between us and pulled me aside.

"George?" I whispered in a panic. "Did you just call him George?" I looked back at him with as much subtlety as I could muster, which was frightfully little.

"Livi, I need a favor. A *huge* favor. I'll owe you forever."

I spoke through tightly clenched teeth. "Fi, tell me that's not George Clooney."

She threw a casual look behind her at the man who was now taking a sip of some masculine-looking drink that I knew probably tasted like cough syrup and who was still looking straight at me with amusement.

"It is. He's a big supporter. Now, listen—"

"He was about to hit on me, Fi! George Clooney was walking over here to seduce me!"

"Seduce you, huh?" She smiled and bit her lip. "Well, I am truly sorry to have interrupted the great Clooney seduction, but this is important . . ." Her voice trailed off, and she paused for a moment, and I could see her wheels turning. As was the norm when I saw Fiona's wheels turning, I felt a rush of fear and excitement. "This is perfect! Oh, Livi, you have to do this for me."

"Do what for you?"

"Make him pay!"

Oh no. Did Fi have a past with George Clooney of which I had somehow never been aware? I wouldn't find that too surprising. Had he cheated on her? That dog! What kind of friend was I? I had almost fallen for another of her men! I had almost done it again! Although, in fairness to me, I'd had no idea they shared any history. Also in fairness to me, the last time I had fallen for one of Fiona's men, he had been my man first. He had not been hers when I fell for him. But that was no excuse.

Stay focused, Liv.

Fiona and I were strong enough to survive that, and we would survive this. If Mr. Clooney thought he could come between the two of us, he had another think coming. Or did he have another *thing* coming? In this situation, both options seemed appropriate.

"Yes," I calmly and somewhat sinisterly stated. "Let's make him pay."

"Great! Oh, thank you, Livi! You won't regret it."

She grabbed me by the elbow and turned me around, and we marched past George. As we did, I shot him a glance that I hoped was a glare but feared may have ultimately been nothing more than a disappointing puddle of attraction, melted by the warmth of the very Clooney-ness of his eyes.

Fiona was decidedly less affected than I. As we passed, she looked straight into those delicious, ooey-gooey eyes and said, "Pull out the checkbook, Clooney. The auction is about to begin."

The disappointing puddle of attraction vanished, and I was once again committed to making him pay. *Pull out the checkbook, Clooney!* I'd never heard that expression, but I liked it. I wanted to add my own personal spin to it, but nothing good was coming to me.

Hope you brought your AmEx, Clooney.

I'll put it on your tab, Clooney.

Nope. Nothing else worked as well.

Hang on . . .

"Auction?" I asked with fear and urgency.

"Yep. This auction is so successful for the Lakeside Society every year that it has its own clause in my contract. I have complete oversight and creative control over all events—as long as I keep the auction."

She continued to rush and weave through A-listers and wannabes, but I didn't see anyone who seemed to be an impostor like myself.

"Is this like a bachelorette auction, Fi? If it is, that's a degrading and reprehensible way to treat a human, and I want nothing to do with it." I wanted to add that I thought those things only existed as plot devices on *The Nanny*, but I didn't want to detract from my moral-high-ground stance.

She kept pulling me forward as she responded to me over

her shoulder. "Trust me, this is no big deal. It's not like when one hundred bucks got Tony for the weekend on *Who's the Boss?*"

Had *every* show used that storyline?

"As soon as the auction wraps up, the dancing begins. Your first dance goes to the highest bidder. That's it. You dance with someone for four minutes, and a village in Yemen gets a well."

We arrived backstage where bachelors and bachelorettes alike were having numbers pinned to their evening gowns and tux lapels. Right off the bat I spotted any number of actors and actresses whose names I didn't know but whom I recognized from awful movies Fiona had dragged me to.

"This is ridiculous! I love you, Fi, and I'd love to help build a well in Yemen, but this is the worst idea you've ever had in your life. Look at these people! Who is going to bid on me?"

She smiled as she grabbed a number from one of her passing staffers and attached it to my gown with great care. "I'm sorry to ask you to do it. I am. But Charlize Theron has the flu. Someone has to step in, and you know what, Livi? You look gorgeous! I've known you since before you had boobs, and I assure you, this is the most beautiful you have ever looked in your life. You're going to knock their socks off, and you completely deserve to be up there with the rest of these beautiful people. And as for who will bid on you? Well, I'm pretty sure George Clooney will."

The thought of that was somehow so much more terrifying than the thought of no one bidding at all.

A young man with a clipboard and a headset ran over to where we stood and politely interrupted. "I'm sorry, Ms. Mitchell. I need her bio."

Ha! My bio. Yeah . . . okay. If there had been any chance of George Clooney—or anyone else—bidding on me, "lifelong writer of sappy greeting cards; working on the same screenplay for more than six years; currently mourning the loss of the man who was probably her soulmate; deathly allergic to wasabi" being included in my introduction should do the trick.

"Olivia Ross, graduate of Boston College, impressive history of work for Heartlite, Inc., screenwriter of upcoming major motion picture."

Then, information in hand, he ran off before I could stop him.

"Fi! You made it sound like I write for the Heartlite Network or something!"

"Hmm. Did it sound like that? I just spoke the truth."

"The truth?" I enunciated through my teeth. "'Screenwriter of upcoming motion picture' is the truth? Fiona!"

"No," she corrected me. "I said '*major* motion picture.' And yes. It's the truth. You just don't have a release date yet."

"Or a production company. Or a script. Or any real reason to think I will ever have any of those things! Oh, Fi . . ."

"It will be fine, Liv. I promise. You're next, as soon as Robert Downey Jr. leaves the stage. Just have fun with it. I assure you, you are a worthy replacement for Charlize Theron. And if that isn't enough for you, just know that there is a lot of free-flowing champagne out there tonight. And even more free-flowing money. Every person out there is here to either make a difference or be seen looking like they care about making a difference. Someone will bid on you. I have no doubt."

Out of the corner of my eye I saw Robert Downey Jr. return backstage, just as I heard the announcer say something about Heartlite.

"Please welcome Ms. Olivia Ross."

Fi gave me a quick hug followed by a gentle shove, and before I could turn and run the other way, I was on the stage, in the spotlight. For the first time in my life, I was so grateful for the spotlight. I had always avoided it at any cost, but never before had I realized that when you are in the spotlight, you can't see the crowd. I realized how much symbolism existed in that epiphany, and I got lost in my thoughts and social commentary. So lost, in fact, that I began to feel at peace as it dawned on me that celebrities couldn't *help* but be self-centered. After all, when they are in the spotlight, how can they possibly be aware of those around them in the dark?

"Five thousand dollars." The deep voice came from the audience, but I couldn't see who it belonged to.

"Alright, gentlemen," the auctioneer spoke, and I was glad that I could at least see him. "Mr. Ralph Fiennes gets the bidding started at five thousand dollars."

Ralph Fiennes. *Ralph Fiennes?* He was a little old for me, but he was a good-looking guy, best I could recall. And in *The English Patient* he had been positively dreamy, when it came right down to it. I couldn't think of what else I had seen him in, but—

"Mr. Fiennes," the auctioneer continued, "is perhaps most well known as Lord Voldemort in the Harry Potter films."

Oh, that's right. Well, I could get past thinking of him as an evil wizard if I had to. Surely his real nose was much less snakelike.

"And, of course, his critically acclaimed and award-winning role in *Schindler's List*."

As the audience applauded to show their appreciation, I couldn't help but pout. *That's* what I knew him from. Yeah, a snake nose and a creepy voice were one thing, but being the bad guy among a whole army of Nazi bad guys in *Schindler's List* was something else entirely. Why couldn't Liam Neeson have bid on me? Even so, he was simply an actor, playing a role. And if he wanted to bid five grand to dance with me, I would just focus on *The English Patient* and all the water we would be responsible for in Yemen and have a lovely time.

"Don't let him win so easily, gentlemen." The auctioneer spoke once again, overpowering the silence in the room and *The English Patient* visions in my head. "Who will raise the bid for a chance to spend some time with Ms. Ross? Mr. Fiennes was *Maid in Manhattan*. Let's see if he's made of money."

Oh *no*. You portray the man who killed Harry Potter's parents, and I can look past it. A sadistic Nazi, and I will remind myself our time together is all to benefit a good cause. But lowering yourself to a stereotypical rom-com with a pun-based title alongside J.Lo? No. Some things can't be overlooked.

"Ten thousand."

I breathed a sigh of relief as an appreciative giggle seemed to overtake the crowd. I was offended. Were they sympathy bids? Was the audience in on the joke? But as my eyes began to adjust and I followed the eyes of everyone in the room to the guy with the salt-and-pepper hair in the back corner, smugly holding up his bidding paddle, I realized that those appreciative giggles were just the soundtrack that accompanied George Clooney wherever he went.

It was the next bid that caught me off guard. You know . . . because George Clooney offering up more than my share of the rent for half a year, just for the chance to dance with me, happens every day.

"Twelve-five." I sensed more than saw all of the heads turn their focus from one side of the room to the other. "No, actually, let's go on up to fifteen thousand. What are these nights for if not to make Clooney pay through the nose?"

The room erupted in laughter, but I stood there in stunned silence, straining my eyes to see if what I thought to be true could actually be true. Or did my dialect-challenged ears deceive me yet again?

"Well said!" The announcer laughed as he waited for quiet to once again overtake the crowd. "The gauntlet has been thrown! The current bid is fifteen thousand dollars by Mr. Hamish MacDougal."

I didn't mean to gasp, but I couldn't help it. I knew then that my cover was blown. It had to have been blown. I had managed to play it so cool while the first two Hollywood heavyweights bid ridiculous amounts of cash on me. But I could have no doubt that any belief I actually belonged there had been washed away by my gasp. I couldn't even make myself care about that, though. I strained my eyes to get a look at Hamish. I'd been so distracted by George Clooney wanting to marry me and make lots of babies, I'd forgotten he was there. I was no longer worried about being onstage, or even who would eventually win me. My only concern was whether or not he knew it was me. Was he bidding on some supposedly successful screenwriter, or was he bidding on the girl from the coffeehouse?

Ralph dropped out early, thank goodness, but the bidding between the other two gentlemen continued on. As the money got ridiculous, I reminded myself that they were making huge tax-deductible contributions, and that it had nothing to do with dancing with me. But I also found myself falling into fantasies, which I so rarely allowed myself to do. I knew that I would likely be able to talk with both guys after the auction, regardless of who won. So who did I want to win? Did it even matter? What if Hamish was bidding on the girl in the unflattering sweatshirt and the even less flattering first impression? That would mean something, right? Had he been thinking of me for the past six years, toying with the idea of rushing down to our couch each February 4, just in case?

February 4. It was February 4! It had been six years to the day, and there he was, bidding fifty-five thousand just to dance with me. Hold on . . . *Fifty-five thousand dollars?* Could I have heard that right? Hamish MacDougal on February 4.

Talk about ironic.

And then, of course, my thoughts went to Liam.

Not now, Olivia, I lectured myself sternly. *It's time to move on.*

I heard the crowd laugh as George demonstrated extreme cool and humor by sitting down and ordering another drink as he raised his bid to sixty thousand. He seemed to be saying he had nowhere to be and could do this all night.

"Livi!" At first I didn't realize that the calling of my name had come from just offstage left, but once I did, I turned to see Fiona waving her arms in an attempt to get my attention. "I'm sorry. I didn't know."

I easily heard her over the crowd noises, if only because her lips were moving so emphatically, but I knew I was probably the only person able to make out what she was saying. Not that I had a clue *why* she was saying what she was saying.

I shrugged my shoulders as I glanced at her.

"I didn't know he would be here. I'm so sorry!"

I raised my eyebrows. She didn't know he'd be here, and she was sorry? If I knew Fiona Mitchell, I knew the odds were pretty good that she did, in fact, know Hamish would be there—and that Charlize Theron was never even scheduled to participate.

Well played, Fi. Well played.

I winked at her and smiled, grateful for once for the overly dramatic way she had of taking matters into her own hands. Then I turned back to the crowd, ready to fully enjoy the conclusion of what I knew would go down in the history books as the most surreal night of my life.

"One hundred thousand dollars," a voice rang out from a far corner of the room, far surpassing George's last bid, and suddenly it was time for everyone else to gasp.

"Well, well, well!" The auctioneer shuffled through the papers on his podium as the Los Angeles elite burst into applause and whistles. "Mr. Clooney? Mr. MacDougal? Shall either of you be outbidding the gentleman?"

"The gentleman" was clearly some unknown, or the man responsible for selling me would have referred to him by name. No! I didn't want an unknown. I wanted Hamish! Or I at least wanted George. Yes, that would be fine. I would settle for George Clooney if I had to. I would somehow pull myself up by the bootstraps and make lemonade out of lemons. But the unknown gentleman was not welcome.

I took turns looking at each of them, imploring them not to give up on me now. It was George who first raised his hands in surrender, laughing good-naturedly as he joined in the applause for the mystery man. I turned to Hamish, hoping against hope that he thought four minutes with me, a few years ahead of schedule, was worth more than one hundred thousand dollars—but knowing how ridiculous that was, even in the context of the evening. He winked at me as he lowered his paddle to the cocktail table in front of him and gestured that the man in the back was the victor.

No! What if he was ugly?

What's gotten into you, Olivia? You don't care about that.

What if he wasn't a movie star?

Good! Snap out of it!

What if he was pervy and creepy?

Okay, that's an actual concern. But it's four minutes in a room full of people. Do it for Yemen!

The auctioneer glanced back at the highest bidder, though I was afraid to do the same. He then looked at the papers in his hands, matching the paddle number to the list before him.

"Sold! Ms. Olivia Ross, for one hundred thousand dollars, to the representative from the law firm of Boynes & Madison!"

Liam? Liam was there? Liam had bid on me?

Liam had bid on me!

That made so much sense. *That* was why Fiona had apologized. She hadn't known he was coming. In all that time that neither of us had heard from him, he'd been working through some things and waiting until the time was right. He'd wanted to return and pledge his eternal love to me through a grand, romantic gesture that hinged entirely upon Charlize Theron coming down with the flu. Brilliant!

Except that actually made no sense whatsoever. Liam no longer worked at Boynes & Madison . . . unless I'd made the wrong assumption. When I called on his birthday and the voice of some lawyer named Simon sounded on the office voicemail, maybe I shouldn't have rushed to judgment. That was it. Liam hadn't left. He'd been promoted. And contrary to my egocentric belief, he hadn't moved out of his apartment for the sole purpose of making sure I could never contact him again. With that promotion came a lot more money. Of course! He'd been blissfully planning our long-awaited reunion from a house in Bel Air.

"Oh, my apologies." The voice from the podium spoke once again. "I believe I had an outdated reference on my master list. The representative is from the law firm of Boynes, Madison & Larcraft. Congratulations to Mr. Malcolm Larcraft. Mr. Clooney and Mr. MacDougal, you were worthy adversaries for the attention of Ms. Ross. Well done."

I stood in a fog until Fiona rushed onto the stage to help me off, just as Matthew McConaughey took my place on the auction block.

"Livi, I'm so sorry," she whispered as tears formed in her exquisitely made-up eyes. "I had no idea he would be here. They just handed me the final guest list. He was a late addition."

As Liam's girlfriend, Fiona had been forced to socialize in Malcolm's vicinity a few times—at various company gatherings and such. But since then she'd been filled in on all the good, the bad, and the lying, cheating, heartbreaking deceit of my relationship with him, all of which had occurred while Fi was in Paris. Needless to say, between cheating on me and forcing Liam to work overtime on Valentine's Day, Malcolm Larcraft was not on Fiona's fan list.

I sighed and felt a few soft tears of my own fall. "Hey, it's okay," I said sadly. I tried to be reassuring as I pulled her to me for a hug. "There's no way you could have known. It's not a big deal." I knew that was just a hypothesis until I laid eyes on him.

"You know what, though?" I pulled away and smiled at her with determination and, for the first time in ages, hope. "I'm going to go talk to Hamish. How long until that first dance?"

Her face lit up. "You've got at least ten minutes. How can I help?"

I didn't know how she could help because I had no plan whatsoever. All I knew was that February 4 was not a fluke. I didn't understand what caused it or even what the point of any of it was. All I knew was that I was on the seventh February 4 in a row made up almost entirely of confusing emotions and opportunities—none of which I had previously seized to satisfaction—and for whatever reason, Hamish MacDougal was usually at the center of it all. Well, Hamish MacDougal or Liam Howard. Now, apparently, we were throwing in a recurring Malcolm Larcraft component. Whatever. I'd sort all that out later. Right then, Hamish and I were in the same building, and rather than wait four more years, he'd just offered up five figures for four minutes with me.

"Do you think there's a way you can stall Malcolm?"

She squealed with menacing delight. "Sure!"

"Okay." I took a deep breath and ran trembling hands over the abdomen of my Vera to smooth out the silk—and to try to settle the butterflies. "Okay. Wish me luck."

"You don't need luck, Livi. You're the most gorgeous woman in the room, and this is your night. He's probably wandering around looking for you right now! I'll stall Malcolm. I'll even stall the dance if I can. Now go!"

I grabbed either side of my dress at the knees and hiked it up a little higher above my ankles. I contemplated whipping off my slingback heels and carrying them, but decided it was more dangerous to scurry across a marble floor in pantyhose. *Okay, Hamish . . . where are you?* I surveyed the packed room. So much black and white! How was I ever supposed to find one tuxedo-clad needle in this haystack?

And yet Clooney kept finding me time and time again.

"Any other time, George. Any other time," I muttered as he began heading once again in my general direction, and I took off the opposite way.

I tried to keep myself from getting discouraged by imagining how it was all going to play out. I would walk outside and look around aimlessly, despite the fact that I was eagerly searching for something—much like Cinderella when the clock strikes midnight—and then I would see him. He would be leaning up against the same well-loved classic convertible from so many years ago, his bow tie undone and the top two buttons of his shirt freed from their formal captivity. He would stand up straight, and a smile would overtake his face as he began to walk slowly toward me.

"This seems like as good a time as any to confess that I have no idea where Sri Lanka is," I would say. He would look down at his feet and try to hide the width of the smile that consumed him as he realized just how much he had missed our banter . . . but he wouldn't succeed.

At that point, I knew one of three things would happen. Possibility One: He would gallantly offer me his arm and we would walk the gardens of the Getty for hours, talking and laughing. Possibility Two: He would gallantly—but mischievously—open the passenger door of the convertible. I would get in, and we would drive off to the Mulholland Drive overlook, where we would park and make out until sunrise.

Possibility Three: George Clooney would somehow break in there, and either Possibility One or Possibility Two would happen with him instead of Hamish.

Except all of that was how it would happen in the movies. Not real life.

But then, in a moment that really did feel like a scene from someone's imagination, a song ended and the crowd parted, and I spotted Hamish MacDougal standing thirty feet away from me talking to Michael Keaton. I made a quick mental note to remember to ask Fiona if all the Batmen had been invited or just Michael and George, and then I set off toward my destiny. And I was almost there when I ran smack into Ralph Fiennes, who seemed to materialize out of thin air. How very Voldemortish of him.

"Olivia, isn't it? Yes. Olivia Ross," he said in a voice that, I must admit, was manly and sexy and nearly enough to make me view him through the sensuous sepia hues of *The English Patient* rather than the monochromatically contrived filter of *Maid in Manhattan*. But either way, I had to keep my eyes on the prize.

I turned away from him, back to where Hamish had just been standing. The crowd was no longer parted, but I could just make out Michael Keaton over a few heads. Michael Keaton. Alone.

"Sorry, Ralph. No time!"

I pushed through the bodies in my way and saw Hamish's wavy hair and broad shoulders in silhouette as he neared the door. He was going outside! Or possibly the bathroom. No. Outside. Possibilities One and Two were still on the table.

My eyes struggled to adjust to the dimmer lights as

I followed him toward the exit, but by the time I could see clearly, I had lost him. I had a choice to make. Did I continue on straight ahead and chase the outdoor cinematic ending? Or did I turn left and pursue the less romantic but more realistic scenario in which I would be waiting in the hallway for him when he finished up in the men's room?

Against my more rational judgment I stepped outside, and real life crashed down upon me as I snagged the lace hem of my Vera Wang gown on the stem of a bay laurel topiary. I struggled to catch my breath while I looked around aimlessly. No one was waiting for me. That was it. It was official. I was meant to possess neither love nor designer clothes.

I could run back in. I could go down the hallway. I could take a chance that I would get there before Hamish exited the restroom, just in case he was actually in there and a car hadn't already driven him away. But the very concept of waiting for him while he finished up at the urinal was the wakeup call my perception of reality needed.

I looked out over the beautiful gardens and wanted nothing more than to run to them and get lost. A lifetime of not caring about romance. Of not fantasizing my days away. Of refusing to get caught up in emotions that were destined to lead to disappointment. This was why. This was what I knew about life—certainly about my life—that no one else seemed to understand. It just wasn't in the cards for me.

I'd been okay with that—and then they'd ruined me. Hamish and Liam and Malcolm. They'd each done their part to chip away, little by little. I hadn't asked for it. I hadn't asked for the pain that came with knowing no one would ever care enough to fight for me. The pain that came with wishing they would. Why was it that men accepted the end so easily when it came to me? Why did they accept with such finality little hiccups like having to rush off to auditions and breakups and being told I didn't love them and the bidding getting up to six figures?

"Ladies and gentlemen," a loud voice boomed across the property. "The dance is about to begin. Will all first-dance participants please report to the ballroom at once?"

My brain told me it was over, but my heart somehow convinced my eyes to appraise the grounds one more time. Just in case.

Nothing.

No one.

The cold washed over me as quickly as if I had cannon-balled into a swimming pool full of blue raspberry slushie in Death Valley in the middle of summer, and I found myself welcoming it.

I ignored the desire to run to the gardens and hide away and instead turned on my heel to go back inside. I would dance with the lying, cheating cretin who had spent a hundred grand of company money for the privilege of holding me in his arms for four minutes. I'd try to disregard the memory of when I'd wanted nothing more than to beg him to hold me for a life-time—no charge. I'd do it for Yemen. More importantly, I'd do it for Fiona. And then I'd get out of there as quickly as I possibly could, before anything else could trick my weakened resolve into believing, for even a moment more, that I had been cast into any roles that I hadn't been born to play.

He was waiting for me on the fringe of the haystack, the fact that he was the needle I had once loved making him stand out in a class all his own. In every other way, he blended in. He belonged there. He spoke the same language and sported the same style as all the other people in the room who had paid exorbitant prices to see and be seen.

"Nice tux," I greeted him. "Armani?"

"Tom Ford."

"What are you doing, Malcolm?"

"You look gorgeous, Liv. I would try to guess who made your outfit, but you know I have no idea."

"Vera Wang."

"It suits you."

Note to self: don't turn around and let him see the topiary damage.

"What are you doing, Malcolm?" I repeated.

"What do you mean—"

I scoffed. "You know what I mean. You threw away a lot of money on someone with two left feet."

"That's not true. If I recall, you and I had a lot of fun on the dance floor together."

"It's always fun when you're dancing with someone you like."

He shrugged and inched closer. "Then I'm going to have fun."

"Does it matter at all to you that I'm not?"

He cleared his throat and shuffled his shiny black shoes. "Look, Liv, I'm sorry. Not a day has gone by in the past three years that I haven't wished—"

"That you hadn't slept with your secretary?"

The amplified voice came across the sound system again. "Ladies and gentlemen, the Lakeside Society wishes to thank you, once again, for your benevolence. As you know, the Lakeside Society exists to bring attention and awareness to the plight of the many countries of the world where there is not enough water to sustain life."

I *knew* Fi was quoting that from a pamphlet.

"Because of your generosity here tonight, you are part of that important mission. Your impact will sustain communities for generations to come. Thank you. And now, would all first-dance participants please find their way to the dance floor."

I took Malcolm's offered hand and walked with him to the center of the room. We passed Robert Downey Jr. escorting Thandie Newton, who had apparently been his highest bidder. Matthew McConaughey was already sambaing around the floor with Tilda Swinton, and they quickly took the award for my favorite pairing of the night. George Clooney had Betty White in his arms, and even that coupling made better sense than me with any man in the building.

Hamish was nowhere to be seen, and as the opening chords of Eric Clapton's "Wonderful Tonight" began playing, I convinced myself to stop looking.

"Katie isn't my secretary," Malcolm spoke into my ear as my cheek lined up with his.

I pulled back and looked at him as he twirled us with expertise. "I'm sorry, what?"

"She's not my secretary, Liv, and you know it. You make it sound so . . . I don't know . . . cliché. Tacky."

I did a double take. "Hang on. Katie Bronson? The junior counsel you were working on that case with? The case that was so important we couldn't go to Italy? The Katie who set me up with that great caterer for the New Year's party you and I threw? *That* Katie? *That's* who you slept with?"

He froze, and the twirling ceased until Matthew and Tilda, oblivious to all life outside of their delightful bubble, bumped into us. Malcolm pulled me against him and found the rhythm again.

"You didn't know?"

"No, I didn't know! I just said it was your secretary because, well . . . you know . . . because it was cliché and tacky."

That was the moment when I, at least momentarily, lost my mind. I began to laugh maniacally, and I couldn't control it at all. He, on the other hand, looked terrified. Olivia Ross was sensible, for the most part. Olivia Ross did a pretty good job of keeping her emotions in check. Olivia Ross was not typically prone to mental breakdowns in a roomful of celebrities.

"I'm sorry," he said softly. "I assumed he told you."

I shook my head, trying to make sense of it all. "You assumed *who* told me?" Of course, as soon as the words left my mouth, I knew.

"Liam. He never seemed to like me as much after all of that, and I figured that was probably because the two of you were better friends than either one of you let on."

The tightness in my chest worked its way up and constricted my throat. "Yeah, it couldn't have had anything to do with him realizing you weren't, in fact, likable."

"Actually," he began with a casual tone, though his twitchy fingers against my waist gave away the gravity he was feeling. "I always wondered if it was you."

"If *what* was me?"

"If you were the one who broke him."

It had been a long time since I'd had any desire to be back in Malcolm's arms, but in that moment I knew they were the only thing keeping me upright.

"'Broke him'?"

He loosened his grip on my waist and leaned his shoulders back to look at me. "Smart money was on Fiona, I guess. I mean, one day they were this perfect, happy couple, and the next he was giving his notice. But when I tried to convince him to stay, it was suddenly all about you."

"What do you mean?" I whimpered. I was desperate for information and clinging to every painful word, but I had no faith whatsoever in my ability to get through the conversation in one piece.

He shrugged again. "He said he couldn't work for someone like me. Someone who had treated you the way I had."

I cleared my throat. "It sounds like that was about you, Malcolm. Not me."

Eric Clapton's final notes rang out, and I pulled out of Malcolm's grasp as people all around us began to clap.

"Larcraft! I thought that was you!" I heard the voice from behind me as an elderly couple rushed toward us.

"Rick, Kathleen, how good to see you." He shook the man's hand and kissed the woman on the cheek. His voice was in control, but his eyes seemed to have a mind of their own as they darted from me to Rick and Kathleen and back again. "May I introduce you to Olivia Ross?" He gestured toward me, and they seemed to notice me for the first time. "Olivia's an old friend. Liv, this is Rick and Kathleen Boynes. Kathleen is one of the founding members of the Lakeside Society and on the board here at the Getty, if I'm not mistaken. And Rick married up and is the luckiest man alive."

Rick laughed uproariously and Kathleen put her hand on Malcolm's arm and said, "Oh, you!" I feigned a smile and shook their hands as Malcolm added, "Rick is also the senior partner at the firm."

Why had I ever found him or any of this attractive? Even his

The Way We Were hair annoyed me. How had it not changed at all in three years? How had *he* not changed at all in three years?

"Lovely to meet you, Olivia," Kathleen said as her dainty little hand shook mine. "It's nice to see Malcolm with a friend outside of the office."

"Yes." Rick laughed. "We didn't know he *had* friends outside of the office."

"We're not friends," I replied. "He paid one hundred thousand dollars to dance with me. That's all."

Malcolm laughed uncomfortably. "Well, technically I suppose Rick's signing the check."

Rick slapped him on the arm and joined in the laughter. "Money well spent!" And then with a wink he tagged on, "To support the Lakeside Society, I mean. See you on Monday, Larcraft. Don't have too much fun."

Ick. Ick, ick, ick.

The moment we were alone—apart from the dozens of rich people all around us—Malcolm shifted into a more intimate gear. "Look, Liv, this didn't go the way I had hoped."

"How did you hope this would go? What did you think your money was going to get you?"

He groaned. "This has nothing to do with the money. I was tasked with donating a hundred thousand to the Lakeside Society tonight, and when I saw you up there, I decided to be done with it all in one fell swoop. I didn't know you'd be here. I didn't have any plans. I just saw an opportunity and took it. I thought it would be nice to reconnect—"

"'Nice'?" I blurted out. "Do you know what a mess I was when we broke up? Do you know that I went to Italy—"

"Good! That's what I wanted you to—"

"For a year, Malcolm. I went to Italy for a year. I . . ." I sniffed and willed the tears to stay in place. "I lost a year of my life. And no, that wasn't your fault. Not entirely. But forgive me for not wanting to 'reconnect.'"

His eyes broke away from mine, and he began looking from side to side, as if one of the passersby would, perhaps, be able to help him out.

"I'm sorry about everything, Liv," he said as his feet began slowly retreating from the uncomfortable intimacy between us. "I truly am."

"Hey, Livi." Fi was suddenly by my side, her arm looped through mine. "Everything okay?"

"Yep, everything's great." I grabbed her hand and smiled at her. "I was just going to take off."

"It's good to see you, Fiona," Malcolm said with that same schmoozy tone he'd used with Rick and Kathleen. "When was the last time? I suppose at the firm's Christmas party—"

"Oh, shut up, Malcolm," she seethed.

His eyes widened. "Excuse me?" Who knows how long it had been since he had failed to charm even one woman. Much less two.

Fi sighed as she threw her arm over my shoulder. "You're right. That was rude. Forgive me." She adopted her sweetest voice. "On behalf of the Lakeside Society, please allow me to pass along our sincere appreciation for the generosity of Boynes, Madison & Larcraft. But if you ever come near my girl again, it won't matter how much attention and awareness you bring to the plight of the many countries of the world where there is not enough water to sustain life. I will destroy you. Do you understand me?"

We didn't wait for him to snap out of his stunned silence. We just turned and walked toward the door, arm in arm.

"You okay?" she asked as we parted the crowd.

"I am. I do have a question, though."

She smiled at various patrons, and they smiled back. "Fire away."

"I'm just wondering . . . Could you tell me one thing about the Lakeside Society that isn't printed in the pamphlet? Even one?"

She stopped in her tracks, and I had no choice but to stop alongside her. She thought for a moment and then smirked. "Nope. I've got nothing."

As children we played here, with abandon and glee,

While dreaming of "someday" and what we would be.

The sky was our limit. We were untethered and free.

It was all possible for you and for me.

Now we are older and amazed how time flies.

We're busier. More hurried, with eyes on the prize.

But something about coming back to this place,

Of once more experiencing, face-to-face,

The joy of our childhood, the freedom of then . . .

It helps me remember the magic of "when."

When possibility was big, and problems were small.

When we welcomed a challenge, accepted them all.

When rather than bury us, trials made us stand tall.

When we knew that together, we never would fall.

Welcome home.

Heartlite® Greeting Card Co., Number 10-Y76Co

FEBRUARY 4, 2010

On the day I was born, my brother, Brandon, who was six at the time, was hit by a car. He was pretty much fine, apart from a broken bicycle and some bruises. But it was scary enough that when my dad received the call at the hospital from my grandmother, on whose watch the accident took place, he left the hospital where my mother had just given birth to me to travel across Boston to the hospital where Brandon was.

That was the first of countless times my big brother stole my spotlight.

While I was recovering from chicken pox, Brandon contracted meningitis. I was left quarantined with chicken soup and old episodes of *The Andy Griffith Show* while all of the constant, loving attention I had been receiving from my mother was redirected his way—simply because his disease was more life-threatening than mine and there was a chance his brain might explode or something. He chose the evening of my senior prom to announce he was dropping out of grad school to enlist in the Air Force, the afternoon of my high school graduation to tell us he was getting married, and he called our parents from Kirtland Air Force Base to inform them he was getting a divorce just moments after I told them I was leaving Boston and moving to Los Angeles.

Therefore, it came as no real surprise to me that the day Fiona and I arrived in Boston together for the first time in nearly a decade, for a surprise visit, was the day Brandon arrived in Boston on leave. His visit was also a surprise—and, obviously, a better one.

I don't believe my parents have ever tried to love him more. It just naturally happened along the way.

"That's ridiculous." Fi laughed as we bundled up in our eleven layers of clothing in preparation for leaving our hotel to join our parents and Brandon for dinner. "They do not love him more."

"No, they do." I nodded complacently, having long ago come to terms with my position as the second favorite Ross child.

"But you have the best parents—"

"Oh, I know. They *are* the best. And I know that I am well loved. And if they ever realized they love him more they would be horrified and live out the rest of their lives in full guilt mode." I shrugged. "It's not intentional. It's just circumstantial."

We braced ourselves for the painful Massachusetts winter air and began walking the four blocks to the country club Landon and Jocelyn were members of. I'd never pictured the Rosses as country-club people, but the Mitchells most assuredly were.

I hadn't been to the club myself since I was a little girl. For as many years as I could remember, Fi had had her birthday parties there. She was never impressed by any of it—that was just a part of her life—and I think she would have given anything to have a party, just one year, at the bowling alley or the ice-skating rink like the rest of us always did. The grass is always greener, I suppose, but I thought she was crazy for feeling that way. I loved the country club. Everything was made of luxurious solid wood and marble, and everyone who worked there was always so nice. As a child I didn't realize they were paid to be nice; I just knew that they were nice. The bowling-alley people weren't as nice, as a rule—though presumably they were paid to be nice as well. Well, be nice and spray the insides of the shoes—a task of equal importance.

"Remind me . . ." I shivered as we approached the opulent entrance to the club. "Why did we decide to leave the warm coast for the frigid coast in the dead of winter?"

"To take back control!" Fi muttered with exuberance through her scarf. "You're going to finally conquer the absurdity of February 4 and show this date who's boss!"

I rolled my eyes at her and laughed. "That's right. Now I remember."

In truth, for all her current enthusiasm, Fiona hadn't been easy to convince. After all, she was fascinated by the absurdity. She loved the idea of there being no control over love's influence in our lives. She enjoyed getting caught up in what she perceived as fate or serendipity or destiny . . . or something. But I couldn't take another year of wondering when Hamish would pop around the corner. I couldn't suffer through another twenty-four hours of waiting for some sort of heartbreak that would inevitably be associated with Liam. And after Malcolm staked his claim on the day last year . . . Yeah. No more.

The formal doorman greeted us, and we stepped into the warmth.

"We're looking for the Mitchell party," Fi said with a smile as she handed him her coat.

The doorman's assistance in locating our party ended up being unnecessary.

"Darling!"

We stole a quick, sardonic glance at each other before turning to the voices of our mothers ringing out in unison. My jaw dropped, and I heard Fi stifling a giggle beside me, and I realized I had accomplished my mission. The absurdity of this February 4 would have nothing whatsoever to do with Hamish MacDougal. Not when I got to spend the evening with Susannah Ross and Jocelyn Mitchell dressed up from head to toe like 1920s flapper girls.

Fi took a step toward them, but I grabbed her elbow and pulled her back. "Hey, Fi, wait a second."

"What's up?"

"I'm serious, you know. I don't want anything about this day to have anything to do with Ironic Day. If we so much as walk past a movie theater and there's a Hamish movie playing, we're hopping in a cab and going to the Boston Massacre site or something. If an unlisted number calls my phone, I'm throwing it right into the Harbor, just to be safe. And so help me, Fiona Mitchell, after this moment, the name Liam Howard is just a string of gobbledygook letters that means nothing in our language. We're clear on this, right?"

She placed her hands on my shoulders and squeezed gently as she smiled. "We're clear. As of this moment, no Hamish, no Liam, no Malcolm, no romance, no fun, no adventure—"

I groaned. "You promised. Seriously, Fi. Today we let this go. I just need, on this one February 4, to prove that it's all been a fluke. An odd little series of coincidences that stops now. This year is what's going to keep me—"

"From being institutionalized. I know, Livi. I get it." She dropped her hands from my shoulders. "I'm here, aren't I? Would I have given up my post-gala forty-eight hours of sleep and junk food to get on a plane to Boston with you if I wasn't all in?"

Fiona's second Lakeside Society fundraiser had been an even bigger success than her first, at least according to her own report. I would have to take her word for it. For reasons understandable to all, she hadn't fought me too hard this time when I declined her invitation to attend.

"I know. You're right. Thanks, Fi. I'm just . . . over it. You know?"

She nodded. "I do. So stop thinking about it and come on. Clara Bow and Thoroughly Modern Millie are waiting for us."

"Hi, Mom," I said with a smile a few seconds later. A smile that quickly transformed from slight apprehension to total disbelief. "What are you wearing?"

"It's costume night, sweetie!" She leaned in and kissed me on the cheek and then did the same to Fi. "Didn't we tell you? I could have sworn we told you this morning at breakfast."

I heard Fiona snort, and I looked at her to confirm that we'd been told no such thing. I was certain that if we had, we would have remembered. We still wouldn't have dressed up, of course, but we would have remembered making the conscious choice to disregard our mothers' impassioned pleas.

"Did the two of you get together ahead of time and decide to be twinsies? Or was that just a happy coincidence?" Fi asked with a smirk.

It was so odd to both of us. Our parents had lived nearly an entire lifetime circling each other. Their daughters had been inseparable for three decades, and yet all it took, apparently, was the two of us getting out of their way for them to start spending time together. Over breakfast they had regaled us with tales of golf outings and canasta parties and the cruise they had booked for June.

"Well, of course it was intentional, Fiona." Jocelyn laughed. "And just wait until you see Henry and your father. They look like Jay Gatsby: The Later Years."

"If only that whole getting murdered in the swimming pool thing hadn't gotten in the way," I muttered to Fi, and she chuckled.

"Come along, girls," my mother chirped, hooking her arms through ours and forcing us to walk farther into the club. "Brandon is already here, and I'm starving!"

"Did Brandon dress up?" Fi asked, but we didn't have to wait long for an answer to that question.

"Ahoy, there!" he shouted toward us, jumping up onto his chair and pulling a telescope to his eye—the eye that wasn't covered by an eye patch, of course. "Arrrgh, there be ladies here!"

Everyone laughed at him and all his ridiculousness. Well, everyone except me. I just rolled my eyes, though I couldn't fight the slight smile that made its way to my lips despite my best efforts.

He jumped down from his chair and rushed over to hug us both in a way befitting neither a pirate nor a country club—but it was all overwhelmingly Brandon. I'd never been able to deny that the guy was insanely lovable. In fact, despite my lifelong feelings of inadequacy, I'd always been his biggest fan. He was a complete dork, and he drove me crazy more than anyone else on earth, but he was my big brother, and I was in awe of him.

"You do realize you're a forty-three-year-old child, don't you?" I asked him as I leaned into his embrace.

"I prefer man-child, actually." He grinned at me and my stoicism melted. "I'm glad you're here, sis. Best surprise ever."

Before long, Henry and Landon Gatsby joined us, and we sat down to a strange, wonderful, first-time-ever full Ross and Mitchell family dinner. Conversation was rich, sentiments were real, the food was delicious, and apart from Brandon's incessant booty puns, the humor was hysterical.

At one point when the conversation turned to the second retelling of a you-had-to-be-there story from the parents' recent night at the theater, Brandon leaned over to whisper conspiratorially to Fiona and me.

"Hey, so some friends are meeting me here in a little bit, and we're going to take off. You two should come with us."

"Friends?" I asked. "You've been back in Boston for two days and you have *friends* you want to hang out with? When your sister's only here until Sunday?"

"Don't give me that guilt trip. I invited you! Besides, it's only one friend." He blushed. Brandon Ross blushed. "And then she's bringing some friends."

He had always been fun to tease. "Are you going to invite

your parents, who worry like crazy when you're away fighting for our freedom—"

"Behind a desk in Albuquerque."

"—and treasure every moment that you're safely back home within their grasp?"

He chuckled. "Um, no. I am not taking Scott and Zelda over there out dancing at Club Uey. And besides, they're not going to have to worry as much anymore about the possibility of me being injured in some act of office-work heroism on distant New Mexican shores."

He winked, and I felt my stomach sink in a familiar way. I had no idea what he was alluding to, but I knew that my surprise visit home was about to be further overshadowed.

"Why? What are you talking about?"

"Hey, let's get back to what matters here," Fiona interjected as she leaned around me to get closer to Brandon. "Who's this one friend? You said 'she.' Spill it, Ross."

The color crept up his face again. "You'll meet her when she gets here."

"What's her name?" Fi pushed.

"Sonya."

"And how'd you meet?"

He rolled his eyes, but his joy was evident. "I forgot how annoying you are." When Fi didn't reply but simply rested her chin on her knuckles and kept staring at him, he gave in. "We went to high school together. We reconnected last year on this online message board for our twenty-five-year class reunion. They tried to stage an online party for those of us who couldn't make it to the actual thing. There were only about six of us who bothered to sign in at all, and by the end of the night it was just

Sonya and me." He shrugged, but the joy remained. "She's been out to visit me on the base a few times since then, and during my last leave I met her and her kids—"

"'Her kids'?" Fiona's eyes grew even wider.

"Yeah. Matthew is seven, and Maisie is five. Her husband died in a car accident in 2007. Sonya and the kids and I spent a few days at the Cape, getting to know each other." He pointed his finger at me. "Don't you dare tell Mom and Dad I was in Massachusetts and didn't see them."

"Brandon!" Fiona squealed quietly. "You're going to marry this girl, aren't you?"

The goofiness and any lingering annoyance with his little sister's pushy best friend melted off his face. "If I have anything to say about it, you bet I am." His eyes flashed to me, and I measured my reaction. I'd never seen him regard me so earnestly.

I swallowed down the emotions I didn't quite understand. Yes, everything was all about Brandon, and that always pushed my buttons. But that wasn't it. Not this time. I was used to not being in the spotlight. Apart from fleeting moments here and there, I'd never wanted to be. But this time my brother had something I did want. I wanted to feel for myself the certainty and the happiness and the love—all wrapped up in one earnest and goofy package—that were radiating from him.

For thirty-seven years he had outshone me, but true jealousy was just now imparting on its maiden voyage.

"Oh my gosh, Bran," I whispered through the frog in my throat. "I'm so happy for you."

And I was. I wouldn't have taken his happiness away from him for anything in the world. I just wouldn't have minded having some of that for myself.

He grinned at me like a schmuck. "Thanks, sis. I can't wait for you to meet her."

Fiona glanced around the big, circular table to verify that our parents were still in their own little world. Indeed, they were. I heard murmurings of plans to visit DC when the cherry blossoms bloomed. Fi's interrogation resumed.

"Tell us more. What does she do?"

"She works in the communications office at Harvard. She used to be an assistant metro editor at the *Globe*, but after her husband died . . ."

It wasn't that I wasn't interested in hearing all the details about the woman my brother loved. I was. But I was unable to focus on anything he was saying. Random details about Sonya's career and how smart and cute Matthew and Maisie were intermingled with comments like, "Oh, but you have to see the Jefferson Memorial at sunset, surrounded by all that pink."

Snap out of it, Liv. Wonderful things were happening for the people I loved. My parents and the Mitchells were living their best life. Brandon was in love. Fiona was singlehandedly saving Yemen. And it sounded like I was about to become an aunt.

Maybe it just wasn't in the cards for me. Any of it. Love, fulfilled dreams—*my* best life. Then again, maybe this *was* my best life and I needed to get busy living it. I had it pretty good, overall. I got to write for a living. I got to live vicariously through Fiona's fabulous adventures without ever having to put on a bra or makeup. I got to go to the beach whenever I wanted.

When was the last time I had gone to the beach? How stupid! I loved the beach. I loved the ocean. Why did I never go? Why didn't I spend my days there with my laptop? And when was I ever going to finish my blasted screenplay?

"This year," I muttered to myself, and of course I'd spoken during the one millisecond of silence that had occurred all evening.

"What's that, dear?" my mother asked.

I shook my head. "Nothing. Sorry." I smiled at Fi in response to the questioning in her eyes.

The chatter picked back up as a waiter approached our table and began gathering empty plates.

"You okay?" Fi asked.

"I guess I'm just tired of never being the one with exciting news. Does that make me petty?"

She squeezed my hand and shook her head. "Not at all."

Once the waiter had departed, Brandon stood up and clinked his glass. "If I could have everyone's attention for a second, I have an announcement to make."

I laughed softly. Fi looked at me with concern, but I shook it off.

He smiled and took a deep breath. "Mom, Dad, I wasn't completely truthful with you guys when I said this was just routine leave. The truth is I've been reassigned."

Ah. His earlier wink began to make sense. The spotlight was his. I attempted to dissipate the inexplicable bitterness I was feeling by thinking about how happy my parents were about to be.

My mother gasped, no doubt bracing herself for the worst. "Oh no. They don't need you back in Afghanistan, do they?"

Back in Afghanistan? He had been part of the administrative team of a two-day supply mission nearly a decade ago. Still heroic and patriotic? Absolutely. Befitting of the reverence and veneration with which my mother regarded those uneventful forty-eight hours? In my opinion, not so much.

Brandon smiled at her across the table. "No, Mom, it's okay. This reassignment is a bit closer to home."

"So, tell us, son," my dad said as impassively as he could as he placed his arm around my mother.

"Before I tell you, I just need to thank you. You've always encouraged us to follow our dreams, and I know that Liv and I are both so grateful for the ways you've supported us, even when we've done crazy things like join the military or move to Hollywood. I'll never forget what you said when—"

"Oh, good grief, Brandon. Just get on with it!" I exclaimed, startling everyone. No one more than myself. I cleared my throat and adjusted in my seat. "I am so sorry. I, um . . . I agree. With everything you're saying. I'm just . . . Well, I'm just so anxious to hear the news!"

"Nice save," Fiona chortled through clenched teeth.

Brandon quirked his eyebrow at me as he continued. "Well, I guess I should get to it, then. Effective immediately, I've been reassigned to Hanscom." Everyone continued staring at him. "Hanscom Air Force Base." Silence. "You know . . . in Bedford." Nothing.

"You guys, he's moving home," I said.

It finally clicked.

My parents jumped up in a torrent of squeals and lots of flapping, courtesy of my mother's sparkly garb. Landon and Jocelyn were a little more refined, as always, but even they seemed thrilled. And Brandon soaked it all in as he always had. He thrived on being the center of attention. He needed it, like sunflowers need sun. And he had it, once again.

I didn't move. I couldn't. Fiona wrapped her arms around

me and leaned her head against mine as she said with a sigh, "Okay. I get it now."

"Hey, Liv, you okay?" Brandon asked, taking me off guard. I was shocked. He had never before seemed to notice how his big announcements knocked the breath out of me. Then again, maybe I'd always had the energy to cover it better than I did this time.

All eyes were on me, and I had no choice but to suck it up, once again. "Of course. I'm so happy for you. And for them!" Again, I meant it. I smiled as valiantly as I could as I stood and hugged him. "I mean, you're ridiculous, of course." I flicked his clip-on gold-hoop earring. "But I am so happy for you."

"Hey, everybody," Fiona interrupted the reverie a bit too loudly. "Livi has an announcement too."

Wait, what? Pulling back from Brandon, I looked at her with terror in my eyes. What was she doing?

"What is it, hon?" my dad asked with all the interest he could possibly muster, considering all of the energy being diverted to the celebration that his baby boy was moving back home.

"Oh, I don't know . . ." *Seriously. I really don't know.*

"She's just being modest," Fi pressed onward. "It's huge. And I, for one, am immensely proud of her, and I know you all will be too."

"Well, let's have it, Liv," Brandon said, I think genuinely excited to hear what wonderful thing was happening in my life.

"I mean it. I don't have anything." I hoped no one noticed the tears in my eyes as I slid back into my seat. "I think Fiona is just—"

"Her screenplay is getting made into a film starring Hamish MacDougal!"

My head snapped toward Fi, while everyone else's heads snapped toward me. Well, everyone's except the bearer of the unbelievably exciting and extraordinarily false news. She avoided my eyes and kept on spewing the lies. "She doesn't want to talk about it, because there are still a lot of details being worked out, and of course she doesn't want to steal the moment from Brandon, but—"

"Liv!" Brandon ripped off his eye patch as he ran to the back of my chair and squeezed me from behind. "How dare you try to keep that from us! My little sister's a star!"

"Oh my goodness," my mom said, her hand covering her mouth. "I didn't even realize you had finished your screenplay. That's incredible! Does this mean you'll be leaving Heartlite?"

"Of course she'll be leaving Heartlite!" my dad boasted. And then, to complete the paternal moment, he added, "Though you still need to give two weeks' notice, of course."

"That's remarkable, Olivia," Jocelyn chimed in. "Congratulations. I'm not quite sure I know who Hamish MacDougal is, but it's all very exciting."

"Champagne all around!" Landon said, flagging down a waiter.

"I'm so proud of you, kiddo," Brandon said with emotion in his voice, and then he kissed the top of my head before returning to his seat. "Okay. Tell us everything."

I looked around the table, and every eye was on me. I had the spotlight. In a moment that had been all about Brandon, I had the spotlight. It was just too bad that the spotlight was cheapened and, in fact, meaningless because it was acquired through ill-gotten means. I had to confess the truth before things got any further out of hand, but I knew that in their eyes I was about to go from a star on the rise to the suspected victim of a midlife crisis.

"Sure." My voice trembled. "I'll tell you everything, but I need to run to the restroom first. Fiona, will you accompany me?" I didn't look at her, and I didn't wait for a reply. I just stood up and walked toward the ladies' room, needing to escape as quickly as possible.

She began to speak as we entered the beautifully feminine restroom, which was roughly the size of our apartment. "Livi, look, I'm—"

"What were you thinking?" I hissed as I finally turned to face her. "How could you do that to me? You just . . . You made it all so much worse."

I didn't know if I was angry or hurt. Both, probably.

"I'm sorry," she whispered, and tears rolled down her cheeks. "I didn't think. I'm just so proud of you, and I wanted you to have your moment."

"But there's nothing to be proud of!"

"That is not true."

"It is, Fi! I have an incomplete screenplay I've been working on for seven years. *Seven years!*"

"But it *is* getting made into a film starring Hamish MacDougal! I believe that."

"It's not even a great story, much less a well-written one, and the only reason I've never moved on to something else is because of the stupid, nagging idea in my head that maybe February 4 actually means something. And all I wanted for today was for it not to mean anything. That's all I wanted, Fi. And you said you'd support me in that."

She sniffed before walking to grab tissues for us both. "I know. I'm sorry."

"We were here to wash away the February 4 madness. And now . . ." I sighed.

"I know," she repeated. "So let's wash away the madness—but not the reality. It's been seven years. You have three years left to—"

I growled at her. I hardly recognized the sound as my own as it echoed around the cavernous space. "Let it go, already!"

"No." She crossed her arms and planted her feet. "No, Liv. I won't let it go. I can't. You've just happened to be in the same room with him twice since you met him. Always on the same date. How is that even possible—"

"We live in Los Angeles. I've seen Bette Midler three times at three separate Trader Joe's in the last year. How is *that* possible?"

She stared at me, gearing up to argue, and then her eyes melted into amusement and she began to laugh. "Well, yes. That does seem somewhat unlikely."

"See?" I smiled at her as the tension between us dissipated.

She took a deep breath and leaned against the velvet settee. "I really am sorry. I didn't mean to throw it out there, and I didn't think about the repercussions. I just . . . Sheesh, I thought you were exaggerating about Brandon. How have I never noticed that before?"

I shrugged rather than tell her the reason I suspected she wasn't usually clued into Brandon's propensity for the spotlight. It was because when it wasn't Brandon overshadowing me, it was her. Between the two of them, I'd developed quite the vitamin-D deficiency through the years. And, again, I usually wouldn't have had it any other way.

"Well, regardless," she continued as she dabbed the tissue under her eyes. "I'm not going to apologize for believing in you."

"I wouldn't want you to." A grateful grin overtook my lips. "Now let's get out there. Brandon's probably about to announce he's been chosen to colonize Mars or something."

I adjusted my top and ran my fingers through my hair as we approached the table. I hadn't been sure how I was going to get out of this one, but it looked like maybe the cavalry had arrived. A new group of people were huddled around the table, and a striking brunette was sticking particularly close to Brandon. Even an actual movie being made with Hamish MacDougal right there in the country club would not have been enough to distract my mother once she put the pieces together and realized her little boy had requested a transfer because he had fallen in love. The woman who got Brandon Ross to move home would be dubbed a saint.

"Liv!" Brandon called out as we approached. "Sonya, this is my little sister, Olivia. Liv, this is Sonya."

She hurried over and hugged me, and I liked her right away. She had warm eyes, and they never strayed from Brandon for long.

"It's so great to meet you, Olivia. You're pretty much all he talks about."

I laughed. "That's terrifying."

Brandon continued the introductions. "And that's my other little sister, Fiona."

Fi looked genuinely touched, and I sort of was too. I'd never heard him refer to her that way.

"Hi, Sonya," Fi said as she got her hug.

"He tells me the two of you have been friends since you were little."

"Yep," Fi confirmed. "We have decades of annoying Brandon together under our belts."

As Brandon talked to our mother, who was predictably beside herself, Sonya introduced us to her friends. There was Sean, who worked in the admissions office at Harvard; Dehlia, an adjunct professor at Harvard; Samantha, a clinical professor at Harvard Law; and Aziza, who was a visiting lecturer at the Harvard Kennedy School.

Surrounded by that group of brilliant academics, it totally felt like the right time to confess that my entire career plan was based around keeping my fingers crossed that a movie star would stop for a cup of coffee in three years.

"Brandon says the two of you are going out with us tonight?" Sonya asked. "I'm so glad. I know you're only in town for a little while, and I'm anxious to get to know you."

"Of course we'll go," Fi replied. "Sounds fun."

Sonya leaned in and murmured, "I told him this wasn't the best way to introduce me to your parents—a quick drop-in with friends, then we take off. But Club Uey is just down the street, so he insisted."

I shook my head. "No, I think it's good. This is perfect, actually. They'll get a little taste and then be left with their friends to rehash and analyze every moment." I had to hand it to him. My big brother was a master of parental influence.

The master popped up behind Sonya. "You guys ready?"

"I think so." Sonya smiled up at him. "Sean and Samantha have friends meeting us there, but this is it for our traveling party."

"You girls are leaving too?" my mom asked as she adjusted her cloche hat.

We each walked over and kissed our parents' cheeks, and I

wrapped my arms around my dad from behind. "We'll see you in the morning."

"I feel bad," my dad said as he patted my arm. "We didn't get to finish your celebration."

Fi and I looked at each other and resisted the urge to laugh. The cork of a second bottle of champagne had just been popped, and not a single member of the younger Mitchell or Ross generation had consumed a sip.

"I have complete faith in your ability to celebrate on my behalf."

"Remind me," I repeated as we walked the six blocks from the country club to Club Uey. "Why did we decide to leave the warm coast for the frigid coast in the dead of winter?"

Even Fiona was shivering now that the sun had gone down in its entirety. Through her scarf and chattering teeth she replied, "Because we're idiots?"

"Ah, yes. That's right."

We arrived—by my estimation mere seconds before the cryogenic freezing process took full effect—and found a table in the back. I was sweating by the time I got to the table, having pushed through a cluster of overheated bodies dancing and shouting to be heard over the pumping bass of the music.

Sean's friend—I think his name was Logan, but it was difficult to tell over the sound of my eardrums bursting—was there waiting and ordered the first round before we'd even pulled enough seats around the table. It was as we were finally getting coats off and struggling with what to do with them—considering we only had barstools standing between safety and sticky floors where they would most assuredly be trampled—that Samantha's friend arrived.

"Hey, everybody, this is Liam. Liam, this is everybody."

My back was to them, but one glance at Fiona was all it took to understand that we already knew this Liam. Her eyes were as wide and glistening as the abundant disco balls overhead. I consoled myself with the knowledge that there was at least a small chance the numbness in my extremities and my inability to breathe were nothing more than symptoms of the final stages of hypothermia. But I knew I needed to consider my options, just in case death was *not* imminent, and wondered if I still had time to sink below the high table and mosey into the crowd before he spotted me. Before I had to look at him. But three things were keeping me in place:

1. The helpless look in Fiona's eyes as she came face-to-face with him for the first time since he'd broken up with her two years prior.
2. My overwhelming desire to take in the sight of him and recharge, one last time, for the rest of my life without him.
3. The thought of just how sticky those floors probably were.

"You okay?" I asked Fi, my back still turned to him.

It was as if someone had snapped their fingers and broken Fiona free of hypnosis. It was so instant that it was almost creepy, and I couldn't help but wonder if for the rest of her life she was going to cluck like a chicken whenever someone said, "Peanut butter and jelly."

"Liam!" she squealed in apparent delight. "What in the world are you doing here?"

Then I had no choice but to turn around, because there could be no doubt that all eyes were going to be on her . . . and by extension us. Liam was blocked by half the current members of the Hasty Pudding Club, but I caught Brandon's eyes. I tried to unlock some special sibling powers to telepathically communicate that this was *the* Liam I had told him about. Love-of-my-life Liam. Most-serious-relationship-Fiona-had-ever-had Liam. Maybe if I got lucky, I could also communicate that Fi had told a bald-faced lie when she said I was making a movie with Hamish MacDougal and that he should break the news to our parents. And maybe, if I concentrated, I could even get him to order me a drink and have it delivered to me somewhere a little farther away from the scene that was currently unfolding—like New Hampshire.

"What?" Brandon mouthed at me as he shrugged, and I silently cursed our wasted childhood in which we had not worked together to develop even one secret language between us.

"Uh . . . Fiona. Wow," Liam stammered. "Wh-what are you doing here? I mean, it's great to see you, of course—"

"You two know each other?" Samantha asked.

"We, um . . ."

"We're old friends," Fiona interjected, cool as a cucumber, and then she hurried over to hug him.

I watched her pass and caught Brandon's eyes again as she did. He got it now. Too little, too late. "Liam?" he mouthed emphatically.

I closed my eyes and nodded subtly.

Brandon knew more than most, but even he didn't know all the salacious details about the strange, dramatic history Liam, Fiona, and I shared. He knew I'd dated him for eight months. He knew he'd become my closest friend while Fiona was in Paris. And he knew that in Italy I'd begun to look at breaking up with Liam as the great regret of my life. But he also knew that by the time I got back home, Fiona and Liam were together. And from that point on, the details I shared with my brother were intentionally vague, evasive, and often downright untruthful.

Brandon didn't know that, and he certainly didn't know why.

"Dance with me, Brandon," Fiona insisted as she pulled him onto the dance floor, and I was left alone in an impossible situation. In true coward's fashion, I swiveled back to the table with lightning-like reflexes that proved my organs were not on the verge of succumbing to hypothermia after all. I just couldn't catch a break!

I wanted to kill her. I'd stuck around and not followed through on my brilliant "slink out like a snake" plan because I knew I never could abandon her that way. She, apparently, felt no such loyalty. Of course the difference, I knew, was that as far as my best friend was concerned, I'd never had any particularly strong feelings for Liam. Yes, the last time I saw him I was kissing him in the kitchen, but that had just been a flash. A mistake. A momentary loss of good judgment. When it came right down to it, Liam and I had never been more than friends, as far as Fiona was concerned. And as Liam's former best friend—and as Fiona's forever one—she knew I would be happy to take the bullet for her.

She was right. I would have to take that bullet. After all, I had been the one to load the gun.

"Olivia?"

I took a deep breath and turned back around. "Oh my goodness. Liam? Wow! What in the world are you doing here?"

His smile faded, though he quickly covered the reaction and forced it to return to his lips. His mouth valiantly acted like everything was fine—though his eyes seemed to tell a different story—and the smile grew larger as he raised his hand in gentle greeting. I forced my face and my hand to mirror his. At least, I hoped that's what I was doing. I hoped that the total demise and destruction of my heart and soul wasn't on display for all the world to see.

I decided I had to take control of the situation, so I circled around the table to him. It wasn't a long walk, but I had far too much time to absorb the sight of him. He looked older, but not in the ways I knew I probably looked older. While I continually found myself having to increase my use of moisturizer and night cream in order to combat the tiny lines at my eyes, his face had simply gone from that of a handsome young man to that of a sexy mature guy. His jawline was accentuated in a new and tantalizing way by the slightly longer sideburns that accompanied his slightly longer hair. He'd clearly gained some weight, though every last pound appeared to be pure muscle.

And he was wearing jeans. Liam had always been as comfortable in a three-piece suit as most people were in their sweats, and his lazy-Saturday-at-home wardrobe had been khakis and a button-up. But in that nightclub—an environment in which I'd never even imagined him—he wore jeans that fit perfectly and a T-shirt with sleeves that didn't seem completely convinced they were strong enough to contain his biceps.

"Well, hey," I said as I approached, determined to appear

relaxed and unaffected. I would refuse to give him any reason to suspect I had been anything less than completely truthful when I had denied loving him.

"Hey, yourself." His smile appeared as genuine as mine. He leaned in and hugged me, and it wasn't nostalgic. Or even warm. It was a formality. Well, for him it was only a formality. For me it was pain and regret and a longing to turn back time.

"So, um, seriously, what brings you to Boston?" It was a feeble attempt to pretend location was the aspect of running into him that was most shocking to my senses.

"I live here, actually."

"Oh, wow. Are you at Harvard too, or—"

He shook his head. "No. Still practicing law. I left LA and spent some time at a nonprofit in New Orleans, of all places, and then one of my old law professors called me with an offer to join his private practice in Beacon Hill about a year ago—"

"Beacon Hill, huh? Not exactly nonprofit work now, I'd imagine."

He laughed. "No. Not exactly. But, hey . . . what about you? Are you and Fiona just here for a visit, or—"

"I'm gonna go dance," Samantha interjected, and I looked at her differently as she silently and effortlessly placed her hand in his. She was tall, thin, blonde, and beautiful—and obviously brilliant too. What had Sonya said Samantha did at Harvard? Some sort of law professor.

Liam turned his head and smiled at her, and I tried to ignore the sting that accompanied the realization that for her his smile was genuine. "I'm sorry. I didn't even introduce you—"

"No, it's fine. We met back at the country club." Kindness and confidence exuded from her as she grinned at me. "You take your time catching up." She kissed him lightly on the lips, and then she was on the dance floor with everyone else, and only Liam and I remained.

The only thing I wanted more than to run away as quickly as I could was to stay right where I was with him forever.

He tore his eyes away from the huddled mass under the flashing strobe lights, where one ex-girlfriend danced about four feet away from his current one. "So, um . . . are you just visiting?"

The music got even louder—somehow. "Yeah," I shouted. "Just for the weekend. We didn't know Brandon would be here too—"

"Hang on!" He whipped his head toward the dance floor and then back to me. "That's *your* Brandon?"

I nodded. "Small world, huh?"

He said something, but it was completely drowned out by the pounding.

"I'm sorry, what?" I pointed to my ears in the universal symbol for "I'm way too old to spend my time at a place like this."

"I said—" But then he stopped and shook his head. "Never mind." He glanced down at the glasses on the table and looked like he desperately wanted to drink something, but there were six glasses and two beer bottles, and he didn't seem too sure that any of them were his.

We stood there awkwardly, not saying a word, just watching—or at least pretending to watch, in my case—the people swirling all around us.

"If you want to go dance—"

His dismissal of the notion came with head-to-toe

vehemence. "I don't, as a matter of fact. I think I'd rather go test the structural integrity of the ice on the Harbor, if you please."

Laughter erupted from my chest. "So you haven't changed *too* much."

"But don't let me stop you if you want to get out there." I just tilted my head and raised my eyebrow, and the corners of his mouth rose. "And neither have you."

Before I could think better of it, I said, as loudly as I could, "There's a Starbucks across the street."

"Yes, please!"

We grabbed our coats and made our way toward the door. He stopped briefly by Samantha and spoke into her ear and pointed across the street. She nodded, kissed him, and then waved at me like we were old friends. Fiona was dancing with Sean and Logan, or whatever his name was, so I grabbed Brandon.

"Tell Fi I'll meet her back at the hotel later, okay?"

"Are you alright?"

"Fine. Just going to grab some coffee with Liam."

He nodded. "Be careful. And hey, sis . . . I'm proud of you. Sorry we got so sidetracked from your big news."

There would be time to clean up that mess later. I squeezed his arm, stood on my tiptoes, and said into his ear, "Sonya is awesome. Don't mess it up!"

Ten seconds later Liam was closing the door behind us, and it was totally worth the price of frostbite in exchange for silence.

"I feel like I'm still yelling," he said as we crossed the street. "Am I still yelling?"

"A little!" I yelled back with a chuckle.

He held the door open for me, and then we were once again enveloped by warmth—but the smell of rum had been replaced by coffee beans, the sound of techno beats had been replaced by soft acoustic folk, and the hip and trendy crowd had been replaced by urban professionals *tap-tap-tapping* on their keyboards. We grabbed a table in the corner and set down our coats, then I began walking toward the counter.

"I've got it." He walked backward to the barista so he could look at me. "What'll it be?"

"Peach Tranquility hot tea. Thanks."

"Okay, I take back what I said. You *have* changed."

I shrugged and bared my teeth in a wide grin. "And a chocolate croissant?"

"That's better."

A contented sigh escaped after he turned away. *Stop that, Liv. There is no contentment to be found here.* Although as soon as I began arguing with myself, I found myself arguing with my argument. Okay, so we weren't going to end up together. He'd clearly moved on, and he looked happier than I had ever seen him. I'd only been in his presence a few minutes, but it was easy to tell his new life suited him. Boston suited him. Samantha suited him. Jeans suited him.

I diverted my eyes to the Ethos Water sign before he could catch me admiring just how much jeans suited him.

He stayed by the pickup window and put his debit card back into his wallet as he waited for our drinks, and I watched him. Goodness, I'd missed him. More than I'd allowed myself to realize. For so long I'd been focused on the heartbreak of it all. I'd been focused on the charade of it all—the charade I would probably continue in forever in order to protect my friendship with Fi. But it had been a while since I'd allowed myself to think about how much I missed my friend.

I couldn't remember the last time I had dared to reminisce about the ritual of our Monday dinners when Fiona was in Paris. About the ridiculous things we would buy at flea markets on Saturdays. About how he so patiently tried to explain baseball to me at Dodger Stadium and then still wanted me to go to games with him even after it became evident that I would never get it.

"Here you go." He set our goods on the table. "One namby-pamby tea and a chocolate croissant."

"Thank you very much. And for the record, I don't *want* to drink namby-pamby tea instead of coffee. I'm just getting old and can't handle caffeine this late at night anymore."

Nice, Liv. Way to defend your bold and sexy choice.

He smiled. "I get it." He pointed to his cup. "Half-caf."

"Wow." I pointed my thumb over my shoulder, back toward the club. "You are dating someone *so much cooler* than you."

I had not meant to dive straight in like that, but if he noticed my embarrassment, he didn't let on.

"No kidding." He took a sip of his coffee. "Let's be truthful: that's always been my type."

I chuckled nervously. I knew he meant Fi. Maybe he meant me, too, whether I would agree with my classification as cool or not. (I would not.) Either way, I wanted to get off the subject of Liam's past relationships.

"How did you and Samantha meet?"

Well, shoot. I hadn't wanted to stay on the subject of Liam's *current* relationship either.

"She's a clinical law professor, so she works with different firms in the area where students can get some on-the-job training. My firm has a tradition of handing off the Harvard Law students to the newbie."

"As initiation?"

"Essentially. It's a lot of extra work and fewer billable hours." He took another sip and smiled. "If they'd known Sam had transferred from Princeton, I think a few of the guys might have sacrificed a few billable hours."

You are a strong, independent woman, Olivia Ross, and you will not sink to the level of disliking another strong, independent woman simply because she was smart enough to snatch up what you discarded.

"And how long have you been dating?"

"Almost three weeks."

"That's . . . great, Liam. She seems just . . . great."

He nodded. "Thanks. She is. But what about you? Are you seeing anyone?"

I bit the inside of my cheek. "Nope. Not right now." That was good enough. He didn't need to know that he had been the last person I kissed. He didn't need to know that I hadn't dated anyone since Malcolm. "I saw Malcolm last year." *What the what?! Why did I say that?!* "I mean, I only bring that up because . . ." *Why? Why? Why?* ". . . because, well, it's a funny story." *For one brief, shining moment, Liam, I thought you were bidding a hundred thousand dollars to dance with me, but when that dream was dashed, I at least thought Hamish MacDougal would be waiting somewhere for me. But in the end, all I got was a torn Vera Wang dress, a whole lot of disappointment, and one epic dance/fight with my cheating ex-boyfriend. Oh, how we laughed!*

"A funny Malcolm story, huh?" He shuffled in his seat. "Well, I'd love to hear it." There was more sincerity in our love for our reduced caffeine tolerance than there was in that statement.

I looked at him for a couple seconds and then dropped my eyes as I shook my head. "No. It wasn't funny. It was just . . . Well, it was just another absurd February 4."

"Hang on. You saw Malcolm on February 4?"

"Yep. And Hamish MacDougal. And George Clooney, although I'm afraid George's involvement may have been a one-time thing."

"That's what I was going to say earlier."

My eyes snapped back up to his face. "You know something about George?"

He laughed. "No. About February 4. You were talking about it being a small world, and I was going to point out that today—"

"Oh. Yeah. Trust me, it's crossed my mind." I watched the tea bag swirl around in response to the circular motion of my wrist. "The truth is the only reason Fi and I chose now to visit our parents was to avoid all the February 4 insanity that seems to follow me around in LA."

"You waited nearly the whole decade to take that flight . . ."

"Hmm?"

"Nothing." He chuckled. "Just adapting Alanis lyrics to fit the situation."

I'd forgotten how comforting it always had been to talk about the Ironic Day madness with Liam as opposed to Fi. Yes, Fi was supportive, and yes, she had indulged my desire—in retrospect my foolhardy, pointless desire—to try to escape it.

But I always knew she loved it. She probably had scars on her lips from all the times she'd had to bite down to keep from encouraging me to "get lost in the magic."

But Liam was sensible. Apart from his insistence that I chase down Hamish in the international terminal at LAX— when, admittedly, the "magic" had been difficult to deny and he had been in the early days of Fiona's romantic influence—he had always landed squarely more in the "Hmm, that's weird" perspective category with me.

"Now here we are," he continued. "You fly across the country, and I agree to go out dancing with people I don't know—and you know how much I love all those things . . . going out . . . dancing . . . people I don't know—all to avoid this day. So of *course* the people I don't know include my girl-friend's friend's boyfriend. Your brother. I mean, when you think about it, the odds were stacked against us *not* ending the evening together at a Starbucks in downtown Boston."

He stared at his cup, and I stared at him. Had he meant to reveal as much as he just had? Two years and three thousand miles away, was it possible that for him February 4 remained Olivia Ross Day?

"I'm sorry about how weird this is," I said, once I felt confident my voice would hold.

"Well, it really couldn't ever be any other way, could it?"

I exhaled. "No. I suppose not."

I watched his shoulders rise and fall with deliberation three times in a row before he appeared to shake off whatever was consuming him.

"How is Fiona?"

Ah. Of course. That's what's eating at him.

Not that I doubted he had all sorts of emotions associated with me swirling around in his mind, but the sadness of his hunched shoulders and the uncertainty of his darting eyes . . . Fiona made more sense.

He'd broken her heart, and he knew it. He probably couldn't allow himself to dwell on the pain he had caused, because if he did, he wouldn't know how to go on. As a result, he had probably spent two years hoping he would never have to face her again.

Just like I'd spent two years hoping I would never have to face him again. Just like I had fought every day to keep myself from dwelling on the pain I had caused him, because when I allowed that to consume me, I didn't know how to go on. Because I'd broken his heart, and I knew it. He had risked, and ultimately given up, everything in order to take a chance on a life with me. And when he did, I had cruelly allowed my kiss to reveal every emotion I felt—and refused to let my words confirm a thing.

As the heartbreaker, he'd probably hoped for avoidance. But as the heartbreakee? Had he prepared himself for the possibility of one day running into me? Was *I* the encounter he had fortified his heart against? We had an entire country between us, but of all places, he'd moved to my hometown. He had to have known there was a chance. Had he comforted himself with the knowledge that there were more than four million people in the greater Boston area while still preparing himself for it—body, mind, and soul? Had he practiced the words he would say and perfected the ability to keep the smile on his face? Had he trained himself in the art of concealed emotions?

As much as I wanted to believe otherwise, maybe Fiona didn't make more sense after all.

"She's good, Liam." I quickly wiped the moisture from my eyes before he looked up at me again. "She's great. It takes a lot more than the likes of you to keep Fiona Mitchell down—don't kid yourself."

He laughed softly and raised his head. "I have no doubt about that." All the same, he exhaled a shaky breath, and I sensed it was a breath he'd been holding for two years.

"She's working at this huge nonprofit—"

"She doesn't work for Shonda Rhimes anymore?"

"Nope. You know—this way she can be fabulous *and* save the world. It suits her."

A warm smile overtook his face. "And how about you? You saw Hamish MacDougal last year. Did you slip him the screenplay?"

I groaned. "We didn't actually speak. Besides . . ."

"Still working on it?"

Laughter burst from me. "I'm never going to finish the stupid thing!"

He joined in, though I sensed he wasn't laughing with me so much as he was laughing at my uncontrollable chuckling.

"Let's see . . . Are we still dealing with new DA Jack Mackinnon racing against the clock to save the first woman he ever loved? What's-her-name? Felicia? Is that right?"

"Alicia. And he wasn't trying to save her. They were trying to save Landing's Edge, together. But regardless, I'm about fourteen drafts away from that."

He squinted his eyes at me. "I think I'd be more into it if he was trying to save *her.*"

"Really?"

"Oh yeah." He downed the last of his coffee, set down his cup, and leaned in. "I know you aren't much for romance—"

I knew what he meant, and he was correct in the way he meant it, but that was still not something any girl wanted to hear their ex-boyfriend say about them.

"—but I think you could write some good stuff there. It can still make you think, and you can still have characters who use their brains and not just their hearts or libidos to solve problems. But if love is at the center of it . . . Yeah, there's always more buy-in, I would think."

"Does Alicia need to die?"

This time he was laughing at me.

"No! Someone doesn't always have to die, Olivia."

The laughter made him cough, and he went to his cup to find relief and came up empty. Without so much as a single conscious thought, I offered him my tea—and I would guess he didn't think any more than I had before accepting the offer and taking a sip. We both seemed to realize in the same instant, as our fingers grazed each other as he passed the cup back to me, that we had fallen back into old comforts. But we were a long way from him finishing off my drink while he waited for his refill.

Don't let this turn awkward. Don't let this turn awkward!

"So if she doesn't die . . . I mean, does love actually win out in the end? You know how unrealistic I think that is. I mean, in the movies. Not, like, in real life. Not that we were talking about real life. We weren't. It's just a movie." I scoffed. "It's not *even* a movie. It's just . . ." I pantomimed writing on the palm of my hand with a pen and then realized it had been a long time since I had actually written by hand. I morphed into a dramatic typing gesture. "It's just words on a page!"

awk·ward | ˈôkwərd
adjective
1. causing difficulty; hard to do or deal with
2. causing or feeling embarrassment or inconvenience
3. not smooth or graceful; ungainly

Nailed it.

He wasn't laughing. I wasn't even sure if he was breathing. What he *was* doing was staring at me with that infamous expression of his that always seemed to get me into trouble one way or another. The one that made me think he wanted me more than he'd ever wanted anything ever. The one that messed up my heart when I interpreted it incorrectly—and messed up my entire life when I got it right.

"What?" I asked, desperate to fill the silence. Desperate to get back to the talking or the laughing or anything that didn't remind me of the last time I'd seen him—when he'd held me like I was still his and kissed me like I always would be. "What's wrong?"

His eyebrows inched up, and then he shook his head from side to side. "Nothing. Nothing's wrong."

Big breath in. Hold it. Big breath out. Again. Again. *Come on, Liv, get hold of yourself.*

"Okay, so . . . tell me a little more about what you're thinking. If Jack and Alicia were—"

"I don't think I'll ever understand you, Olivia."

"Oh, not you too. I just happen to prefer my movies a little more emotionally realistic. So I prefer the friendship of, I don't know . . . Andy and Red in *The Shawshank Redemption* over the friendship of Harry and Sally, or whoever. So what?"

"Because two men becoming best friends in prison and going on to live happily ever after on the beach is definitely more realistic than two friends who get to know each other and fall in love—"

"I said *emotionally* realistic," I interjected, flustered. Was it my imagination or was his chair closer to me than it had been?

"But that's not even what I'm talking about," he went on. "I don't think I'll ever understand *you*."

His chair was definitely closer. I knew for a fact that there had been a table between us in the beginning. Now Liam was on the side of the tiny two-top rather than across from me, and his knee was only inches from mine. And when he leaned over like that, and rested his forearms on his legs like that . . . How far away were his lips? Eleven inches? Thirteen, maybe?

"How so?" I asked through the lump in my throat.

Nine inches. Ten at most.

"You don't think love wins out in the end in real life either."

My lips were tingling. And his were *right there* . . .

"That's not true. I've seen it happen. My parents. Fi's parents. Brandon's first marriage was a disaster, but it looks like he's getting another shot. Paul Newman and Joanne Woodward were married for, like, fifty years."

"And what about you?"

Nervous titters filled the air. "No, afraid not. Paul and I never got the timing right—"

"You know what I mean."

"Liam, I really don't."

Eight inches. There was no possible way his lips were any farther than eight inches away.

He sighed, and I could smell the peach from my namby-pamby tea on his breath. "I guess I wish I knew how to convince you that you're as worthy of love and romance as anyone else."

I closed the gap between us—it couldn't have been more than six inches—and my heart rejoiced as our lips picked up where they had left off two years prior. I placed my hands on either side of his face and shuddered as my senses came alive at the feel of him. One of his arms wrapped around my shoulders and pulled me closer against him while his other hand grabbed the edge of the wooden seat of my chair, just beside my leg, and scooted my entire body forward a couple more inches.

His hand then moved from the chair to my hip, and he pulled me closer still. I was no longer sitting just on my chair. Most of one leg was on his—and it still wasn't close enough. I dropped my fingers from his face to his chest and allowed myself to sink into the kiss. To sink into him.

And then an instant later I was stabilizing myself for a different, much less pleasurable reason as his chair was ripped out from under me.

Twenty inches. Maybe twenty-two.

He muttered a few incomprehensible words—though the tone of them made it pretty clear it was not his undying love for me being communicated through those clenched teeth—and rubbed his face aggressively.

"What was that?" he asked, boiling over.

"I'm . . . um . . . I'm sorry. I—"

"Why did you do that?"

Every nerve in my body stung. "*Why?* I . . . Well . . . I thought . . ."

His eyes locked with mine. Until that moment I'd never seen him look at me in anger. "What right do you think you have to—"

"You kissed me back." The shock and pain began manifesting themselves in rage. "Don't act like you didn't kiss me back."

"*Of course* I kissed you back, Olivia. You know that I . . . What did you . . ." He growled and then looked around the room to see if we had drawn any attention to ourselves. I'd never been so grateful for a society of self-focused, disconnected individuals all caught up in their own little worlds. "What did you think would happen?" he continued, remembering to use his Starbucks-friendly voice. "You had no right—"

"You keep using that word. 'What *right* did you have?' 'You had no *right*.' What right did *you* have to kiss me two years ago, Liam?"

Thirty inches. Thirty-four, easy.

"Oh, so this was payback? Is that it?"

The stinging nerves had been set on fire.

"'Payback'? No, of course not. That's ridiculous. I didn't mean to do it. At least, I didn't *plan* to." I didn't understand a single thing that was happening. "Look, I'm sorry. But when you're looking at me the way you were, and when you're saying things about how I deserve love and romance—"

"Oh, I'm sorry. Did I not play the part you wanted me to play? What was I *supposed* to say, Olivia? Hmm? I really want to know. What were you expecting? What lines had you written for me in the script?"

There had to be at least a hundred miles between us. Maybe a thousand.

I cleared my throat and did my best to choke down the sobs that were about to erupt. "You know, Liam, I have honestly never been clear about the role you should play in my life. I'll admit that. I know that's never been fair to you, and I am so sorry for all the pain I've caused for us both. But never, at any point before right now, did I ever wish I'd never met you." I scooted my chair back and grabbed my coat off the back.

"Olivia, wait." I ignored him and turned to go, but he grabbed my hand. First with one of his hands, then with both. "Please. Wait. I . . ." I turned back to face him and saw the redness brimming his eyes. "I'm sorry. That . . . I shouldn't have said any of that. I'm so sorry. I just . . ."

He growled again, and this time he didn't seem to care if the whole world was watching. "It wasn't just you. I wanted it as much as . . ." He momentarily rested his forehead on my hand. "I can't believe I'm here again. I can't believe that after turning my entire life upside down and starting over and putting as much distance between us as I possibly could, considering there are only so many states where I can practice law without having to take the bar exam again, here I am. Kissing you while my girlfriend is on the other side of a couple doors. And no, you sure didn't do it alone." One of his hands kept hold of mine while the other rubbed his eyes, and the next words were said so softly. "I don't know when I'm ever going to learn."

I sniffed. "Stupid Hamish MacDougal Day," I whispered under my breath before inhaling and sitting back in the chair. "I'm sorry too. I really am. But, hey, at least this time *I'm* leaving. And I promise never to come back again on February 4. Seriously."

"As if you would want to anyway. It's twenty degrees out there."

"But you can tell yourself I'm doing it for you, if it helps."

"Thanks. Means a lot." A sad half smile overtook his lips. "For the record, I miss you. As my friend, I mean. Well, not just . . ." I knew he was about to say he missed me as more than his friend, too, but he thought better of it and shook it off. "I miss my friend. How's that for emotionally realistic? And I wish . . . But . . ."

Oh, Liam.

I reached out and cupped his face, and he leaned into my hand. "I know. Me too."

He kissed the inside of my wrist and then stood up, grabbed his coat, and began putting it on. He gave me his hand to help me up, and I joined him. "Can I walk you back over there?"

I shook my head. "Nah. I'm heading back to the hotel. How about you? Are you—"

"Going to go have an awkward conversation with my new girlfriend, whom I've been dating for about a minute, in which I beg for forgiveness and grovel at her feet so she doesn't break up with me? Why, yes. Yes, I am, as a matter of fact."

"You, Liam Howard, have always known how to have a good time."

We threw away our trash, and he held the door open for me as we faced the bracing wind together. We each bundled up as tightly as we could and crossed the road.

"Can I call you a cab or—"

"No, we're staying just down the street, but thanks. When you get back into the club, if Fiona is still there—"

His eyes flew open, and he stopped in his tracks. "Fiona could still be in there! Oh, Olivia, we have to stop spending February 4 this way!"

I giggled. I couldn't help it. "I was just going to say, if Fiona is still in there . . . Well, don't worry about what she would think about tonight or anything. I'm not going to tell her."

I hadn't put any actual thought into that decision, but I felt confident it was the right one. I told Fi everything, but the truth about my feelings for Liam would have to remain the one thing I didn't.

"Well, she won't hear about it from me," he stated, then rolled his eyes at the "Duh!" factor within that statement.

It was time to say goodbye before we froze to the spot, but I didn't know how to leave. I couldn't shake his hand like we were old acquaintances who *hadn't* just made out at Starbucks. For one moment I considered going all Streisand on him and giving him the full *The Way We Were* send-off. *"Your girl is lovely, Hubbell. Why don't you bring her for a drink when you come?"* But that wasn't good enough. Not for Liam.

He took the decision out of my hands. He reached out his arms and pulled me into a tight embrace. It was laced with history. That hug somehow told me he was sorry and that he forgave me and that he would always care about me and he knew I would always care about him. But that hug also told me goodbye in a way Liam and I had never said goodbye before. It said goodbye, and it meant it. I wanted to hold on for dear life, and I knew I'd never survive if I didn't leave right then.

I pulled out of his arms and kissed him gently on the cheek, desperate to commit the scent and feel of his skin to memory.

"You take care of yourself," he said as he opened the door and the rhythmic bass beat did its part to try to overpower the sound of my heart shattering, once again, into a million little pieces.

"Bye, Liam." I smiled, though I was as sad as I could remember ever being.

You may be out of sight,

But you're never out of mind.

Heartlite® Greeting Card Co., Number 11-8U643B

FEBRUARY 4, 2011

Jack kisses Alicia again as the music swells.

CUT TO

AERIAL OF LANDING'S EDGE—SAME

The scene is idyllic. All the colors of autumn fill the shot. BOYS ON BIKES cut through piles of leaves. A young READING MOTHER sits on a bench, watching her CHILDREN play at the park. An ELDERLY MAN rakes leaves.

THEN

Jack and Alicia enter the aerial shot together, holding hands, laughing. Jack throws his arm over Alicia's shoulder as—

> JACK
>
> I've been thinking.

> ALICIA
>
> Uh-oh.

                    JACK
No, this is good.

                   ALICIA
I've heard that before.

                    JACK
This time it's good.

                   ALICIA
Okay, Mackinnon. Dazzle me.

                    JACK
Private investigators. You and me.

                   ALICIA
                 (laughing)
Jack!

                    JACK
No, think about it! We're naturals!

                   ALICIA
I think . . .
Alicia stops Jack in the middle of the frame,
midway between the Elderly Man and the Reading
Mother. The Boys on Bikes zoom past.

ALICIA (CONT'D)
It's time we hang up our detective
badges—

JACK
You got a badge? I never got a badge!

ALICIA
(laughing)
And maybe we could try living a
normal life. Just for a little
while. Just you and me.

Jack gazes down on her adoringly and brushes
her windswept hair from her face. He gently
brushes her bottom lip with his thumb.

JACK
Just you and me?
Alicia nods up at him as he pulls her close,
and from within the safety of his arms she looks
around at the calm all around them, where chaos
so recently reigned supreme. The expressions on
their faces are heavy with the price they've paid
to save the town they love, and the knowledge that
all the life happening around them is possible
thanks to them. It is a heaviness and a knowledge
they will never share with anyone besides each
other.

ALICIA

Just you and me.

FADE OUT.

THE END

I stared at my screen, not sure if I could trust my eyes. *The End.* They were the most beautiful six letters I had ever seen in my entire life, bar none, and there are a lot of great six-letter combos. Cookie. Butter. Burger. Waffle.

Wow, I was hungry.

I looked at my alarm clock. Six twenty-nine. I knew my alarm would be going off in one minute or less, but that wasn't enough to tempt me away from my spot on the floor—leaning up against the wall, surrounded by empty cups and plates and a bowl that showed the remnants of the few drops of Hershey's syrup I hadn't licked off—where I could keep staring at the glorious words.

The End.

The alarm began blaring, and it startled me, even though I had known it was coming. My reflexes wouldn't allow me to ignore it, no matter how little I wanted to move. I'd had many years to perfect my silence-the-alarm-before-you-have-to-face-Fi's-wrath skills.

I have to wake up Fi!

The obnoxious blaring ceased, and I kicked my blankets, pillows, notepads, and dishes out of the way so I could get to the door. I would face Fiona's wrath for this one. I would break one of our three most sacred friendship vows, as scrawled out in 1985 in a spiral notebook with Wham! on the cover.

1. No boy is worth destroying our friendship for, and if
   George Michael wants to go out with Fiona or Tom
   Hulce wants to go out with Olivia, we won't be jealous.
2. Fiona will always give Olivia the last onion ring or
   French fry if there isn't an even number.
3. Olivia will only wake Fiona up before the sun comes
   up if Fiona will die in a fire or miss seeing George
   Michael if she doesn't.

It was only about fifteen minutes until sunrise. I would risk it.

I tiptoed into her lavender bedroom with actual design concepts that I'd never bothered with and braced myself for the first wave of resistance.

"Fi. Hey, Fi . . . ," I whispered in my sweetest voice. "Hon, can you wake up? I know it's early—"

"Ten more minutes," she mumbled as she rolled over and pulled the fluffy ivory comforter over her head.

"I made cinnamon rolls. They're fresh and hot and gooey—"

"You're lying. I'd smell them. Go away."

"But, Fi, George Michael is here, and he said he loves you and I should wake you up before he go-goes."

She peeled back a corner of the cover, and I saw one sleepy eye appear. "You know I stopped holding out hope for George Michael in the late nineties."

I knew that my Fiona-consciousness window would close quickly, so I put aside the jokes I wanted to make about how she just needed to have faith-a-faith-a-faith. "I know. But this is important enough that I invoked the George Michael clause. So . . ."

She groaned and grumbled as she rolled back over and sat up. Sighing loudly, she reached for her glasses from the bedside table. She looked so cute in her oversized Gucci Wayfarer glasses that she only wore for about twenty minutes each day.

"That's not fair. I don't even remember who your guy was."

"Tom Hulce."

She poked her fingers under her glasses to rub her eyes. "Like I said . . ."

"Fiona Mitchell, you have watched *Amadeus* with me no fewer than twenty times over the course of our friendship. How do you still not know who Tom Hulce is?"

"Olivia Ross, how do you still not know that regardless of whether or not I've been in the room, I have *never* watched *Amadeus* with you?" She yawned. "Since George Michael is not here, can I safely assume something is on fire?"

"Just these." I wiggled my fingers and sat on the edge of her bed.

She crossed her arms. "What are you talking about?"

"I finished."

"You finished? You finished what?"

I placed my hand on her crossed arms. "Fi, I finished."

Realization dawned—just before the sun—and her eyes widened. "You finished? You finished the screenplay?"

I nodded, and she threw her arms around me. "Oh, Livi, that's huge! Congratulations!" She was out of bed in a single bound. "Tell me all about it. Tell me everything! What time is it? Did you even sleep? Oh my gosh, we need coffee. Come on!"

She was out the door and in the kitchen reaching for coffee filters before I stood up from the edge of her mattress.

"I'm going to use the good stuff today," she said as she dug through the cabinet. I didn't know what the good stuff was when it came to coffee grounds, or why the good stuff was hidden in the back behind things we had bought on a whim and would probably never use—things like red-bean flour and powdered milk—but I was wholeheartedly in favor of the best coffee money could buy on this particular occasion.

"Hey!"

Fi's hand froze in midair, holding a bag of lentils. "What?"

"Let's go out for coffee."

She chuckled. "Look, I know you're wide-awake and ready to confront the day—seriously, did you sleep at all?"

"Not yet."

She rolled her eyes. "I'm off work today, and I have no intention of leaving the apartment. You know the next few weeks are going to be crazy for me, and—"

"That's fine. No big deal." I sighed dramatically and walked to the living room to flop onto the couch.

"Oh, good grief, Liv. I'll get dressed tonight, and we can have a celebratory dinner. Don't be such a martyr."

I sighed again. "Yeah, that will be great. It's just that there's this little coffee place I know in Culver City . . . I was thinking we could go there—"

"Are you kidding me? You need to take a nap before you start imagining clowns in the bathroom or something. Why in the world would we fight the morning rush on the 405 just to go to Culver City, of all places, for coffee?"

I stared at her and waited, and then began batting my eyelashes as I flashed an innocent smile.

Her eyes flew open wide. "Are you saying . . ."

I shrugged. "I mean, I guess it couldn't hurt, could it?"

She left the cabinet wide open, and the "good stuff" coffee was forgotten as she ran into her bedroom and slammed the door behind her after shouting, "I'll be ready in ten minutes!"

My innocent smile melded into a more genuine one as I stood from the couch and walked into my bathroom. *"I guess it couldn't hurt."* I wasn't entirely sure that was true. I didn't know what memories would be waiting for me in that old coffeehouse on Venice Boulevard. Maybe they had redecorated so much that I wouldn't even recognize the place. That was probably the best-case scenario I could hope for.

"Except this has nothing to do with Liam," I muttered to myself as I applied some dry shampoo and ran a brush through my hair. It had a little to do with Hamish, and a little to do with nostalgia, but it had nothing at all to do with Liam. It had all to do with me.

In one year I'd finished a screenplay. I considered that as I applied an excessive amount of deodorant. Well, eight years. In *eight* years, I'd finished a screenplay. But in one year I'd gone from zero to sixty. I'd set my mind to completing it in a year, and I'd done it. I hadn't wasted any time. I'd walked back to my hotel that night after kissing Liam at Starbucks and—

No, wait. It had nothing to do with Liam.

On the flight back from Boston, I'd told Fi about my commitment to finish the screenplay within the next year, and the subsequent events in everyone's lives had kept me spurred on. Everyone else was living their best life. Over the course of the year, Brandon and Sonya had gotten married and were living happily with Matthew and Maisie in a beautifully renovated 1854 townhouse in Charlestown. My parents had seen their beloved cherry blossoms and taken an Alaskan cruise with the

Mitchells, and a scuba diving trip to Cancun was supposedly next on the docket. Fiona had dipped her perfectly pedicured toes into new but ever-glamorous waters as a celebrity stylist, thanks to Vera Wang calling in a favor and getting Fiona's assistance on Oscar night just a few weeks after we got back from Boston (assisted by a series of could-only-happen-to-Fi events that followed). And Samantha had, apparently, forgiven Liam, they were madly in love, and they went on double dates with Brandon and Sonya all the time—

Stop that! It had nothing to do with Liam.

Besides, I didn't even know if any of that was true. After Brandon told me he saw Liam and Samantha together a couple months later at some Harvard reception and I threatened to show Sonya some Polaroids I'd held on to from my big brother's perm years if he ever mentioned Liam's name to me again, I'd been left with no choice but to connect my own dots.

But none of that mattered anyway. What mattered was that I had finished my screenplay! I brushed my teeth and splashed some cold water on my face and then went into my bedroom. As I slipped on my favorite pair of jeans, I said the words aloud again. "I finished my screenplay." I reached for a comfy Boston College hoodie but then thought better of it and instead grabbed a short-sleeved white peasant top that made me feel like Baby Houseman from *Dirty Dancing*—admittedly not a style I usually aspired to or a movie I thought of often. But it was a day to soak in the sun and celebrate the world and refuse to let anyone put me in a corner.

I finished my screenplay.

I couldn't quit saying it over and over in my mind, and I couldn't wipe the stupid grin off my face. It wasn't just that I had finished it. Although that was momentous, I had finished things before. Greeting cards, articles, columns, even some super crappy pseudo-screenplays that I never would allow to see the light of day. But *this*. It wasn't the story I had set out to tell, but I genuinely loved it. Jack and Alicia were engaging characters with a fantastic story arc, if I did say so myself. Most of the dialogue was fresher and more engaging than half the movies I had seen in my life, and it packed in all the emotions. Even the romance was pretty great in the end, I had to admit. By making Jack and Alicia's undying love the centerpiece of the story, I'd been able to increase the impact of every other aspect. It was time to acknowledge that Liam had been right.

Not that the day had anything at all to do with Liam, of course.

"Liv! Hurry up!"

I opened my sock drawer, then closed it again. Sun. Celebration. No corners. It was a sandals sort of day. I slipped them on, grabbed my purse, and met Fi in the living room.

"How were you ready before me? When has that ever happened?"

And of course she wasn't just ready *before* me. She was ready *better* than me. Contacts were in, makeup was simple but flawless, and she wore a summer dress that, once again, made me feel like Baby Houseman. Not in a good Patrick-Swayze-thinks-I'm-like-the-wind-through-his-trees sort of way. More in a Fiona-looks-like-Penny-who-makes-so-much-more-sense-for-Johnny-Castle-while-I-look-like-I-just-carried-a-watermelon way.

"You look cute!" Fi looked up from her compact, lip gloss perfectly in place. "So, tell me, what are we hoping for? Do you think he'll be there? Are you *counting* on him being there? Or is this just in case? I'm good with it, regardless, I just want to make sure I'm in the right frame of mind."

I shook my head. "No way. Hamish won't be there." My reaction was instinctive, but something felt different. Something I couldn't quite put my finger on. "I just thought it would be fun. It feels like a nice little way to wrap up this part of the journey. Honestly, I don't even know why I thought of it. It just . . . I don't know . . ." I'd just blurted it out without giving it any thought.

I *was* sort of tired. Considering it was Friday and I'd only slept about twelve hours since Monday, I guess that wasn't surprising. Adrenaline and caffeine had kept me going, but for the first time in a while, my body was running low on both.

"Well, I think it's a brilliant idea." Fi grabbed her keys off of the hook by the door. "And you know what? I think he might be there."

"He's not going to be there." Again, something felt different. It was almost like I wasn't convinced I was correct.

"It's February 4, so something's going to happen. That something might as well be you bumping into Hamish MacDougal at Mugs & Shots two years early."

She opened the door, and I followed her into the hallway and locked the door behind us.

"I'm not even going to argue with you this time. Maybe he'll be there. Maybe he won't. Regardless, I have a completed screenplay, Fi. Can you believe it?"

"Of course I believe it. I'm so proud of you."

Outside, we climbed into her yellow ("It's not yellow, Livi—it's *solar*") Mitsubishi Eclipse as she continued. "So how did you end it? Did Jack watch Alicia die and then walk off into the sunset alone with only his existential thoughts to keep him company?"

I laughed and buckled my seatbelt. "No, but only because I didn't think of that. Why didn't you suggest it sooner?"

She backed out of her parking spot and pressed on. "How *did* you end it? I want to hear all about it."

"Well, believe it or not—"

The ringing of her cell phone cut me off. "Sorry. Would you look and see who that is?"

I dug into her bag and pulled out the phone. "It just says 'Giselle.'"

In one fluid motion Fi maneuvered the car to the side of the road and snatched the phone out of my hand. "Amy, hi. Is everything okay? Oh no. Well, that's okay. We'll just let Emma have the Valentino. I've had my eye on an Elie Saab . . . Yes, exactly. The one from fashion week. No, of course it's no problem. I'll have a few different options for you to try on tonight. Yes, of course I can be there. I'll see you then."

She ended the call and threw her phone back in her purse with a heavy sigh. Then she faced me slowly, a disappointed expression on her face. "I'm sorry, Livi. I have to go to work."

"No problem. What's going on?"

After checking her mirrors, she pulled back into traffic and began circling the block to get back to our parking garage. "I claimed this gorgeous Valentino for Amy Adams months ago, and now, apparently Emma Watson is wearing it to the BAFTAs next weekend." She shrugged. "It's fine, except I don't actually know for a fact if the Elie Saab is still available. Hopefully it is. If not . . ." She began talking more to herself than to me. "I guess she could go ahead and wear the de la Renta next week. But then what for the Oscars? Oh . . . of course. The L'Wren Scott."

I stifled my giggles. It was all so extravagant and unimaginably cool, but Fi talked about it all with the same tone and enthusiasm with which we *all* talked about our jobs. Our much less extravagant, much less cool jobs.

There's an uptick in St. Patrick's Day cards.

Cleanup on aisle fourteen.

Market projections have slowed in the third quarter.

Emma Watson stole Amy Adams's BAFTA dress, and now I have to work with the world's top designers to find a new one-of-a-kind gown for the Academy Award nominee to wear.

It was all the same.

"Why is Amy Adams in your phone as Giselle?" I asked as she shifted the car into Park.

"Princess Giselle. *Enchanted.*" I kept staring, and she sighed. "I know. You didn't see it. But Amy played her." And still I stared. And again she sighed. "If anyone ever hacked into my phone, I wouldn't want them to have access to celebrities' phone numbers."

My mouth gaped. She was just so stinking cool. "Who else do you have?"

"I've got to go, Livi. I really am so sorry to bail."

I grabbed her phone from her purse again and entered her passcode. "I'll forgive you if you give me thirty seconds to look through your contacts."

She smiled and raised her hands in surrender, and I began scrolling. There were dozens of mysterious names.

J. C. C.

Mr. D.

Liz L.

Henry V.

"Who *are* all these people?"

She laughed. "I've got to go!"

"Fine," I grumbled and handed her the phone.

"Call me if Hamish shows up," she said as I opened my door.

"Nah, I'm not going by myself."

"Oh yes, you are!"

I scoffed and scrunched up my nose. "I'm definitely not. I think I'm just going to go to bed."

"No way, Liv. You have to do something special. You have to! I think he's going to be there today. I have a good feeling about it. Please go. Please. I can meet you there when I get all my work stuff sorted out. And if he doesn't show up, I'll buy you lunch or dinner or whatever you want, and we'll still celebrate. Please," she pleaded.

"Oh, you're pathetic."

She held up her phone and fixed her eyes on mine as she scrolled through her contacts list. "I'll tell you one."

I wanted to act like I didn't care. In fact, I wanted to *not* care. But curiosity had gotten the better of me. It wasn't even that I was all that impressed by celebrity—though, admittedly, over the course of the past few years, I had taken a new interest thanks to the unexpected star encounters in my life. But it was the mystery of it all that I found irresistible.

"Okay, but I'm staying long enough for one cup of coffee. Maybe a pastry. That's it."

She was so cocky. She hadn't had any doubt she would win that one. "Which one do you want to know?"

"Henry V. I can't think of any characters with a last name that starts with V. Is there a Henry Valentine or something?"

She gasped in mock horror and true delight. "That's probably the *one* I thought you had a chance of knowing! It's not a *V*. It's a five."

I tilted my head in confusion. In retrospect, I blame it on the lack of sleep.

"Henry Five? Was that the robot in *Short Circuit*? I can't remember who was in that. Steve Guttenberg?"

Fi shook her head in dismay. "That was Johnny 5. And no, Steve Guttenberg is not one of the top-secret celebrities in my phone." She added, "Although . . . yeah, I think you're right. I think he was in that. You didn't recognize Hamish MacDougal when you spent thirty minutes with him, after he'd already been in a Bond movie, but by golly you remember the cast of *Short Circuit*."

I stepped out of the car and shut the door, and then talked to her through the open window. "Alright, smart aleck. So who's Henry Five?"

"Good grief, Liv. It's Henry the Fifth. Kenneth Branagh."

"Shut up! You have Kenneth Branagh's phone number?"

"I met him at a Harry Potter event when I worked at Grauman's. His wife doesn't always trust his fashion sense. I advise. No big deal. Now get out of my way so I don't run over your toes."

Cleanup on aisle eleven. Repeat, cleanup on aisle eleven.

She drove away, and I pulled out the keys to my much less sporty—and plain silver, as far as I was concerned—Toyota

Corolla, parked three spaces away. For a moment I contemplated betraying my commitment, but I now knew that my best friend had Kenneth Branagh's number in her phone. A friend like that deserved better.

I drove through a Starbucks on Laurel Canyon Boulevard to grab a coffee to help me hang on until I could get some coffee and then hopped onto the 101, which would take me to the 405. Even with the morning rush, I knew I would be in Culver City in about a half hour. For the first time ever, I found myself hoping that Los Angeles traffic would live up to its infamous reputation. I had a full tank of gas, a venti latte, and a Lilith Fair CD from 1998 that I had discovered a few weeks prior in a box in the back of my closet during one of my more legendary writing procrastination spells of the past year. It was a day to enjoy life. To enjoy California. To enjoy the smooth musical stylings of Sarah McLachlan. And maybe it was even a day to be reunited with Hamish MacDougal.

Four hours later I had traveled eleven miles, and if Sarah McLachlan made one more comment about all the peace and comfort that could be found in the arms of angels, I was going to jump out of the car and take my chances on foot. Maybe one of those angels would come in the form of the safety officer who would tackle me to the ground and cart me away. At least then I'd probably get to ride in the HOV lane in which vehicles kept zooming past while the rest of us watched time slip through the hourglass of our lives.

"No more," I muttered. Or I may have screamed it at the

top of my lungs like William Wallace shouting "Freedom!" in *Braveheart*. Who remembers?

I began the arduous process of maneuvering two lanes to the right to get off at the next exit. Whatever it was. Wherever it would take me. I got there about an eighth of a mile—or approximately six days and three hours—before the turn off to N. Sepulveda Boulevard. I knew I could take Sepulveda down to Wilshire and cut through Beverly Hills to get to Culver City, but my caffeine had long ago quit working its magic. Besides, if Hamish was there when I got there, I didn't revel in the idea of walking in and immediately saying, "I'll be right back. I have to pee."

That was it. I was going home. Fi couldn't possibly be upset with me. I really had tried. I had welcomed the madness and mayhem of February 4. Invited it in, even. And a car accident on top of construction on top of a mudslide had said, "Not today, Olivia. Not today." Even Fi couldn't argue with that.

I had myself convinced and was ready to turn back onto the 405—since the loose northbound traffic heading toward my apartment in Studio City seemed to be laughing at the southbound schmucks in a way that indicated *they* certainly weren't listening to Lisa Loeb and the Indigo Girls—and then I stopped at a red light. For my bladder's sake, I surveyed the area around me and spotted a safe- and clean-looking gas station.

And I also realized where I was.

"Oh, you've got to be kidding me," I whispered in good humor. Or I may have given one of any number of angsty and spellbinding cinematic Nicolas Cage temper tantrums a run for their money. Again, it's just so hard to say.

The Getty Center.

"So is this it, February 4? Is this how you're going to play this today? Are we doing this?" I flipped on my turn signal and scoped out the situation behind me via my rearview mirror. "Who's there waiting? Is it Hamish? Or is Liam here? Ooh, I know! Maybe Liam and Samantha are getting married in the gardens. Maybe Malcolm's his best man!" I felt myself unhinging (so, yeah, probably more Nicolas Cage) as I turned onto Getty Center Drive and snaked my way up the hill.

I stopped at the admissions kiosk and half expected to see George Clooney clocking in for his shift, but instead it was some elderly man named Ned.

"Sorry, ma'am. We're currently closed to visitors."

I shook my head. "No. You must be mistaken. I'm supposed to be here."

"Oh, I see. Are you part of the team working on the Obsidian Mirror-Travels exhibit?"

What the heck is Obsidian? Or Mirror-Travels, for that matter. I've moved to about eight different apartments with Fiona Mitchell through the years. Does that count?

"Um, no. I'm not. All I want to do is walk around the gardens a little." And pee.

Ned nodded. "Ah, yes. You can feel free to do that—"

"Excellent."

"—beginning at 5:00 p.m."

I stared at him. "Ned . . . seriously. Are you really not going to let me in?"

"I'm really not."

"No matter what I say?"

He smiled apologetically. "I'm afraid not."

I shifted into Park and turned more toward him so I could rest my folded arms on the windowsill. "What if I said it was my dying wish to walk through the gardens, and I only have right now—this moment—to make it happen before I leave Los Angeles and fly to Switzerland for last-ditch treatment efforts? What would you say?"

"I would say I'd be honored to give you directions to the Mildred E. Mathias Botanical Gardens on the campus of UCLA, which are *also* lovely and just about three miles away. And I'll say a prayer for you tonight at mass."

"I knew I liked you, Ned." I felt the weight of Ironic Day melting away, and I felt thirty years old again. Like my life was once again my own. It was as if it was a day just like any other. It was as if I'd never even heard of Sri Lanka. "And do you mean to tell me that if I told you my soulmate was in there waiting for me and you were the only thing standing between me and my long-awaited happiness . . ."

"I would tell you that unless your soulmate is part of the team working on the Obsidian Mirror-Travels exhibit, you are mistaken. Either about them being in there, or about the identity of your soulmate."

"Love it!" I squealed and shifted back into Drive. "Thank you! You've given me my life back!"

I circled around and drove back to Sepulveda, pulled over at a 7-Eleven to take care of business and pick up a Dr Pepper and some little chocolate donuts, and then climbed back into my car, feeling like a new woman. It was over. I had won. Until then, I hadn't known that it was a competition, but *I had won.* It hadn't been about love or romance or fate or destiny or any of that. It had been about finishing my screenplay.

"That's all it was!" I laughed to myself in the silence of the parked vehicle. "I was doing it to myself! All this time!"

Again, sleep deprivation may have played a role in some of my enlightenment. But in that moment, it all made sense. I knew I had been in control all along. I'd been playing mind games with myself, and it had all worked together to get me where I needed to go. Jack and Alicia's story had been completed because of the journey. And now it was time for a new journey.

But just to be safe . . . the journey and I were going on one last adventure together.

"Where have you been?" Fiona asked me at 11:03 that night when I finally walked through the door of our apartment. "I've been worried sick! You were supposed to call me. I've been calling you all day—"

"I'm sorry, Fi. I had my phone off. I've been driving."

"All day?"

"All day." I couldn't wipe the ecstatic smile off my face. "It was incredible. Seriously. One of the best days I've ever had. I mean, it was a hard day, but it was *amazing*."

She gasped. "Hamish? He was there, wasn't he? I *knew* he would be! Tell me everything, Livi. Tell me every last thing!"

I plopped down on the couch and kicked off my sandals as she sat down beside me. "Nope. No Hamish. No . . . anyone. Except for Ned. And this guy at the front desk at William Morris. I spent a little time with Chip. Or was it Dale? But other than that—"

She stared at me like maybe I'd finally gone off the deep end and she didn't know if she should go get help or sit there and enjoy the show. "What are you talking about?"

I told her about the endless traffic and the coincidence of ending up at the Getty. "I couldn't get there, Fi. It was like everything that had been pushing me toward all these ironic things for eight years was suddenly pulling me away, in the opposite direction. So I decided to test it. Just to be sure." I jumped up from the couch with as much energy as I had collapsed onto it seconds prior. "Do you want to order takeout?"

"Um . . . no, you go ahead if you want. I ate." She turned her head, her eyes following me into the kitchen. "Tell me what you mean. What did you do?"

I grabbed a leftover lo mein carton from the fridge, sniffed it, and began picking up noodles with my fingers. "Well, I quit my job, for one thing."

"I'm sorry, you *what*?"

I shrugged and slurped up a noodle. "That's what I'm saying, Fi. The whole day was so clarifying. *Cathartic.*"

"But you quit your job?"

I walked back in and sat beside her again. "It'll be fine. You've had so many jobs, and I've pretty much just had the one. It's time for me to be the impetuous one for a change, don't you think? I've probably missed out on so much by having a degree in Decided all this time."

She cleared her throat and looked like she was leaning more and more toward placing that call for help. "Sure, sure. Um . . . you haven't been drinking, have you?"

"No! I'm just finally thinking clearly!"

She nodded, her eyes still wide open and wary. "Cool. So, um, what are you going to do?"

Dangling a long noodle over my open mouth, I said, "I'm going to sell my screenplay."

"And that's why you were at William Morris? You just cold-called a major talent agency? I mean, points for audacity, I suppose."

I shook my head. "Nope. I was there to try and get in touch with Hamish."

We had morphed back into the portion of the evening in which Fiona was willing to overlook the evidence of my disintegrating mental wellness. She was too addicted to the show to turn it off.

"You're not making any sense!" She laughed, and I understood the subtext. *I don't understand what's happening, but I love it!* "Okay . . . You quit your job. You're going to spend some time trying to get your screenplay sold—"

"One year. I'm giving myself one year. I have money in savings, and I'll pick up freelance jobs if I need to—"

"And you know I've got you, so no worries about rent and stuff." I didn't know if her eyes could grow any wider. "Now, how did we get to looking for Hamish at William Morris?"

"Do you want some of this?" I offered her the three or four remaining noodles—that my fingers had touched every inch of—but she shook her head. I quickly finished them off and bounded back into the kitchen to see what else I could rustle up. "Once I realized that all of the February 4 stuff had lost its power, I decided I had to be sure, once and for all. So I could finally move on, you know? I stopped at the library and used one of the computers to google Hamish's agent—"

"You do know you can do that on your phone, don't you?"

"It was some guy at the William Morris Agency, so I went

there. But guess what, Fi? He moved to the New York office last month! There was more proof that it was over. Then I went to LAX, because that was the other place I had seen Hamish."

She was giggling uncontrollably and sitting on her knees and bouncing up and down. "And, what? Because he didn't parachute down into the parking garage . . ."

"Ah, no, no, my friend. Today was not about leaving things up to fate. It was about taking *control* of fate!" I sat back down with a tuna-salad sandwich in my hands. "I was going to buy a ticket to Bandana . . . Bandcamp . . . whatever. The airport in Sri Lanka. But I didn't have my passport."

"And you'd just quit your job."

Sure. Because *clearly* reason and logic played a role.

"But there was a flight coming in from there an hour later. I decided to wait at baggage claim at least that long. And guess what?"

"No Hamish?"

"No Hamish! But then I decided I needed to factor in Liam and Malcolm, too, since they'd both been mixed up in the weirdness. I went to all the significant places I could think of. Places we'd eaten, beaches we'd visited, Dodger Stadium, Disneyland—"

"You went to Disneyland?"

I brushed off her enthusiasm—and a wheat-bread crumb—with a wave of my hand. "Just long enough to walk up and down Main Street, U.S.A. and eat a turkey leg. And catch 'Great Moments with Mr. Lincoln,' obviously."

"Why do I keep feeling the need to remind you that you are without gainful employment?"

I chuckled. "It was worth it, Fi. It was all worth it. Because they never showed up. Hamish, Malcolm, George Clooney, Liam . . . They never showed up. I went an entire February 4 without seeing any of them. I'm free!"

Freedom!

If I could have given a good William Wallace yell without spooking Fi and waking the neighbors, I would have.

I mean, I wasn't naive about the damage I had done to my heart that day—and I don't just mean with the seriously dangerous amounts of caffeine—but it didn't matter. It had been necessary to finally gain a fresh start. It had been worth the forty-minute drive to Redondo Beach, where Liam had told me for the first time he loved me, on New Year's Eve in 2003. And I didn't have any difficulty at all justifying the time spent at Griffith Observatory—made longer due to the "40th Anniversary of Apollo 14" crowd—remembering the night in April 2007 when Fiona had to work late and she sent me in her stead as Liam's escort to an important law society dinner. Remembering how we had skipped out early to watch the most beautiful sunset I had ever seen, surrounded by the Los Angeles skyline and the Hollywood sign. And how we'd talked about the places we each wanted to visit before we died. It had hurt in 2007, because all I had been able to think about was how wonderful it would have been to visit those places with Liam, but it hurt even more in 2011 as I sat alone and cried and realized I'd have been just as content to never leave the Hollywood Hills if I could still have him to laugh and talk with.

But now it was done. Once and for all. I had exorcised the power the day held over me, and the best years were ahead.

"So let me get this straight," Fiona began with an amused but cautious grin on her face. "You spent an entire day running all around Southern California to prove that February 4 no longer has anything to do with Hamish MacDougal or Liam Howard or Malcolm Larcraft—"

"Or George Clooney!" I added (helpfully, I thought). "Yes. Exactly."

"Or George Clooney." She nodded. "Okay, great. But by doing so—please correct me if I'm wrong—didn't you sort of make the day all *about* Hamish and Liam and Malcolm . . . and maybe even just a little bit George?"

I opened my mouth to argue with her, but no words came out. I shook my head as my mouth closed, and then it opened again. I froze and thought a moment. My mind frantically flipped through options.

I had nothing.

"Oh, honey," she said, full of compassion, in response to the tears that began pooling in my eyes. "Come here." She scooted closer to me and pulled my head down onto her shoulder. "I'm so sorry. I didn't mean to burst your bubble."

"I didn't mean for that to happen," I whimpered.

"I know, honey. I know. Aww, just forget I said anything."

"I used two tanks of gas."

"That's okay." She stroked my hair. "We'll get you more tomorrow."

I sobbed into her shoulder. "But I can't afford more. I don't have a job. I put Disneyland on my credit card. And I had, like, three of those Mickey Mouse soft pretzels."

"Don't you worry about any of that right now. You just need some sleep, and that's free. Okay?"

She helped me to my feet and guided me into my bedroom and proceeded to tuck me in like I was four. My eyes were as heavy as I could remember them ever being by the time she flipped off the light switch by the door.

"Hey, Fi?"

"Yeah, what is it, Livi?"

"The day really didn't have anything to do with George Clooney at all."

"Well then, there you go. That seals it," she replied lovingly. "You showed February 4 who's boss."

Does regret come more from the things we say,

Or the things we should have said?

Does regret come more from the things we did,

Or the things we should have done?

As we remember the people we lost,

Or wonder about the people we never found?

I wish I knew.

I could never regret you—

What I said, didn't say,

Did, didn't do,

Lost, found—

It has all joined together to create

The Story of Us.

A story I tell with no regrets.

Heartlite® Greeting Card Co., Number 12-9B5R23W

FEBRUARY 4, 2012

By the time Fiona and I rang in the new year of 2012, we had christened 2011 "The Year We Got Our Stuff Together." Well, that's what I was calling it, anyway. Fi was calling it "The Year We Got Our Stuff Together 2: How Liv and Fi Got Their Grooves Back." She refused to be persuaded when I insisted that made no sense because we had never gotten our stuff together before and therefore couldn't put forth a sequel. Rather, she insisted that any cinematic adaptation of our lives that evoked thoughts of Taye Diggs received precedence, and the other details didn't matter to her in the least. When it came right down to it, I found it difficult to argue with her ironclad logic.

Inspired by my impetuous decision to leave Heartlite—which I had deeply regretted and tried to renege on every day for at least a month, once I awoke from my bearlike state of hibernation—Fiona had decided it was time to figure out what she wanted to be when she grew up. All of her jobs had been wonderful, she knew, but she'd bounced around so much because she didn't have a goal she was working toward. At least that's what she decided. My theory was that she'd bounced around so much because time on earth is limited, and the world needed as much Fiona Mitchell influence as it could get before it was too late.

I think we were both right.

She decided she wanted to be a film producer, but that wasn't a job they posted Help Wanted ads for in *Variety*. So she enrolled in the master of arts Producers Program at the UCLA School of Theater, Film and Television. It was one of the most competitive programs in the world, but apparently the combination of letters of recommendation from Shonda Rhimes, Kenneth Branagh, and Arne Mankekar, the executive director of the Lakeside Society, as well as just Fiona being Fiona, made her an irresistible candidate.

With a full-time graduate-level course load on her schedule, she also took on a new job. When Fi had called about the recommendation letter, Shonda told her she wanted to connect her to a friend of hers named Gus Walsh, whom she had known since they'd worked together on the cinematic masterpiece *The Princess Diaries 2: Royal Engagement*. Gus, apparently, had made as much of that career springboard as Shonda had, though he had taken the slow milk train into film success as opposed to the Shonda Rhimes television express.

Gus and Fiona were a natural fit. He ran his production company like a start-up, and he valued creative ideas, hard work, and unique personalities more than huge box office returns. Of course, what Gus seemed to know and count on was that creative ideas, hard work, and unique personalities, combined with some decent connections, were going to lead to huge box-office returns sooner or later. He wasn't there yet, but his 90 Craic Films did put forth one of the most critically lauded darlings of the 2012 awards season. Fiona didn't join Gus's staff in time to have her name listed in the credits of *Exquisite Agony*—a thoroughly depressing tale of unrequited love and heartbreak that I went to see four times in the theater—but she would be listed as an associate producer in the studio's 2013 follow-up film. What's more, by the time she finished grad school, she would have a more impressive résumé than a few of her professors.

It was more work than I could ever have kept up with, but I think Fiona felt like she was on vacation. Not only did she finally have a defining sense of purpose, she also got to leave behind what she considered the most stressful job she'd ever had in her life. Overseeing production schedules for hundreds of people, coordinating high-profile premieres with an endless menagerie of things that could go wrong, and raising millions of dollars to send water to Yemen were apparently nothing compared to making sure no one ran out of boob tape on Oscar night.

And I, for one, definitely worked harder than *I* ever had before. I loved almost every single moment of it. Again, not right away. The enjoyment began *after* the soul-crushing regret and questioning of every decision I'd ever made. But once I moved on from all of that, it was incredible. For the first time in a decade, I didn't have to come up with new ways to express condolences for lost pets or to congratulate teenage boys on the day of their bar mitzvah. Instead, when I spent time writing, I wrote things I cared about. And then I stepped way outside of my comfort zone and actually spoke to people about the things I had written. Every day I queried agents and production companies, and each rejection—and there were many—spurred me on to the next attempt.

Yes, "The Year We Got Our Stuff Together" was more liberating than I ever could have imagined. And by February 4, 2012, I can honestly say that, well . . . absolutely nothing had come of any of it. At least not for me.

"I'm out of time, Fi," I said softly as I stared out the east window of our Mar Vista apartment, transfixed by the sight of nothing at all. We had moved south to Mar Vista when our Studio City lease ran out last April. It was much less expensive, and Fi cut her commute time to UCLA nearly in half. It added time to her 90 Craic Hollywood commute, but we always chose to overlook that part in a way that would make Taye Diggs exceedingly proud of our grooves.

"Yes," she replied, and then paused, no doubt allowing herself a moment to come up with one more somewhat believable platitude. "Isn't that exciting?"

Lately she had been spending more and more time encouraging me less and less sincerely. I knew she still believed in me, and I knew she was still proud of me. But even an eternal optimist like Fiona had to be discouraged by a year of doors being slammed in my face and the sound of being told no at every turn. Rejection had lost its charm.

"Well, frankly, no. I don't find it exciting." I groaned. "I need to start looking for a job. I need to figure out if I should try to go back to Heartlite or give something new a shot. Although, let's face it—I think I've learned my lesson about trying new things. Besides, I've realized there aren't nearly enough 'Sorry it took you so long to realize you're a talentless hag' greeting cards, so maybe I can corner the market. Or maybe a special rejection line, so that agents don't even have to bother trying to sound sensitive? They just pull out one of their rejection cards and stick it in the mail. 'Thank you for your film proposal. It's now in my garbage disposal,' perhaps?"

"No, Liv, listen to me." Fiona had been lying on her stomach on our carpet, feet in the air behind her, open laptop on the ground in front of her, but she jumped up and sat down next to me on the couch. She pasted on her glass-half-full smile, which had become an indefatigable visitor in our home in recent weeks. "You're almost out of time. And that means a 'yes' must finally be imminent! Your screenplay is so brilliant, and *you* are so brilliant. And you took a huge leap. I believe that leap is going to pay off. You gave yourself a year. Well, the year's not up yet!"

Sweet, supportive, delusional Fiona.

"It's literally been a year, Fi. Today. The year could not be more up than it is."

"But . . . but . . . it's February 4, Livi!"

"Oh, trust me, I'm fully aware—"

"Then you know that anything can happen today!"

I took the pillow I had been squeezing against my stomach and pulled it over my face. "I can't do this again, Fi! Please don't make me. Just let me suffer in peace."

"No way. What are we going to do today?" She pulled the pillow away from my face and threw it across the room. "And choose carefully. You're on year nine. This is the last year you have to soak in all the magic before you meet Hamish at that coffee shop and he takes you into his arms and kisses you— hopefully like he kissed Jennifer Aniston in that awful movie last year—and tells you he never stopped thinking of you."

"You were just telling me yesterday that you saw him in *People* magazine with some new girlfriend."

She shrugged. "It's only year nine."

"I'm sure Hamish's girlfriend would be touched to know you have such great expectations for their long-term happiness."

"So, what are we doing today?" she continued, undeterred by my lack of enthusiasm. "Do you want to send more query letters? Or should we try something new? Impromptu readings of your screenplay at coffeehouses? That's one we haven't tried before. You be Jack and I'll be everyone else."

"As delightful as that sounds, I would actually like to do the one thing I've never gotten to try on this date—I mean, apart from our rousing two-woman action/adventure/romance at open-mic night, of course."

"You bet. Just name it."

"I want to stay home. I want to lock the door and turn off my phone and close the blinds and maybe take a nap. And with any luck, when I wake up it will be February 5, and I can figure out the best way to start my career over from scratch at thirty-nine years old. I can dwell on the fact that I have no job and no realistic idea of what I even want to do with the rest of my life. That I haven't been on a date in . . . oh, I don't know, a century or so. And yet I will be able to look at my calendar and know that I have 364 days until I have to hide under the blankets one last time. And you know what? I think I can find joy in that." I was so tired. I was so tired of all of it. "That's all I want, Fi. I don't think that's too much to ask."

She squeezed my hand. "Okay, Livi. If that's what you want." She smiled at me and squeezed my hand one more time before going to pick her laptop up off the floor. She brought it back and sat on the opposite side of the couch from me, and the only sounds I heard for several minutes were the birds outside the window and the tapping of Fiona's fingernails on the keyboard.

The peacefulness had nearly cajoled me into a false sense of February 4 security when I heard her sharp intake of breath. When I turned to her to see what had caused the reaction, she was staring at her screen. I could see her eyes scanning back and forth, reading quickly.

"What?" I asked, not sure I wanted to know the answer.

Her eyes kept scanning for a few more seconds, then she looked up at me, back to her laptop, and then at me again. She slammed the computer shut and stood with it in her arms. "Get dressed. We're going out."

I didn't have time to argue with her before she was gone, into her bedroom to get herself dressed. Then again, I knew arguing wouldn't do any good anyway. She had probably concocted some hairbrained scheme to pull me out of my funk—and knowing Fiona, it would probably even work. But I didn't want it to work. I wanted to give in to the gloom. Just for the day.

So I sat, staring out the east window at absolutely nothing.

I thought back over my life, allowing myself to get caught up in the melancholy. It wasn't just the year that had been wasted. My entire life had amounted to absolutely nothing. Oh, sure, I had my health and my family and my friends—well, Fiona anyway. But I was nearly forty years old, and the one chance I had taken in my life had amounted to nothing more than the complete decimation of my life savings.

"Liv, what are you doing?" Fi interrupted my depressing reverie with a disappointed groan. "You need to get dressed."

I looked at her and knew I didn't want to ruin her positive outlook, wherever it was coming from. I also didn't have any fight left in me, so I just whispered a defeated "Okay." Then I stood and walked to my room. I followed her lead and matched her style of clothing—though of course I never could quite manage to match her style—and I returned to the living room ten minutes later in a casual dress and sandals.

"Where are we going?"

Her smile widened as she answered, "You're coming to work with me."

"No way," I stated with an ardent shake of my head. "I've told you, I don't want you pulling any strings or using any connections to get my movie made. I have to do this on my own. And if I can't make it happen because of the quality of my work, then it's just not meant to happen. I'm not going to let you make all my problems go away by slipping my screenplay onto your boss's desk—"

"Livi, I love you. And you know that I would do anything for you. But two things: number one, no one in this industry makes it on their own. I mean, I guess Charlie Chaplin was capable of doing it all himself. Oprah, maybe. Other than that . . ." She shrugged. "And second, I know you're my biggest supporter and I adore you for it, but I don't have slip-a-screenplay-onto-a-desk-and-make-the-problems-go-away clout just yet. Thank you for the vote of confidence, though. I just want you to go with me and get your mind off things for a little while. Maybe you'll be inspired. I mean, it's a Hollywood production company. It's exciting!"

"Even on Saturdays?"

She nodded. "Especially on Saturdays. There'll hardly be

anyone there, and we can put Post-it Notes on all the assistants' desks telling them that the project Gus wants more than anything is some sort of epic Civil War vehicle for . . . I don't know . . . Adam Sandler and William Shatner to star in together. It will be fun today. But seeing their reactions when they come in on Monday?" She grabbed her purse as she sighed indulgently. "Well, you'll have given me the gift that keeps on giving."

Forty-five minutes later we were pulling through the security booth of a movie studio. I don't know why, but I think I'd expected to be taken to some offices in a strip mall or something. I hadn't imagined that Fi actually worked on a sound stage.

"Is that Viola Davis?" I asked as I nearly gave myself whiplash turning around to confirm for myself.

"Yes," she replied without looking.

"This is a huge mistake," I whispered as my eyes grew large at the sight of Fiona waving to Daniel Craig as he got into his car, and even larger at the sight of Daniel Craig smiling and waving back. I found myself sinking lower and lower in the passenger seat, as if removing my visibility would remove the reality.

I felt the movement as she made a couple of turns and occasionally braked, but I didn't open my eyes until the car finally came to an extended stop and I heard her take the keys out of the ignition. What I saw, once I allowed myself to see, was not nearly as glamorous or intimidating and therefore much more welcome. Though we still weren't anywhere near a strip mall, the building before us did look much more like a regular, nondescript office complex. In fact, nothing about the building, or the people entering and exiting, would give you any clue as to the entertainment powerhouse that functioned from within, including the understated sign that read "90 Craic Films."

"What is 'craic'?" I asked, pronouncing the word phonetically.

"It's pronounced 'crack,' actually," Fiona replied as she bounded out of the driver's seat and I was forced to follow. "It's Gaelic. It basically means the level of fun. So, if it's at 90, you're doing pretty well."

I laughed. "Well, it seems so obvious now. I mean, this is the company that brought us *Exquisite Agony*. And if that isn't at least a million on the craic scale, I don't know what is."

With a defensive but good-natured smile, she said, "To be fair, it was originally called *La Douleur Exquise*, but they didn't want anyone to think it was a foreign film."

"How is that better? Isn't that just the French way of saying you're in love with someone you can't have?"

"Yes, and that even though you know you can't have them, you refuse to quit trying to be with them."

She paused as if the discussion had reached its natural conclusion, but I wasn't yet done being obstinate. "Okay . . . So how is that any better?"

She sighed, and then with a dismissive wave of her hand said, "It's French. Everything sounds more fun in French."

"I'm not sure what language all the people around me in the theater were crying in, but it must not have been French."

"Come on," she replied. Her words indicated she was ignoring me, but the smirk on her face let me know she was amused.

I had made the mistake of getting in the car with her, so I figured I had no choice but to follow her, no matter how much I wished to be back home in bed. We walked past the security guard at the door and then through another checkpoint where I had to have my handbag investigated and my every nook and cranny wanded. I was finally given a visitor badge and allowed to follow Fiona into the elevator, which took us to her fourth-floor office.

We stepped off of the elevator into a workspace that was surprisingly quiet and calm. I'm not sure what I had expected, though probably something more based on the newsroom of the *Daily Planet* in a Christopher Reeve Superman movie than any actual movie-studio ideals. There was no frantic pace as dozens of frenzied workers, one deadline away from a heart attack, ran from side to side, seeking approval and accolades. It was somewhat disappointing.

"Hey, girlie." Fiona was greeted by a woman who appeared to be slightly younger than we were, dressed in a flattering blue-pinstripe pencil skirt, stylishly paired with a men's button-up shirt and dangerously high heels. "I thought you were off today."

"I don't intend to be here long at all. Just showing my best friend around. This is Olivia Ross. Liv, this is Cricket Oppenheim. She's 90 Craic's vice president of development and the genius responsible for nailing down the rights to *Exquisite Agony*."

"Well, equal credit needs to go to every other genius in this town who passed on it before it got to me, but still, I'll take it. Nice to meet you, Olivia."

"You too. I genuinely loved the film."

"She's not just saying that either," Fi chimed in. "Liv is probably responsible for 10 percent of the domestic box office."

Cricket laughed and shook my hand. "It's a great little film, isn't it? As Fiona has probably told you, the critical appeal hasn't exactly translated to mainstream success yet, but because of fans like you, we were at least able to pay the catering service. Thank you for that!"

"My pleasure. Truly. And I'm sure with the Oscars coming up in a few weeks, more people will discover it," I said, as if I had any idea what I was talking about. It made sense, though. "And if not, I'm sure I can go see it again enough times to at least pay for the director's dry cleaning or something."

"I may hold you to that," Cricket replied. "None of the nominations have done anything yet, but yes, the Oscars should give us a little boost, even if we lose."

"Which, let's face it, we probably will."

I looked at Fi in shock after her pessimistic declaration, and she smiled at me.

"Gus doesn't want us to jinx it, so anytime the Academy Awards are mentioned, we've been instructed to downplay our chances."

Cricket smiled and grabbed a hot-off-the-presses fax from the machine next to the reception desk where she stood. She skimmed it quickly, then looked back up at me, the smile still on her face.

"He's not normal, our boss. But we like him."

"Is he around, by the way?" Fi asked.

"Just left. He had to meet Keanu in the Valley." Her groan was accompanied by an eye roll. I wasn't sure if the groan and the eye roll were evoked in the name of the Valley or for

Keanu, but Fi's sigh and nod indicated she fully understood the meaning.

"Even better, then," Fi said as she grabbed some papers out of her inbox just beside the fax machine. "I was telling Liv it might be a good day for some Post-it fun."

Cricket's eyes flew wide. "Yes! What did you have in mind?"

"I was working on an Adam Sandler–William Shatner Civil War epic."

"Brilliant!" Cricket chuckled and then looked at me. "Last week we had them convinced Gus wanted to produce a Chumbawamba musical biopic starring David Schwimmer and Jackie Chan. When will they ever learn they can't trust the Post-its?"

A couple minutes later we were in Fiona's office, and as she closed the door behind her, she whispered, "And that's how it's done!"

"That's how *what's* done?"

"Networking."

I scoffed. "What are you talking about? I didn't even tell her I'm a writer."

"I know. You were charming and kind, you're a fan of her work but you acted like a peer, and you were part of a simple but memorable conversation. Now, in a few months, when the moment is right and your screenplay somehow crosses her desk, she'll take note." Fiona tapped on her keyboard as she sat behind her desk. "Not only because she remembers you, but because she remembers that you didn't come on strong or exploit the situation. And that's how it's done."

That made some sense. Besides the part where my screenplay would somehow cross her desk, of course. But I decided to trust that Fiona knew what she was talking about and take it as a win.

"Well . . . thanks."

She looked up and smiled. "You know, Livi, I'm sorry your year is nearly up—"

"My year is *completely* up."

"—but I still don't believe this is over. Okay, so maybe you have to get a job. If I wasn't paying for grad school I would offer to—"

"No way!" I interjected. "Thanks for that, but you've already done so much."

"I guess we could take in another roommate or something."

I laughed. "Because *that* will make us feel better about entering our forties. Seriously, Fi, it's fine. I had the year, and it didn't happen. I won't give up. I may just . . ." I took a deep breath and leaned against the door. "Well, I think I'll probably just need some time to figure things out."

"You take all the time you need." A sly grin spread across her face. "I mean, rent's due on the first, but until then you do whatever you need to do."

Just then, the door flew open as a beautiful man rushed in. He was tall, but not too tall. Tall enough to help me grab things I couldn't reach from the top shelf, but not so tall that I would get a cramp in my toes if I wanted to wrap my arms around his neck and never let go. His dark-blond hair was strategically unruly, and he wore glasses with dark frames, which made his blue eyes sparkle—reminiscent of a day at the beach when the sun is so bright that you don't realize how blue the ocean is because all you can see is the reflection. Those eyes were further accentuated by his bold blue shirt and even bolder blue tie, in that style I had always tried to hate after Regis made it popular on *Who Wants to Be a Millionaire?* but that I actually found quite attractive, in spite of myself.

Unfortunately, I didn't get to observe any of that at first, having been knocked to the ground from my position leaning against the door.

"Oh my gosh, Livi!" Fiona rushed over to me, as did the beautiful, beautiful man.

"I am so sorry," he said softly as he helped me up, not by simply giving me a hand, but rather by guiding and assisting me. One hand was on my elbow, and then it was on the small of my back. It was while each hand was on an elbow, and my hands were resting on his muscular forearms, that I finally got a good look at him. "Are you okay?"

Truthfully, I wasn't okay. I wasn't okay at all. And it had nothing to do with my tailbone, which I was fairly certain was bruised. And it wasn't because of my pride, which struggled to hang on as I adjusted my skirt and wished I had fallen in a more dignified way.

"I'm fine," I lied with a smile I didn't recognize from myself. "I'm Olivia, by the way." I added this in a breathy voice that I also didn't recognize. Before I could stop myself, I involuntarily applied just a little bit of pressure to those amazing forearms, which were still within my grasp.

"Caleb," he replied, one corner of his mouth tilting upward, perfectly mirroring the opposite eyebrow. "Are you sure you're okay, Olivia? I feel awful."

"Okay," Fi bellowed, not at all subtly. "Caleb, did you need something? Caleb! Did you need something?"

He hesitantly pulled his gaze from mine and turned toward

an impatient Fiona. "Oh, sorry . . . Yeah. I have a message for you from Gus. I was going to e-mail you, but since you're here . . ."

"Well?"

"Yeah. Right. He said to look for a romantic comedy for Keanu Reeves."

She crossed her arms. "And that justifies bursting into my office at a hundred miles per hour?"

Caleb's confidence was teetering on the edge. *Mean Fiona.*

"Well—"

"What?"

"He said it was urgent."

Her laugh was loud and cynical, and I made a mental note never to mess with professional Fi. Professional Fi was scary. "Urgent? Why does Keanu Reeves urgently need a romantic comedy?"

"He didn't tell me—"

"Fine. You can go."

Caleb looked frustrated but not surprised. This was not his first run-in with scary, professional Fi, I was guessing. He turned to leave, as he had been ordered, but as he did, he caught my eye and winked. "So, if I can somehow make it up to you—"

"I said you can go, Caleb!"

He walked out the door and shut it behind him without another look at me.

Caleb was gone, Fiona was pacing, and I was bruised and confused.

"Why were you so rude to him? He seems nice."

She looked at me and laughed, and then the laughter stopped abruptly. She hurried to the door and opened it. "Caleb! Was this message from Gus on a Post-it Note?"

"Um . . . no . . ."

She shut the door again and resumed her pacing.

"Fi?"

"Yeah."

"Why were you so rude to him?"

She laughed again and rolled her eyes. "Caleb flirts with every woman in this office, and every woman in this office has a thing for him."

"Even you?"

"No, not me. Clearly not me."

Yeah, I guess after what I'd just witnessed, that was a stupid question. Unless Fiona was a fan of the Kathy-Bates-in-*Misery* style of flirtation.

"I'm his boss, first of all. But more than that, he's a child, and I'm not just talking about his age. Trust me on this one, Liv. He's not your type."

See, I'm not so sure about that . . .

I looked through the glass and watched him at his desk, typing away and adorably pushing his glasses up once in a while. "How old is he? At least thirty, I would guess. That hardly qualifies as a child."

Before I realized it, she was behind me. She grabbed my shoulders and turned me around so that I was facing her. "Focus!"

"I am focusing. I'm focusing on him. I'm just gonna say it. I am besotted with him."

"'Besotted'?" Fiona's lips repeated me, but no sound accompanied the movement.

"I mean, I can actually hear my pulse. Is that normal? And there's this strange ringing in my ears. Did I hit my head when

I fell? Maybe I hit my head so hard that I don't even remember hitting my head. I guess that could explain all of this. It's like a butterfly thing. But not in my stomach. Hang on . . . Is it butterflies? Is that what flies around Yosemite Sam's head when someone hits him with an anvil? Or is it birds? Whatever. It's kind of like that, but minus the five-inch bump on my head. It all feels like a—"

"Romantic comedy."

"Yes! Exactly! You know how I feel about those things, but I think this may be as close as I have ever come to understanding the appeal." I snuck another peek at Caleb through the glass. Sure, he was younger than me. But if he was thirty, that still made him a full-fledged, professional adult. I wasn't old enough to be his mother or anything. Just a young, hip aunt who was more like a sister. *Okay, Liv. Enough with the family analogies. You do not want to be like a sister to Caleb.* "I think I get it now, Fi. I think I understand why Meg Ryan feels inexplicably drawn to Tom Hanks, like a magnet. I get it. I do."

Laughter exploded from her. "Okay, two things." It was a big "two things" day for Fiona. "Number one, you do realize that Tom Hanks and Meg Ryan haven't made a movie together in more than a decade, don't you?"

"Really? I just thought they were kind of always together."

"And number two, that's not what I meant. I wasn't completing your sentence. I was telling you that what we need to focus on is romantic comedy."

"Oh yeah, that's right," I muttered in a hushed tone. "That did all sound pressing and dire, but also, well, ridiculous, frankly. Keanu Reeves needs a romantic comedy now! The future of the free world depends upon your ability to find

Keanu a romantic comedy, Fiona. Don't let Keanu down. Don't let the world down."

She chuckled as she grabbed my arm and pulled me away from the sight of Caleb. Once I was safely placed in a chair by her desk, she returned to the window and closed the blinds.

"What are you going to do?" I asked with a sigh, once my distraction had been removed. "How does one go about finding Keanu Reeves a romantic comedy that will rescue all mankind?"

"Believe it or not, I think I've already got one. It needs some edits, but I think we can make it work."

"Oh. Good," I replied, not sure what else to say. Sure, I was relieved for Fi, but I was a little disappointed for me. The situation had presented such interesting comic potential only seconds prior, but apparently Keanu's romantic comedy needs would be met. The world could sleep soundly once more.

She sat down in the empty chair next to me. "It's about this dashing hero named Jack Mackinnon who returns to his hometown, Landing's Edge, Vermont."

I seemed to process what she was saying in slow motion, and I think my face communicated each thought as it occurred. A more subdued, unintentional mirroring of each expression I made appeared on my best friend's face at the same time, although each of her expressions carried the added emotional depth of held breath.

"What in the world are you suggesting?" I asked with an uneasy laugh.

"Okay, now, just hear me out. What if we tweaked some things? What if there wasn't quite as much corruption and intrigue, but we kept the romance and made it a bit zanier?

What if Jack and Alicia didn't have to *literally* save Landing's Edge so much as they have to *metaphorically* save it?"

I couldn't tell if she was joking or not. I mean, she *had* to be joking, *right*?

"I'm sorry . . . Did you just say we could make it a bit *zanier*?"

She didn't smile. Instead, she stood from her seat and began pacing the length of the room, squeezing the bridge of her nose as she did.

"Hey," I continued gently, not sure why she wasn't smiling, "I appreciate the thought. I do. But Keanu deserves better."

"Do you think this is funny?" she asked as she continued to pace.

"Sort of."

Regardless of what I thought, I suddenly understood that I wasn't *supposed* to think it was funny.

"Well, you're wrong." She turned to face me, and I saw the tears streaming down her beautiful face, across her flawless-as-ever makeup.

Right there in that moment, I couldn't remember the last time I had seen Fiona cry. My mind quickly ran two inventories simultaneously: one of all the times I could remember seeing her cry, and the other of everything that had been said in the last few minutes, seeking out anything that would explain her emotional reaction.

Strangely, the second inventory took longer to compile than the first. More than thirty years together, and I could only remember four times she had cried. Not crying because she was rereading *The Notebook* for the nine hundredth time or because we stayed up too late laughing until we couldn't breathe or at a funeral or a wedding. *Really crying.* And in the few seconds that I thought through our history in an attempt to remember Fiona crying so that I could potentially figure out what was happening and what I needed to do about it, I found myself focusing more on all the times she *hadn't* cried. Times when anyone else would have, but Fiona held it all in. What was it about this moment that was worse than all those times?

"I'm sorry, sweetie," I said softly as I stood and began walking toward her. "I don't know what I said, but I didn't mean to upset you. I shouldn't have made jokes about Keanu." *I guess.*

"It's not always about you, Olivia," she said with curtness as she directed her pacing away from my general direction.

"Excuse me?"

"You heard me."

"Yes, I heard you, but I have no idea what you're talking about. What is your problem?"

"My problem," she shouted, facing me head-on with her feet planted in front of me, "is that I just handed you everything you've ever wanted and everything you've worked for, and you decided to make jokes."

"So it *is* about me . . ."

She exhaled with a bit of a growl, and I couldn't help but flinch. "Sure, Liv. Sure. Yes, it's about you. Is that better? Do you feel a little more comfortable now? Is that more like you're used to?"

Well, that did it. "Fiona Mitchell, what in the world are you talking about? I don't know where this passive-aggressive crap is coming from, but would you please just tell me what this is about? I appreciate you trying to make the screenplay work, but you know as well as I do that it's a ridiculous idea. Ridiculous! The script needs some 'tweaks'? We could make it 'zanier'? You and I both know I probably couldn't write a romantic comedy if Keanu Reeves's life depended on it. And frankly, how dare you?"

"How *dare* I?"

"Yes! How dare you? How dare you take something I've spent nearly a quarter of my life working on and treat it like it doesn't even matter? Like this is all just about getting a movie made rather than actually seeing work that I love made into a film I can be proud of."

She smiled, but nothing about the smile indicated there was a thaw taking place. If anything, it indicated that winter was just beginning.

"You're so pretentious."

I swallowed down the hurt, determined to continue the fight. After all, a third inventory had begun taking place in my brain, and I was realizing that fewer than the things I might have potentially said that I shouldn't have in the last few minutes, and even fewer than the times I had seen her cry, was the number of times Fiona and I had fought. We'd disagreed, and we'd not spoken for extended periods of time, but I could only think of two times we had ever had an actual fight. The first fight had ended with Fiona going to a New Kids on the Block concert without me, and the second had ended with her moving to Paris. I couldn't imagine how this one would end.

"I'm pretentious? *I'm* pretentious? Are you kidding me right now?" The words cascaded out of me, seemingly beyond my control. "This, coming from the spoiled princess who has always gotten every single thing she has ever wanted? This, coming from the daddy's girl who got her degree in Undecided? *Undecided*, Fiona? Has that never seemed strange to you? But at least you've put your degree to good use. You've been undecided your entire life. But that's okay, because now you finally know what you want to do, and the rest of us are supposed to roll over and make it happen for you, I guess. I'm sorry if I'm not willing to throw away my dreams so you can make your boss happy. But sure . . . Okay. That makes *me* pretentious." I started to turn away from her but rushed back and spewed, "It's never been called freaking *Untitled Keanu Reeves Project*, you know!"

For about five seconds, we each appeared to be completely driven by our convictions and unrepentant. For about five seconds, we stood our ground, convinced we were saying what needed to be said. For about five seconds, she held my determined gaze. Of course, no matter how my gaze appeared, I became less determined with each passing moment. By the time five seconds had passed, I was ready to apologize for everything I had said, that day and ever, and rush home to watch the seventeen films Tom Hanks and Meg Ryan had made together so that I could educate myself in the art of the romantic comedy. If that's what it took to make Fiona happy again, I would do it.

But before I could do any of that, I saw her crumble before me. It began in her eyes, and then it presented itself as a tremble in her lips.

"Oh, Fi, I'm so sorry," I cried as I threw my arms around her. "I didn't mean any of that. Really, I didn't. I just needed something to say. You're not a spoiled princess. I'm so proud of you for all you're doing, and *Untitled Keanu Reeves Project* has a nice ring to it, actually—"

"He's getting married, Livi."

"Oh. Okay," I stammered, thoroughly confused. "Is that why he's in the mood to make a romantic comedy, or—"

She looked up at me in confusion and then laughed through the tears when she realized what I thought she meant. "Not Keanu, doofus."

I smiled, relieved by her laughter. "Okay, then I have no idea what you're talking about."

"I thought . . . Well, when I got the e-mail . . . That's why I thought we should come here. I wasn't going to talk about it today, not on February 4, that's for sure. I thought coming here would be a good distraction for the day. But I'm not distracted. *That's* distracting me from everything else, and—"

"Fi, you're scaring me. What's happening?"

She took a deep breath, and then in one fell swoop she caused my heart to implode upon itself.

"Liam."

"Liam?" I pulled away from her and steadied myself against the wall. "Liam's getting married?" My jaw tightened, along with every other muscle in my body, as the old cannonballing-into-blue-raspberry-slushie sensation washed over me.

"Yeah."

"Liam?"

"Does Heartlite have the perfect card for congratulating an ex? You may be on to something with that rejection line you were brainstorming."

How was she able to make jokes while I was struggling to breathe? "And . . . and . . . he e-mailed you? Or . . . Why would . . . How do you . . ."

Color rose to her cheeks until they matched the scarlet-leather wingback chair behind her desk.

"We've been in touch."

I shook my head, not understanding. "What do you mean you've 'been in touch'?"

She sighed and for a moment looked around the room like she was trying to figure out the best place to sit. Or maybe she was wondering if it was too late to escape the whole conversation. She could have been trying to figure out if she could craft a time machine with the supplies available to her in her office so she could go back and rewind the whole thing. Regardless, it must have all been too taxing for her, because in the end she just sank down onto the floor and tucked her legs underneath her.

"After Boston, I felt like such an idiot. I didn't handle it well. Seeing him, I mean. I was embarrassed." She shrugged. "So I wrote him a letter, apologizing. Explaining, more like, I suppose. He wrote back. And we've e-mailed a few times since then. It's . . . Well, it's nice."

"It's nice?" Fiona got to share *nice* e-mail correspondence with Liam while I had to act like the thought of him never even entered my mind?

I sank down against the wall that was still providing me the support I desperately needed and joined her on the floor. "What was there to explain? It was the first time you had seen him, and he was there with someone else. It was uncomfortable and painful—" I balled my hands into fists in an attempt to stop the trembling. "I mean, it must have been so uncomfortable and painful for *you*. It must have been hard . . . seeing someone you loved so much . . ."

She scrunched up her nose and shook her head. "Nah, I don't think that was it."

"I—I—I mean . . ." Hands balled up: not helping. Teeth biting inside of cheek: ineffective. Fiona's words: not making sense. "You don't think *what* was it?"

She dabbed at elegant tears. "I'm pretty sure I never actually loved him."

It was as if she'd spoken the sentence in a hybrid of Welsh and binary code, but the moment the translation became clear in my mind, an instant and flaming-hot rage flooded through me. "You *what*?"

"I mean, I loved him. Of course I *loved* him. But . . . was I ever *in love* with him?" She shook her head again. "I don't think so. I thought I was, but that night—"

"What night?"

"In Boston. When I saw him, I think all I felt was hurt pride."

I was dying.

I was dead. That's all there was to it. I had died. That was the only possible explanation. I had suffered a horrible stroke or I'd been hit by a bus or a meteor had crashed into me, and I was no longer living. And anytime now the jarring effects of the inciting incident would subside, and I would pass into a peaceful eternity. Anytime now. Any minute . . .

"So let me get this straight. You acted weird and rushed over and hugged him and then pulled Brandon onto the dance floor and danced the night away to cover up your bruised ego—"

"I said hurt pride."

"—because . . . what? Because Liam was the only guy who had ever dared to break up with you? *That* was why your ego was bruised?"

She stared at me with a mixture of confusion and

indignation. "That's why *my pride was hurt*, I think, yes. Livi, what's going on?"

I felt like a caged animal. I jumped up from the floor and began pacing the room as Fi had a few minutes prior, grumbling to myself all the way. "All this time. I went to Starbucks. I drank tea. And then . . . then!" I laughed, because I didn't know how else to express anything I was feeling. "And you didn't even . . ."

I stopped and faced her. "I took the bullet for you that night."

"You went to Starbucks. I wouldn't exactly call that taking a bullet for me."

"He was my ex-boyfriend, too, Fiona!"

She was on her feet and inches from my face within two seconds. "Yeah, for a few months a million years ago, and then *you* broke up with *him*."

"I know, but—"

"And then *he* broke up with *me* after *you* kissed him. Do you remember that part, Liv? With my parents in the next room, while you were waiting for me to get home from work, you kissed my boyfriend—the longest relationship I've ever been in—and that was the end!"

"I know! And I was so sorry about that. I am *still* so sorry about that. You know I am. But you *just now* said you weren't in love with him, so don't act like that's even what this is about."

"I'm not acting like anything. I'm just saying that maybe, just maybe, you owed it to me to take that bullet in Boston!"

I panted and tried to catch my breath as all the memories and all the emotions got tangled up in my mind. Everything Fi was saying . . . That was what I had thought too. I'd owed it to her. It was the least I could do.

I took a step back. "I can't," I whimpered. "I can't talk about this anymore."

She crossed her arms. "So that's it, Liv? You're done, huh? All this stuff we've never talked about—" She threw her hands up in the air. "That's just how it's going to stay, huh? Because you say so?"

"I just . . . I mean . . . I can't, Fi. I'm sorry. It just . . . It hurts too much."

She raised her eyebrows, and though her face was still covered in the wet mascara remnants, all other signs of sadness were suddenly gone. "'It hurts too much'? It hurts *you* too much? You mean to tell me it hurts you too much to give me the benefit of closure from that time my boyfriend cheated on me with my best friend? That hurts *you* too much?"

For four years I had managed to walk the line. Without ever telling an actual lie, I had somehow kept her believing that, sure, I'd had feelings for Liam—without ever letting her know that I had gone to Italy in a panic and stayed for a year to escape him. I'd convinced her that I was thrilled the two of them had found each other while I was gone—without letting her know I wouldn't have thought twice about leaving her behind and running away with him when my judgment was clouded by mango margaritas but my heart was unafraid. Sure, she knew as well as I did that kissing Liam in the kitchen had been a mistake that I would undo in a heartbeat if I could—without ever having any idea just how fiercely I'd had to fight to keep from choosing him when the only thing standing in our way was my love for her. And she knew I'd taken a bullet for her that night in Boston—but I'd never wanted her to know that from that moment on, the theory that I would never not want him had become indisputable fact.

"Let's not do this," I whispered as I began searching for a tissue and a way out.

"Let's not do what? What are we not doing?"

"Please, Fi," I begged.

"Livi, what are you not telling me?"

I couldn't. I just couldn't. I was so afraid of what would happen if I ever said any of it aloud. I didn't know how I'd possibly be able to go on. How would I ever act like things were normal ever again? I'd never considered the possibility, but now that it was there before me, I couldn't allow it to come out. I'd never once said it. Not in the eight months we'd dated, or the year we'd been friends, or the year we'd been *best* friends, or the year I'd run away from him, or the year he'd been in my life as Fiona's boyfriend, or the two years it had been *his* turn to run from *me*, or the two years since my theory had become fact.

"I'm in love with him!" I blurted out, despite my best efforts to keep it in. And once I began, I realized that trying to keep it in would have had all of the impact of putting one of those drain stoppers you buy at the hardware store over Old Faithful. "I've always loved him. He was the love of my life. I have absolutely no doubt that he was the great, stupid love of my stupid life. I'm nearly forty years old, and I'm just now coming to terms with the fact that I will never love anyone else like I love him, ever again. I wanted him to kiss me, not just that day when it shouldn't have happened—*of course* it shouldn't have happened—but every day. Every single day the two of you were together, I was in love with him. Every single day, Fiona. Every time I talked about how perfect the two of you were together, and every time I was the third wheel, and every time I was sitting there as you kissed him good night and told him you loved him, *I* was in love with him. Every single day."

She said nothing; she just stared at me. Tears were streaming down my face again, and I didn't know how to reconcile the sense of relief I felt with the betrayal I knew she had to be feeling.

"But nothing ever happened while the two of you were together, except for the one kiss. I swear to you, it didn't. I never tried to get him to choose me, or—"

"But he *did* choose you," she said softly.

"No, he didn't," I tried to assure her, though I wasn't sure of that at all. "No matter how he felt about me, once upon a time, I know he loved you. And I think he just panicked." I blew my nose. "That wasn't his best day, of course. Or mine, needless to say. But, man . . . Liam and me . . . You talk about two people who probably needed closure and never got it . . ." I fell back against the wall again, more tired than I had ever been.

"He took all the blame."

"I know."

She shook her head. "No, Livi, you don't understand. It's not like . . . I mean, I believed you when you told me it was a mistake because I'd just gotten done listening to him talking about how he'd never gotten over you. But he said you'd never felt the same way about him. He told me that. Why did . . ." She released a frustrated groan, startling me. "Why didn't he fight for you? Why didn't he tell me? I mean, I would have been hurt. I *was* hurt. Of course I was. But if I'd known you were in love with him—that it wasn't just a mistake—I'd have . . . I don't know what I would have done, but if I'd known you loved him as much as—"

"He didn't know, Fi. As hard as I worked to hide it from *you*? Yeah, that was nothing compared to keeping it from him. I just . . . I couldn't do that to you." I bit my lip. "Of course, if I'd known you didn't love him after all . . ."

There was silence as her breath caught, and then it released with a *whoosh*. "I don't think I knew that then."

I nodded. "I know."

"Still, I guess we both could have stood to be a little more transparent."

"Yeah. I'm sorry."

"Me too."

We stood there without saying a word for the longest time, and I'm sure she was analyzing every misunderstood moment and neglected opportunity like I was.

"You know," she eventually began with a sigh, "when you were in Italy, he was . . . different."

I stood up straight again, bracing myself for another journey into the unknown. Fi and I had always talked about everything, and yet in the course of that conversation, I could barely keep up with all of the topics that were being broached for the first time. What was happening in California while I was in Europe had always been carefully avoided—certainly by me, but I had always suspected by her as well.

"How so?" I asked, hoping the answer didn't break me further. I didn't know how many more times I could withstand being pieced back together.

"He was angry. Bitter. Resentful."

I exhaled, grateful for an unsurprising response. "Well, yeah. I left without saying goodbye."

"But it wasn't that." She shook her head as she looked off into the distance, as if she were seeing it reenacted before her. "I think he was hurt that you left that way. But the anger? That was different. I think he was angry at himself. He never understood what you wanted, but I think as long as you were still in his life, he felt like he would figure it out. Eventually. But then . . . you *weren't* in his life. He didn't know what to do, so for a while, all he did was wonder what he *could* have done." She paused, and I hoped she didn't expect me to say anything. I was afraid that if I opened my mouth, all that would come out would be pain and regret. But then she added one more thought, and it was one to which I had no difficulty constructing a reply. "He never could figure out what he would have to do to be good enough for you."

"What?" I shook my head and crossed my arms in defiance of the notion. "That's the most ridiculous thing you've ever said."

"I didn't say it, Liv. He did."

He didn't think he was good enough for me? How was that even possible? "He was *too* good for me, Fi. He was a Redford."

She smiled at me quizzically, as she had countless times through the years. "A Redford?"

I sighed and walked back to sit in my spot on the floor, against the wall, and she followed. "You're going to think I'm crazy."

"I already do."

I had no doubt that was true. "A Redford. A leading man. There are certain people who will never play the quirky side character or be the supportive friend who cracks jokes and detains the detectives while eating cheesecake and wiping away the main character's tears."

"That movie sounds horrible—"

"Robert Redford would never play that role."

"*No one* would ever play that role, Liv."

"But don't you get it? Liam became a Redford. And a Redford never ends up with a Cusack," I stated definitively, certain that I would soon be contacted by some grad student who wanted to pursue my theory as the subject of their thesis.

Fi seemed slightly less confident. "What does John Cusack have to do with this?"

"Not John. Joan. But now that you mention it, Liam was more of a John Cusack until the end. Until he became a Redford. If he hadn't become a Redford, maybe we would have stood a chance."

"Because you're a Joan Cusack?"

"Yes."

"And you stood a chance when he was a John Cusack?"

"Exactly."

"But aren't they brother and sister?"

My brilliance balloon was losing a lot of air. "The point is it was never a question of Liam not being good enough for me. Quite the opposite, I assure you."

She seemed to ponder my hypothesis for a while, then she crossed her legs in front of her and sat up straight. "The problem with everything you're saying is that I don't think he changed."

"No, he did. He developed a sense of humor and became more confident. And that was all it took for my demented mind to say, 'Well, now. That won't do at all, will it?'"

Fiona was not convinced. "But Liam was always pretty funny."

My jaw dropped. "This is coming from *you*? The woman who told me I shouldn't settle for Liam because I needed a man who made me laugh?"

She held her hands up in front of her in surrender. "I know, I know. But I didn't know him then. And really, I don't know if *you* knew him then." She chuckled as a memory washed over her. "Remember how he'd say his name when he called the apartment?"

"He was such a dork. 'This is Liam Howard. Your boy-friend.'" I laughed in spite of the pain. "Did he do that with you?"

"You mean when I was dating him?"

"Yeah."

She shook her head. "Nope. That one seemed to be reserved for you." She thought for a moment. "I think it just took him a while to let his guard down around you. You made him nervous."

"Nervous?" I raised my head from my crumpled stature to look at her, a confused scowl on my face. "Why in the world would I make him nervous? That's absurd."

She turned her head to look at me, and the bewilderment on her face mirrored the confusion on mine. "You're kidding, right? Of *course* he was nervous around you! Think of how different he was with you than he was with me. I mean, let's face it: he was immeasurably cooler when he and I were dating than he ever was when the two of you were."

"Well, yeah." I lowered my head back into my hands. "That's because you bring out the cool in people."

"That is simply not true. I've been trying to bring out the cool in you for years, and I have failed in splendid fashion."

"Hardy-har-har."

She wrapped her arms around me, and I rested my head on her shoulder. I felt safe and loved, and I knew that no matter how many men let us down, or how many times in however many ways we let ourselves down, Fiona and I would always have each other. And sure, maybe we would fight every few years, and maybe some guy would occasionally cause us to be less than our best with each other, and sometimes it might even be so bad that one of us missed the Hangin' Tough Tour, but when all was said and done, we would be there for each other, to offer support and love and kind, encouraging words.

"Livi, you know I love you, right?" she asked sweetly.

I nodded as my eyes grew misty, more certain of her love for me—and mine for her—than anything else in my life.

"Okay, then hopefully you'll know that I mean it with complete love and devotion when I say you're an idiot, Olivia Ross. Seriously."

"Excuse me?"

She held me tighter as she groaned. "You don't get it, do you? You ended things with Liam just when he finally felt safe enough to be who he is. I think he was always nervous and played it safe because he didn't want to lose you. Don't you see that? But finally, something clicked. I've always thought that he finally believed enough in what the two of you had to stop trying so hard."

I thought back to that evening at the coffeehouse when his good mood spilled over into Alanis lyrics. I'd known for a long time that I was an idiot for letting him go, but was Fi right? Had that been the moment when rather than *becoming* a leading man, as I had always believed, Liam had finally felt safe enough with me to let the leading man he had *always* been shine through?

"And that's the precise moment I decided I couldn't be with him," I whimpered as I saw it for the first time. "But it was because . . ." It was incomprehensible. "Are you saying he decided to be himself with me for the first time and then thought I didn't like what I'd seen? Is that what you're saying, Fi?"

That didn't even make sense in my head, but if that was true . . . *Oh, Liam.* What I wouldn't give to go back and do every single thing differently.

"Who he was, who he wasn't, who he tried to become, who he became . . . I think it was all for you all along, Livi. If he was a Redford, he was always a Redford. A Redford who believed you were the leading lady he'd been looking for his entire life."

I spent the next few minutes crying my eyes out, not at all understanding how I could have possibly gotten it so wrong for so long.

Finally, Fiona broke the monotony of the sound of my sobbing by asking, "Do you want to read what he wrote to me?"

I sniffed. "Will it make me feel better?"

She gave that serious consideration and then replied with a sigh, "No, probably not."

"Does he ever mention me?"

"He does."

"Did he tell you we kissed in Boston?"

She sucked in air so fast she nearly choked on it, and I pulled away from her and patted her back while she coughed herself nearly to death. Once her eyes were red and watery but still staring at me as if she were in a horror movie being terrorized by something from beyond the grave, I added, "Can I take that as a no?"

"Why didn't *you* tell me?" she croaked.

She stood and walked to the little refrigerator behind her desk and grabbed a Diet Coke. When she offered me one, I nodded. "What happened?" she asked as she handed me the can and then sat in her desk chair while I stayed put on the floor and cracked the drink open.

"I took the lead on that one." Embarrassment washed over me at the memory. Well, embarrassment and other emotions that made the heat rise to my cheeks and made my pulse quicken. "He was talking about how I deserve love, and . . . I thought it was a declaration. I thought he was being romantic. Of course, you have to keep in mind what you know now. That I was madly in love with him at the time." At *all* the times. "So I . . . Well, I kissed him."

"And?"

I shrugged and maneuvered myself up with my soda in one hand and two legs on the verge of falling asleep and then joined Fi at her desk. "And . . . it was . . . Well, it was amazing."

"Did he kiss you back?"

I'd had two years to cement the memory in my mind, and I had complete, comprehensive, full-sensory recall of his hand on my hip as he pulled me close. Of my chair being moved across the floor with me in it. Of his peach-scented breath against my mouth. Of his lips battling with mine in a dance of desperation.

"Oh *yeah*, he kissed me back." But then I was ripped out of my reverie by an aspect of the memory that I didn't look back on with nearly as much fondness. My eyes snapped to Fi's. "Who's he marrying? Is he still with—"

"Yep. It's Samantha."

"Good," I breathed.

"'Good'?"

"Yeah, good." I grabbed a tissue from the box now sitting prominently on Fi's desk and dabbed at my eyes almost with spite. "That means I didn't ruin another relationship for him."

"Hey, now!" She stood from her desk, walked around to join me in the chairs on the other side, and placed her hand on my knee. "You did not ruin my relationship with Liam."

I took a deep breath. "Look, Fi, I know he took most of the blame, and I let him because I didn't want you to know that . . . to let you know that . . ." My chest began heaving with sobs again. "I didn't want you to know how miserable I was. I wanted you to be happy. Really. And I wanted him to be happy. And, well, if you could be happy together—the two people I love most in the world—well then . . ."

If she was able to decipher anything I was saying through the blubbering, it was a miracle. I ended my unintelligible blabbering by lifting a soaked tissue in each hand, like pom-poms. "Then . . . yay!" I collapsed into her open arms.

She stroked my back and spoke against my hair. "Olivia Ross, you listen to me. You did not ruin my relationship with Liam. Sure, the two of you making out in the kitchen nudged the timing along a bit, but . . ." Her shoulders rose and fell. "I don't know. I don't think he was ever in love with me either. In some ways we made sense. On paper, I guess."

"I always thought you would have made beautiful, brilliant babies."

She laughed and kissed the top of my head. "That's probably true. But don't you see? The heart of our relationship was *you*. That's what we talked about that night on the beach in Santa Monica, when we broke up. We only ever talked at all because we were worried about you. Because we were missing *you*. And then when you came back? Well, the truth is it was *still* about you. It was like you were our kid or something, and every evening we'd get caught up on whether or not you'd had a good day at school." She placed her hands on my shoulders and pushed me up to face her. "He's not married yet, you know. Maybe you should contact him. Maybe if you told him—"

"Look, I'm glad you and Liam were able to make your peace. I am. And that's great if you want to be in touch with him, and that's abso-freaking-lutely fantastic if he wants to write to you and tell you he's getting married. But there's nothing there for me anymore. And I can't keep pulling him back in every time he moves on." I sniffed and settled back into her arms. "We said goodbye in Boston. Now I've got to let him go."

We sat in silence until there was a knock on the door.

"Oh, crap!" Fiona exclaimed quietly as she pulled a mirror from her desk and attempted to make herself presentable. "Just a second," she called out, though we both knew it was going to take more than a second.

The knock grew more incessant and impatient. "I'll take the bullet," I groaned, figuring it was the least I could do— partially because I hadn't bothered with makeup and partially because I considered it my great privilege to take bullets for her whenever necessary.

"Oh. Hi, again." Caleb smiled at me when I opened the door, but my impression of him the second go-round conflicted strongly with the first.

"What? Why are you looking at me like that? Did you

forget I was here?" I asked in a tone I was pretty sure never could be mistaken for flirtatious. "Fiona will be just a minute."

"That's fine. I just have a message for her from Gus. But while we wait—"

"How old are you, Caleb?"

"Um, twenty-eight."

"And how old do you think I am?"

"Now, that's dangerous territory—"

"No, seriously. I need to know. How old do you think I am?"

"I would say, maybe, thirty-eight?"

Oh. Well, I hadn't expected him to be that close. Or that honest. I had to step back and try to remember what I was trying to accomplish. I had expected him to guess either way too low, in which case I would point out that he was blind and ridiculous and I was far too old for him, or way too high, in which case I could be offended and slap him or throw a glass of wine in his face like I was Sue Ellen Ewing or something. Instead, I just hemmed and hawed until, thankfully, Fiona was ready to present herself.

"What is it, Caleb?"

"Gus is wondering if you have a script for Keanu."

She looked at me and smiled as she said, "I do. A Nancy Meyers script came across my desk last week, and I think Keanu will be perfect for it."

The beautiful Caleb nodded that he would pass along the message, then he looked at me one more time, with mischievous intent in his eyes—and it did nothing for me. I'm not sure if I was too exhausted or if I'd grown up in the past hour or so. Maybe I'd just been reminded of my heart's high standards.

I shook my head. "This will not be happening. But thank you for your interest." Then I closed the door on his beautiful, confused smile.

"I'm proud of you," Fi said with a grin. "I do believe you just slammed the door in a Redford's face. If that's not a leading-lady move, I don't know what is."

Some days are worth waiting for,

Much like this one.

You worked with abandon to get the job done.

You struggled and wrestled.

You endured quite a bit.

You never gave in, and you refused to quit.

Now look at the payoff,

Just look what's in store!

You found opportunity. You opened the door.

The day you've awaited is finally here.

We wish you success in your brand-new career!

Heartlite® Greeting Card Co., Number 13-4RB67S

FEBRUARY 4, 2013

I awoke three minutes before my alarm went off. And that was the ninth time I had opened my eyes to glance at the clock throughout the course of the night. It was a night that felt eternal—and isn't it funny how therapeutic and refreshing that feeling is when the endless night consists of sleep, and how torturous it is when it consists of restlessness? The one that finally ended three minutes before my alarm went off was nothing short of torture.

After I rolled over and turned off my alarm, I stood and walked to the calendar pinned to my wall. February 4, 2013. How long had I waited for this day? Sure, I could pinpoint exactly how long, if I wanted to be literal, but how long had I been waiting *really*? A decade? Since I was a little girl? My entire life?

I walked around my bedroom in the West Hollywood apartment Fi and I had been living in for about a month and wondered how everything might be different the next time I was in there. The next time I awoke. I wasn't deluding myself that everything was going to change overnight, but I knew beyond the shadow of a doubt that something would. For better or worse, my life would never be exactly the same again. Regardless of what the day held, it was the end of one era and the beginning of another, and that prospect excited me in a way I had never experienced before. I was on the precipice of change. That thought terrified me, but it was a terror I welcomed.

I went to my closet and pulled out the outfit I had chosen for the day—the outfit I had purchased for the day—and laid it out on my bed, ready to get moving. But before I could make any progress, I smelled a fascinating, intoxicating aroma coming from outside my door. It was a scent I knew well and one to which I was enslaved, but in its current context it made no sense whatsoever. It was almost certainly the scent of fresh coffee, but the sun was not yet up, and I knew *I* hadn't brewed coffee yet. So how could there be coffee?

"Liv? You up?" Fiona questioned softly from the other side of my door.

I was so startled that I screamed, which made her scream and then giggle. I threw open my door, bewildered.

"Fiona Mitchell! Do you know what time it is?"

"Well, yes. Of course I do." She stretched out an arm to hand me a full mug.

"Thank you," I said as I warmed my face in the java's steam. "What are you doing up? I was beginning to think we had an amicable burglar who wanted us to be caffeinated when we filed our insurance claim."

"Well, aren't you the funny one. If this is the treatment I

receive at this time of day, is it any wonder I usually choose to wait it out a little?" She took a gulp of her own coffee, enveloping the cup in both hands for warmth. "But I knew you would be leaving early, and I didn't want to miss you. I'm so excited for you, Livi! Can you believe this day is finally here?"

I just smiled, having already gone through that entire sequence of emotions alone in my bedroom.

"Well, I'll leave you to it so you can get ready," she continued. "What are you going to wear? Oh, that's right! You and Stella have finally become friends."

I rolled my eyes at her as I sipped on the surprisingly delicious coffee she had made for me. She must have used the good stuff. "Don't be getting any ideas, Fi. I have not become friends with Stella McCartney. Or any other designer, for that matter. I don't wear designer clothes. I'm just wearing this one amazingly beautiful dress, which just happens to be from Stella McCartney's fall line."

"Admit it. Just saying that sentence made your heart beat faster."

I couldn't deny it, but I also refused to give in to her belief that every self-respecting woman in the universe should wear designer labels whenever possible. I would go back to normal clothes with a normal price tag on February 5. Regardless of how good I felt in that dress. Regardless of how good I *looked* in that dress.

"Fi, this coffee is amazing," I diverted. "I wasn't entirely sure you knew how to work the coffeemaker. I'm super impressed right now."

"Well, I'm glad you're super impressed. I, for one, am super offended. Of course I know how to work the coffeemaker,

Olivia. Having said that, this is Los Angeles, and coffee can be delivered hot and fresh anytime, day or night. But I placed the order all by myself."

Whether or not she or I were what one might consider "domestic," I had no doubt that in the year since our frank discussion about Liam, Fiona and I had grown in about a million different ways. Once we were able to stop skirting around our mutual misery and hidden subtext and actually talk about the things we'd been avoiding, life went on. Without Liam. I'd had a life before him, I'd had a life with him, and I had a life after him—but I had no recollection of life without Fi. We had survived some of the worst things friends could do to each other, and we had come out on the other side stronger and more bonded than ever before.

Turns out Fiona Mitchell and I were actually the loves of each other's lives.

About three weeks after I refused to let Fi show my script to Gus or rework it into a riotous laugh fest about love, loss, and espionage starring Keanu Reeves, *Exquisite Agony* finally picked up its first victory of awards season—the Academy Award for Best Picture. No one could quite explain how it happened, but it didn't matter. The little film that critics had loved all along, but that audiences had avoided like a depressing, heartbreaking plague, pulled off one of the biggest upsets in Oscar history. And those thirty-nine million Oscar viewers were so curious about the winner they'd never heard of that it soon became a box-office smash.

Its mainstream success made me lose a little bit of respect for it, obviously, but it was a good turn of events for Fiona. As Gus became more in demand, and hot on the heels of her impressive, cool-under-pressure (as far as anyone apart from me knew) selection of a Nancy Myers romantic comedy for Keanu, she became 90 Craic Films' most valuable asset. By the time she'd gotten halfway through the UCLA Film School's Producers Program, she had a major Hollywood production credit under her belt. Within six months Gus had handed her the reins of her own slate of films for 90 Craic, and there had been no looking back since.

Thirty minutes after I finished the coffee that Fiona had ordered for me—all by herself—I was standing in our living room, obsessively twirling and contorting in front of the mirror, making sure that each and every angle was worthy of the day. Fiona was also dressed, ready for work, in Vivienne Westwood from head to toe. On her, designer made sense.

"You look sensational, Liv. Stop fidgeting. You're ready. What time do you need to be there?"

"They open at nine, so shortly after that. I don't want to be seen waiting for them to open the doors, but I don't want to lose any time either."

"Smart." She nodded. "And you'll call me after?"

"Of course."

"Although, maybe rather than talking about it on the phone, we could just meet for coffee . . ."

I laughed so hard that I had to run back to the mirror and check my eye makeup again. "That was good, Fi. Subtle. You held out a lot longer than I thought you would, actually. My money was on there being a note on my pillow when I woke up."

"What do you mean?" she asked, exuding naivete. "I just thought—"

"I know what you thought, but no. I'm not going anywhere near that coffeehouse today."

"Are you sure?"

"Yes."

"But it's finally been ten years, Livi! Wouldn't it be a shame, after all this time and all the drama of the last decade, not to even see if he showed up?" With each and every word came more pleading in her eyes and voice, and I began comprehending the real reason she had set her alarm for a pre-sunrise world. She was running out of time to convince me.

Smiling, I put on my light coat and pulled my hair out from under the collar. "Is it not enough that I begin writing for television today? Is it not enough that your best friend is the new head writer of dramatic programming for the Heartlite Network?" Man, that was fun to say. "Seriously, Fiona. What else do you need?"

"I need for you to marry Hamish MacDougal and make lots of Scottish babies that we can dress in little baby kilts. I'm an only child, Liv. You are my only chance of ever being an aunt. Do it for me."

"Brandon has nineteen kids now. That should be enough to get you through."

Okay, so maybe he didn't have nineteen. But in addition to Matthew and Maisie, he and Sonya did have five-month-old twins, Felix and Astrid. Of *course* my overachieving brother had found a way to give our parents four grandchildren in the span of two years.

It was all so disgustingly perfect, and I wanted to be

disgruntled about it. After all, in less time than that I had gone back to work writing greeting cards, but had also written and submitted my first script for a Heartlite feature—which had gone on to be the most successful original feature in the Heartlite Network's history. And there was no spotlight to be found. But my sister-in-law and nieces and nephews were all so perfectly lovely that I couldn't bring myself to be crabby about Brandon's perfect life.

"What would it hurt, Liv?" Fiona was undeterred. "We walk in there and we order a coffee, like we have done so many times at so many coffeehouses. If he's there, then you'll know. And if he's not, well, when have you and I ever regretted having coffee?"

I picked up my purse and keys and she did the same, and we headed toward the door together. "I'm starting a new job today. I have better things to do."

"Oh, you're not starting a new job. You're filling out HR paperwork and getting introduced to your staff. You said so yourself. You don't start *working* until tomorrow. So—"

"I'm going to work now, Fiona. And that's the end of it."

With a sigh she muttered, "Fine. Whatever. I hope you have fun today choosing not to marry Hamish MacDougal. I hope you're okay with that decision for the rest of your life. You know, the rest of your life that you will spend *not married to Hamish MacDougal.*"

I laughed as I closed the door behind us and locked it. "I've made my peace with it."

We stepped away from the door together, but I stopped in response to her gasp.

"What? What is it?"

"You are not wearing those shoes."

I looked down at my ballet flats. "What's wrong with my shoes?"

"Most days, nothing. But on this day, with that Stella McCartney dress . . ." She crossed her arms and shook her head. "No way."

"You're going to make me wear heels, aren't you?"

"You *have* to wear heels, Livi. Yes! This is a dress that is made to show off your calves and make you look tall, and you can't do either of those things in ballet flats you bought off the clearance rack at Walgreens."

I rolled my eyes at her. She could be such a snob. Besides, I hadn't bought them at Walgreens. I'd gotten them at Goodwill.

"Fi, the black heels I have pinch my toes, and I don't want to be miserable all day."

She jingled her keys around and found her key to our front door, which she opened up again. "Wear some of mine."

It was my turn to gasp.

Fiona and I had worn the same shoe size since the ninth grade, but ninth grade was also the last time she had let me borrow her shoes. The details were fuzzy in my mind, but I was pretty sure it had something to do with me wearing her brand-new floral Doc Martens while painting sets after school for the upcoming production of *You Can't Take It with You*. Yeah . . . who could say for sure if that had anything to do with it.

"You're going to let me borrow your shoes?"

She looked me dead in the eye. "You're a forty-year-old woman beginning a professional, high-profile job in the entertainment industry. I'm trusting you to handle this responsibility with the gravity it deserves."

"I'm completely prepared to handle this job, Fi—"

"Not the job, Livi. The shoes. Keep up."

"Of course. Okay, you have my word. I will protect them with my life."

"Knock 'em dead today. I'm so proud of you." Studying me with misty eyes, she said, "My best friend, ladies and gentlemen. Achiever of dreams. Conqueror of life's obstacles. Able to accomplish whatever she sets her mind to." She pulled me in for a quick hug and then turned to go, calling over her shoulder, "Anything but the Manolo Blahniks. You're not ready for those yet."

I crept into her room, no matter how unnecessary the creeping was, and turned on the light before navigating through the piles of shoes, scripts, and magazines that completed the look of Fi's natural habitat. Then, with complete and total abandon, I opened her Narnia closet to see what treasures awaited. Whatever closets she'd had throughout her life had always been Narnia closets. You opened one up, expecting a normal storage center for clothing, but what you found was so much more. Each outfit either had a story or *was* a story, packed with intrigue and occasionally peril—as was demonstrated by the height of some of her heels—and I always exited wishing Aslan were there to guide me home.

I took a deep breath and reached to the back of Narnia, where Fi kept her best shoes. I knew not to pick from the top of the heap, since the ones she wore most often were the ones I was most likely to fall from, so I grabbed a box about midway down. When I took off the lid, I was staring at a pair of Christian Louboutin stilettos, trying to make sense of them. "How do you even get your foot in?" I gaped as I surveyed the twisty-turny ivy-like strap circling up from the bottom of the heel to, presumably, the space where your ankle was supposed to go. Morbid curiosity caused me to attempt to slip them on, but after a quick peek into the box to see if they came with instructions, I gave up.

After returning that box to its proper place, I decided to go all the way to the bottom of the pile. "Oh, you're lovely," I whispered to the pair of Jimmy Choo pumps I uncovered, still protected in their Bergdorf Goodman box. "What do you say, Jimmy? Want to join Stella and me at work today?"

I removed the right shoe and set it on the floor in front of me, then set the box on the bed as I slipped my foot in. That must have been what it felt like for Cinderella. The slipper was a perfect fit, and my days of sweeping floors and hanging out with mice were over. I was well on my way to becoming a princess, but with a much more practical patent-leather footwear option instead of that glass monstrosity Cindy had worn. I'd have cracked those babies before I ever stepped out of the carriage.

Once both shoes were on my feet I tested them out, and having confirmed I could walk across the room in them without resembling an ostrich, I indulged in one more fairy-tale princess moment. I twirled and curtsied low to the ground, as if I had just been asked to share a waltz with the prince. My waltz came to an abrupt end, however, when I knocked the shoebox off of Fi's bed and my feet were suddenly surrounded by enough tissue paper to cover the entire castle in pom-poms and other DIY wedding decorations.

Okay, so maybe there wasn't *that* much, but it was enough to cause a little bit of anxiety as I looked from the cloud-like mound of delicate paper to the box and back again and wondered how Fiona had fit it all in there. Even her Bergdorf boxes possessed a Narnian quality.

Still feeling like Cinderella—the somewhat less glamorous version—I knelt down and began picking up my mess and stuffing it all back into the box. One unwieldy handful didn't fold over and stuff down as easily as the rest. It took me a second to realize it was an envelope. It took me a second more to realize it was a letter addressed to Fiona. But it didn't take any time at all for my pulse to quicken and my temples to begin to throb. I ran my finger over the unmistakable handwriting, which I had seen so many times on notes he had written to me when we were dating—notes I had carelessly thrown away after reading.

March 11, 2010

Dear Fiona,

I can't tell you how nice it was to hear from you. Best surprise I've gotten in a long time.

"What am I doing?" I muttered to myself as I stood. I didn't even remember opening it, much less deciding to read it. And yet there I was. Sticking my nose where it didn't belong.

Although Fi had said I could read the letter. As we sat on her office floor, she'd asked me if I wanted to read what had to have been this specific handwritten letter, before they became casual e-mail correspondents. Whether or not my nose belonged there, it was an invited guest.

No.

I returned Liam's letter to its perfect trifold and stuffed it back into its enclosure. I knew better than to revisit.

Finally—*finally*—I had moved on. In the past year I'd even gone out on a few dates. Nothing came of any of them, but for the most part I'd managed not to think about Liam while sitting across from those other guys. And Fiona had moved on too. After his last e-mail, a year prior, in which he'd announced he and Samantha were getting married, she had written him back to congratulate him, and then they hadn't been in touch again. It had been a Liam-less year, and I knew it wouldn't do my heart any good to rehash any of it. To allow myself to read words he had written nearly three years ago. Words that, according to Fiona, mentioned me at some point.

And now he was married. He had to be by now, right? I knew I could find out if I wanted to—I could google him, or search the *Boston Globe* wedding announcements. Brandon had probably been at the wedding. Maybe Sonya had been a bridesmaid. He took my threat of showing Sonya perm photos seriously, so my brother wasn't going to bring it up. But he'd tell me if I asked. I had ways to find out . . . but for an entire year I'd moved on. And I'd moved on pretty well, overall. I couldn't go back.

But the letter seemed to be my Prince Caspian, not only asking me to come back to the hidden world of Narnia, but giving me a credible reason to. Wasn't I letting the whole past with Liam affect me more if I *didn't* read the letter? If I was over him, which I clearly was, wasn't it irresponsible of me to remain uneducated about the past? Fi had said I could read it, and then said it wouldn't make me feel better, but there had been so many emotions between us that day, who could even say what was decided in clarity and what was not?

I sat back down on the edge of Fi's bed, taking a quick peek at my watch to see what time it was. If I left right then, I'd still be too early. The doors didn't open until nine, and I didn't have a key yet. I would have to sit in the parking garage for a while, and that sounded nerve-racking. Instead, I pulled out the paper once again and proceeded to read with emotional distance and nonchalance.

March 11, 2010

Dear Fiona,

I can't tell you how nice it was to hear from you. Best surprise I've gotten in a long time. Seeing you in Boston was a nice surprise, too, of course, but I, like you, from the sound of it, wasn't exactly thrilled with how I reacted to that surprise. I think it was a shock for both of us—all three of us, I guess—but I think we handled it as well as could be expected. If I came across as anything other than delighted to see you, please forgive me. Your apology was so kind and considerate, but completely unnecessary, I assure you. You were as lovely as ever. And it actually ended up being a good thing to have that chance to talk with Olivia, I think.

You're right . . . you and I had said goodbye. You didn't know I was leaving LA (heck, I didn't know either), but walking on the beach that night, I think we both said everything we needed to say to each other. As hard and sad as that was at the time, I'm so grateful for it now. I'm grateful to you. Olivia and I didn't have that, and I always felt like there was more I needed to say. After seeing her in Boston I think I finally accepted that I'll never get to say it all, and I have to be okay with that. The truth is she was my favorite person. I know you understand that, because I'm pretty sure she's your favorite person too. She thinks she's so normal. So average. So unremarkable. But I know that you and I have always known how wrong she's always been. I hope that someday someone will convince her, but I finally had to accept that I'm not going to get to be the one.

Anyway, yes, let's definitely keep in touch, and next time you're in Boston, I'm taking you up on that dinner offer. I should probably warn you that I'm not a big fan of lobster rolls or chowder, but if you say you'll teach me how to eat like a Bostonian, I trust you. If there's anyone who can teach me how it's supposed to be done, I have no doubt it's you. Many people have already threatened to throw me out of the state. Maybe you can save me.

And one last thing. I know that people get carried away with "I hope we can still be friends," and it can be such a line, but I hope you know that when I said it to you in Santa Monica, it wasn't a line. I meant it as much as I had ever meant anything in my life. You're remarkable, and my life is better because of the time you were part of it.

Love always,

Liam

An hour of bumper-to-bumper traffic later, I was pulling into the Heartlite parking garage—a parking garage I had pulled into many times before. But for the first time I turned right instead of left. And rather than beginning the search for any empty spot in the peon section, as I always had before, I drove directly to the executive section and parked in the spot that boasted a sign that let everyone know it was reserved for the "Head Writer of Dramatic Programming." There was a parking spot at Heartlite reserved for *me*.

"Good morning, Ms. Ross," the parking attendant greeted me. "Traffic was a bear this morning, wasn't it?"

"It sure was . . . Terrell," I said as I looked at his name tag. Then I subconsciously looked down at the front of my Stella McCartney to see if *I* was wearing a name tag. Nope. Terrell just knew me. Weird. "Have a good day, Terrell!"

"You, too, Ms. Ross. Good luck today!"

I was going to need it.

I had seen no point in getting there any earlier than when they opened the doors to the public, but my new administrative assistant—who had been quick to inform me he had been standing by the door waiting for me to arrive since eight fifteen—didn't seem to understand or care about that sensible rationale.

"No, no. It's fine, Ms. Ross," Rupert said in a tone that indicated it most certainly was not after I had apologized profusely. "You're the boss. You can get here whenever you like."

"But it's not like that," I advocated on my own behalf. "I'll be the first one here, nine times out of ten. I mean it. I just didn't have—"

"Yes. You didn't have a key. I know. That's why I was standing by the door for the last forty-five minutes. So that I could let you in. But no, it's totally fine." Once again, his tone betrayed him.

He showed me to my office and with a little too much glee

pointed out the stack of papers on my desk, all of which needed to be completed and sent to human resources before noon. I thanked him, determined to win him over with excellent manners and never-again-in-doubt punctuality, and then asked him where I could get a cup of coffee. He offered to get it for me, but I was in complete and utter dread of putting him out again so soon, so I assured him that would not be necessary. If he would just point me in the right direction . . .

That was also the wrong choice.

"Sure, Ms. Ross. Of course. It's right over there in the corner. Now, if you need me, I'll be over here, sitting at my desk, doing absolutely nothing." He huffed off before I could apologize again, though I was certain he would give me plenty of opportunities before all was said and done.

I greeted a few people as I crossed through the galley. They all stared at me, despite being fully aware of who I was. I, meanwhile, knew no one. Rupert hadn't introduced me to a single person on my staff or anyone else's staff. That had probably been scheduled for eight fifteen. Finally, I arrived at the coffee station in the corner and breathed a sigh of relief. At least the next time I had to uncomfortably cross the room of curious strangers I would have coffee in my hands.

And on my dress.

"Oh no, I am so sorry! Here, let me get a paper towel."

I stood in shock, looking down at the brown, amoeba-shaped accent that, though I was not a fashionista, was difficult to imagine as part of Stella's original vision for her fall line. I heard gasps and teeters behind me, and I knew my desire to make a memorable first impression had been achieved with unparalleled success.

"Geez, I'm mortified. I'm so, so sorry. Here. Here are some paper towels. Should you get it wet? Or do you want me to try and track down a Tide stick or something?"

I glanced up at the man who had ruined my dress, prepared to tell him he owed me 279 Tide sticks in order to make up the cost of the most expensive thing I had ever worn, but I hadn't been expecting to see a face I knew.

"Caleb?" I asked.

His eyes squinted as he opened his mouth to speak, but nothing came out. He pushed up his glasses, then crossed his arms before words finally came out. "I'm sorry. You look familiar, but—"

"Olivia Ross. The last time we saw each other . . . Well, it was pretty much just like this, actually." I laughed and groaned simultaneously. "At 90 Craic, you—"

"Oh no!" He gasped. "You're Fiona Mitchell's friend. I opened the door and knocked you to the ground!"

"That's me!" I exclaimed and gave him a big thumbs-up. "I believe you are even worse at first impressions than I am. And that's saying something."

"I feel awful. How can I make it up to you?"

I'd heard similar words from him before, and a year ago I had very nearly told him he could buy me dinner in response. But then my heart had once again stalled out on the Liam Howard Hang-up Highway.

A year later, Caleb was as attractive as ever, but this time he didn't seem to be flirting with me. Could he tell I was in my forties now? That was probably it. He knew I was forty. Maybe single men heard fortieth birthdays communicated to them with a whistle that only they could hear. Although the change in Caleb seemed to go a little deeper than that. He just didn't come across like that same cocky player Fi had warned me about.

"Do you work for me?"

"I don't know." He smiled and tilted his head. "What do you do?"

"First day as head writer of dramatic programming."

"Then nope. I'm marketing."

I nodded. "Okay. Just trying to figure things out. My assistant hates me."

Caleb looked behind me and gestured with his chin. "That guy?"

I turned and looked back and saw Rupert sitting at his desk, staring at me with a mixture of boredom and loathing. "Yep. That's him."

"Yeah, I think he hates everybody."

"Well, that's better, then. Second question: I haven't had a chance to read the employee handbook yet. Is there any sort of dress-code policy that my coffee-stained dress is currently in violation of?"

"Dress-code violations? I don't think so. Fashion violations? Yeah. All of them." He sighed. "I feel so bad. It's a nice dress." He raised sheepish eyes. "Well, it was. Do you have another outfit you can change into, and I can get that one sent off to the dry cleaners for you?"

"Nope. No extra outfit. Although now that I know you and I are going to work in the same office, I'll be sure to have an entire wardrobe brought in." Playful, unabashed, klutzy Caleb had been cute and appealing. Mortified, responsible, klutzy Caleb was pretty irresistible. "Do you happen to have an extra dress shirt in your office? Maybe I can come up with something avant-garde-ish enough to make it look like I'm a style maven."

What would Fiona do?

The words had just begun bouncing around in my head when I heard them come out of Caleb's mouth.

"That's exactly what I was wondering!" I exclaimed.

He laughed. "I think I have a shirt. Be right back."

A minute later he met me in my office, carrying a crisp white dress shirt on a hanger. That, of course, was after I had the pleasure of walking back through the galley wearing the latest in coffee-splat fashion and hearing Rupert's dry, "Oh, that's a nice look."

If you cut yourself off from the outside world apart from your job—which for a long time is done at home—and your best friend with whom you share an apartment, before long there is no outside world. Caleb felt like a nice welcome back to the world. And though I was determined that after ten years I was finally done with all the Ironic Day stuff, it was pretty tough to ignore that Caleb was now part of the motif. Maybe after a decade of drama and angst, there was a lesson to be learned. Maybe Caleb was there at the end to get my attention in a casual, limited-impact sort of way. I had no desire to fall in love again. Malcolm had pretty much ruined me for life in all of the bad ways, and Liam had ruined me for life in all of the good ways. I was forty years old and at peace with being alone. But it couldn't hurt to make a new friend along the way.

"Do you want to have lunch with me?"

"I would like that," he responded.

"Okay." I nodded my head once. "I hope it goes without saying that you're paying."

He cackled but still had that sheepish, regretful expression on his face. "Yes. In fact, I would assume I'm paying for at least the first twenty lunches."

I looked down at my beautiful skirt popping out from under Caleb's shirt. "This is Stella McCartney. And today was the first time I wore it."

"Okay. Fifty lunches."

The next two hours were spent combing through the mountain of personnel paperwork and caring a little bit less all the time about my ruined Stella—and a whole lot less about my annoyed Rupert. I couldn't believe I had the job I had. All day, every day, I would help scripts get made into movies. Sure, most of them were going to be sappy love stories involving a small-town bakery and a Christmas miracle, but I had enough influence to maybe make them a little less sappy. To maybe make the heroines more independent and the heroes less unrealistically perfect. And in the meantime, I was going to make all sorts of connections with agents and actors and directors, and when the time was right, I would say, "Funny you should mention looking for a vehicle for Hamish MacDougal," or "A script with romance *and* intrigue? Well, as a matter of fact, I might have something you'd be interested in."

When all of the forms had been signed and turned in for processing and I had received my key—and assured Rupert I would be on time for work the next morning—I made plans to meet Caleb at a bistro around the corner. Though I was perfectly on time, he beat me there, which was ideal. That way I got to see him light up a bit when I walked in and stand up for me when I approached the table.

"You're more of a gentleman than you were when I first

met you," I said as I sat down in the chair he had pulled out for me.

"I don't know why you say that specifically, but I have no doubt that is probably a fair observation."

It's a remarkable thing what a little touch of contentment can do for a person. I was no longer searching—for anything, really—and so I no longer felt the need to keep a section of myself quarantined so that it couldn't be destroyed. I suppose I'd been that way for a while, but until lunch that day I hadn't taken my new perspective on life out for a test run. Truthfully, I was a bit fascinated by myself. In so many ways it was as if the lunch served the purpose of me getting to know myself, every bit as much as getting to know Caleb.

But there was one thing I already knew about myself by the time I sat down in that chair he pulled out for me: whether or not he and I ever amounted to anything more than a lunch, I was going to be myself from beginning to end. And I wanted the same from him, even if I discovered he wasn't a leading man. Even if I discovered he was.

I smiled. "I'm a lot older than you."

"I know," he said, returning the smile.

"To be honest, though, the age difference felt like a bigger thing a year ago."

"Because you've realized it doesn't matter? Or because the last time we met I had all the depth of a frat boy, freshman year?"

"Oh yeah. Definitely the latter."

"Figured." His chuckle carried over as the waiter approached and took our drink orders.

"So, what's changed?" I asked when we were alone again.

He took a deep breath and sat back in his chair. "I got my heart broken."

"I'm sorry."

"No, don't be. It was for the best. Not only did it make me less of a frat boy, it also made me start a new career. A career I love."

I scrunched up my face. "I don't follow."

"It was someone I worked with."

"It wasn't Fiona, was it?" I asked, fearing the answer. "Tell me she wasn't the one who broke your heart."

"What? Fiona?" He laughed heartily. "No. It wasn't Fiona. Fiona terrified me."

I breathed a sigh of relief and smiled. "Understandably. I've known that woman almost her entire life, but that day at 90 Craic I saw a side of her I hadn't known existed."

"Interesting." His laughter continued. "That's the only side I *ever* saw. I'm pretty sure she wasn't my biggest fan."

A phone began ringing, and it took me a moment to realize it was mine. By the time I did, there were so many eyes on me that I dared not take the time to excuse myself to answer the call, so I just quietly apologized to Caleb and answered.

"You were supposed to call me!" Fiona yelled into my ear. "How did it go? Were you a huge hit? Does everyone love you? Of *course* they love you. Did you get to meet Melissa Joan Hart?"

I rolled my eyes for my date's benefit as I turned away slightly, not wanting to unearth any PTSD symptoms for him by telling him who was on the phone. "Why would I get to meet Melissa Joan Hart?"

"I don't know. Isn't she on the Heartlite Network a lot? If not, she should be."

"I'll see what I can do about that, but listen, now's not a great time—"

"That's fine. I just wanted to tell you I'm heading out for a meeting with Gus in about five minutes, but as soon as that's over, I should be able to get away, and I can meet you—"

I spoke through clenched teeth. "I am not going to Mugs & Shots."

"Fine, then I'll go."

"Fine. It's a free country." She was making me testy. "If you want to waste your day waiting for Hamish MacDougal to show up, you go ahead. But I'm choosing to live in a realm known as reality. Talk to you tonight." I clicked the button to end the call and then silenced my phone before throwing it back into my purse. "I'm sorry about that," I said, returning my attention to Caleb.

"No, it's fine. Though I have to admit I'm curious . . ."

I rolled my eyes. "Yes. That was Fiona. She really is the greatest person in the world, but certain things seem to bring out the worst in her."

He smiled at me and leaned in. "I have no doubt that's true. I think I must be one of those things. But I actually meant I was curious about the Hamish MacDougal comment."

"Oh. It's the stupidest thing." I smiled and waved my hand dismissively. "I met him in a coffeehouse ten years ago today. It was before he was anybody—well, he'd been in a Bond movie—and long story short, we kind of hit it off and made this ridiculous little pact to meet back at the same coffeehouse in ten years. So, today. I was working on a screenplay, and he said he would be in my movie . . . yada yada. It's so stupid."

The waiter placed our drinks in front of us and I sipped

at my iced tea as I began looking at the menu. Caleb just kept staring at me inquisitively. "I probably would have forgotten all about it, except I kept bumping into him through the years. Always on February 4," I added.

"Hamish MacDougal? You kept bumping into Hamish MacDougal?"

"Yes. But I never even talked to him, so it's not like *that's* a big deal. I would just see him places."

The waiter came back to take our order. As soon as that business was out of the way, Caleb resumed his questioning. "'Places'? Like what sorts of places?"

"Oh, I don't know. The airport once. But I don't think I've ever been to LAX and *not* run into a celebrity."

"I sat next to Neil Patrick Harris at the domestic terminal courtyard Sbarro once," he said with a smile and a shrug.

"Exactly! If you can eat stromboli next to Doogie Howser, then anything is possible."

He grinned. "Okay, where else?"

"Well, there was this one time that he bid on me in an auction. But it wasn't like the bachelorette auctions you see on TV or anything. It was just for one dance. And all the money went to build wells in Yemen or something. So, yeah, Hamish bid on me there. But so did George Clooney and Ralph Fiennes, and they all ended up losing to my ex-boyfriend, so nothing came of that, obviously. I think Fiona just gets caught up in it all because she's such a romantic sap at heart. She wants to believe it was destiny or fate or something." I chuckled as I reflected on the absurdity of it all.

He tilted his head and rested his chin on his folded hands. "Can I be honest?" he asked softly. When I nodded that he could, he said, "If I didn't know that Heartlite performs extensive background checks and testing for their management positions, I would question your sanity."

I laughed a little louder than I meant to, and though he smiled in response, he didn't seem any more certain of my psychological wellness. "I know," I agreed. "It does all sound a little crazy, I guess. But I promise it's true."

"No, I don't mean it sounds crazy that it happened—although, sort of. I mean it sounds crazy that you don't think it's any big deal."

"The truth is it *has* been a big deal, Caleb. All of it. I mean, every February 4 for ten years has had this 'fate cloud' hanging over it, and at times it was tough to ignore. But now I feel like it's finally over, and I just want to move on."

Our waiter set my cobb salad and Caleb's turkey club and fries in front of us and we began eating. At least I did. I looked up at him between bites and saw he was staring at me.

"What?" I asked with a mouthful of lettuce.

"He could be there. Right now."

I laughed unenthusiastically. "No. I don't think so."

"But he could be."

Good grief. I had another one on my hands? "I suppose it's possible, but come on. It was ten years ago. He's a big star now. I'm pretty sure he hasn't thought about me once since then."

"Apart from the night he took on George Clooney, Ralph Fiennes, and your ex-boyfriend, you mean."

I winced. "Apart from then."

"It's just like *Sleepless in Seattle*," he said, unwrapping his utensils and placing his napkin on his lap.

"In what way?" I questioned as I resumed my munching.

"You've seen it, right?"

"Eh. Probably. I'm not much of a rom-com girl."

He let out a deep breath, and I could detect his disappointment in me. It was too bad he and Fiona didn't like each other. Just think of all the hours they could spend watching *Miss Congeniality* together.

"Okay, so Meg Ryan hears Tom Hanks on the radio, talking about his dead wife. He's in Seattle, she's in . . . I don't remember. East Coast somewhere. She feels a connection to him and writes him a letter, which his kid intercepts. The kid wants her to be his new mom. But then they keep missing each other."

"Meg Ryan and the kid?"

"No, Meg and Tom. But she had said they should meet on Valentine's Day, on the top of the Empire State Building—"

"Like *An Affair to Remember*!" I interjected, happy to discover something about the conversation I could identify with.

"Yes! Exactly. That's kind of the point, actually." He stared at me as he chomped on a fry. "You do know that *Sleepless in Seattle* is a total homage to *An Affair to Remember*, don't you?"

Don't get all judgy, just because you're cute. "Anyway . . ."

He grinned. "So anyway, she said they should meet at the top of the Empire State Building, but then she convinces herself that he doesn't care, or even know who she is, and that there's absolutely no chance he'll be there, so she decides to forget all about it. Then on Valentine's Day she's having dinner in New York with her fiancé, Bill Pullman."

"He was good in *Sommersby*."

"And they have this great view of the Empire State Building, and the side of it lights up with a heart—I think that was then, but it may have been later—and she tells him the whole story, certain that he'll think she's crazy. But all he says is, 'So he could be there now.' And he convinces her she has to go, just to see."

"And he was there?" I asked, somewhat intrigued in spite of my most valiant attempts at cynicism.

"Of course he was there. It's a Tom and Meg movie. They aren't going to build up to all of that and then—"

"Well, sorry. I thought if it was an homage to *An Affair to Remember*, maybe Meg got hit by a bus or something."

The smile returned to his lips. "Did you seriously just pull out *Sommersby* as your Bill Pullman reference?"

"What's wrong with *Sommersby*?"

"Nothing," he said, momentarily shaking his head, but then he stopped. "Actually, that's not even true. There's lots wrong with *Sommersby*. And when most people think of Bill Pullman, they think of *Independence Day*. Maybe *While You Were Sleeping*." He laughed in response to the disgust displayed on my face at the mention of *While You Were Sleeping*. As I joked every time Fi mentioned the film, while *I* was sleeping was while I was watching the movie. "You weren't kidding. You're *not* a rom-com fan, are you?"

"How can anyone truly identify with those things? They're so detached from reality."

"Unlike your husband going to war as Bill Pullman and coming back as Richard Gere, or whatever *Sommersby* is about. *That's* relatable." He kept his eyes on me as he took another big bite of his sandwich and swallowed it down. "You write for Heartlite."

"Yes, and I'm going to raise the standard."

"Of course. So tell me, what *are* your favorite movies?"

"Amadeus, Death Takes a Holiday, The Shawshank Redemption. The Elephant Man was pretty good."

He laughed and wiped off his mouth, then threw his napkin on the table. "Background check or no background check, you've lost your mind. *Sleepless in Seattle* is literally the plot line of your life today, and you identify with *The Elephant Man*? Look, I know I'm new to this ongoing saga in your life, and I may not have the right to contribute my opinion, but allow me to be your Bill Pullman. He could be there right now, and I think you need to go, just in case." He stood from his chair. "I'm running to the restroom. When I get back, I'm going to convince you. You'll see."

I rolled my eyes and sighed. "If I can withstand ten years of nagging by Fiona Mitchell, I think I can handle whatever you throw at me."

I watched him walk away with a bounce in his step and then pulled out my phone with a resigned laugh. Caleb was cute. I liked Caleb. I was even a little attracted to Caleb. Caleb and I could probably be good friends. And if not for the fact that they couldn't stand each other, I might have been wondering if Caleb and Fiona were MFEO.

"MFEO?" I muttered under my breath. "Where did that come from?" *Made for each other.* I meant made for each other.

I prepared to text Fi to tell her I'd found her a romance junkie brother-in-arms, but before I could get that far I had to read about a dozen texts she had sent to me.

You will not believe this.

Guess who Gus and I are meeting with? Guess! I'll even give you three hints . . .

It's Feb. 4.

We're not meeting with Liam or Malcolm. Or George Clooney.

He's Scottish.

I'm not even kidding, Livi. We're in a car right now on our way to meet with Hamish about a film he wants 90 Craic to produce.

We're in Culver City. FREAKIN' CULVER CITY!!

Why aren't you texting me back??? TEXT ME!!

He's in the car. HAMISH IS IN THE CAR!

Gus said he wants coffee. OLIVIA ROSS, YOU LISTEN TO ME! I'll get him there. You need to be there too. You can walk there from your office.

BE THERE!

Hmm. Well, admittedly, all of that made me a little less resolute about my "Ironic Day is a thing of the past" convictions.

"Now, where was I?" Caleb resumed as soon as he returned to the table.

I leaned in and whispered with urgency. "He's there. I mean, he's going to be there." I looked down at my phone and pulled up Fiona's newest text as I felt it buzz in my hands. It was a blurry shot of Hamish standing across from a barista, ordering coffee. The angle made it clear Fi had snuck the shot from behind. Great. I'd turned her into a paparazzo.

"He's there." I turned my phone to show Caleb.

His jaw dropped. "That's Hamish MacDougal."

I tittered nervously. "I'm aware!"

"Where . . . I mean, how did—"

"Fiona and Gus are meeting with him about a movie, and apparently Gus wanted coffee. From there, I can only assume Fi told them she knew the perfect place." I laughed at the ridiculousness of my brazen best friend.

"That's the coffee shop you met him at ten years ago?"

"Yep." I chewed on lettuce so my jitters would have something to do, but I neither tasted nor swallowed.

"And where is that?" he asked. "You have to go! My car's back at the garage, but I can drive you. Or do you want me to call a cab?" He pulled out his phone, prepared to do so. "Where is it? Where do you need to go?"

I stopped chewing, and heat rose to my cheeks as a few navigational facts dawned on me. I hadn't been there in years—not since my last date with Liam—though it had been my regular place when Fi and I lived on Venice Boulevard. When I had first been going into the Heartlite offices every day. When . . .

I was too embarrassed to speak, so I just pointed behind him. His eyes grew wide and his mouth flew open as he whipped around in his chair and looked out the window at the coffeehouse directly across the street from us.

"You're kidding me!" He leaned in and grabbed my hands. "You have to go. You just *have* to. It's a little too ironic not to. Don't you think?"

That was the moment. Right then. That was the exact moment when I chose to believe my life could be a romantic comedy after all. Because he was right, as Liam had been right, as Alanis had been right. It was all incredibly ironic. And at a certain point, didn't it seem more far-fetched to believe that it was all just coincidence? At a certain point, didn't I have to admit to myself that I didn't even know why I was resisting? At a certain point, didn't it all have to begin to seem . . . possible?

I gasped as the tears began rushing from my eyes, attempting to wash away the romantic-comedy imagery that my mind had allowed me to envision for the briefest of moments. But it would never be washed away. Never again. I knew it was a long shot, but once the gates of impossible scenarios had been opened, they were opened wide.

"What would Meg Ryan do, Caleb?" I asked as I scurried to gather my things.

He smiled the warmest smile and said, "Meg Ryan would go get coffee."

I jumped up and crossed the table to kiss him on the cheek, and then I ran out of the bistro and looked for the nearest crosswalk. I was so grateful that *An Affair to Remember* was fresh in my mind, because as the traffic never seemed to end, I was tempted to run into the street and take my chances. But that hadn't ended well for Deborah Kerr, so I waited.

Finally, I got permission to walk, and I ran across in Fi's Jimmy Choos. When I reached the door, I took a deep breath before going inside and beginning the process of surveying every corner of the crowded coffeehouse.

I wasn't prepared for it to be so unchanged. How had the world and I changed so much, and yet this one building that had been the setting of the events that had shaped the last ten years of my life was almost exactly the same? I looked first to the table where Liam and I had sat and laughed. Where he had sung. Where we had kissed. Where it had ended. Nine years later, another couple sat there and laughed, and the sight stung my eyes. I cast my wet, burning eyes across the room, until they landed on the couch. The couch itself was new, but it sat in the same spot. Gone was Hipster Cowboy, replaced by an elderly gentleman reading a book. Gone was the aspiring screenwriter with her notebook full of ideas, replaced by a businesswoman feverishly typing on her laptop while talking on her Bluetooth. And gone was Hamish MacDougal grabbing a quick cup of coffee and a moment of peace before an audition, replaced by . . .

Hamish MacDougal.

I couldn't believe my eyes. He was actually there. The curls and the sideburns were both shorter but unmistakable. The chiseled physique from the "Holy muscles, Batman" era had been molded into a gentler, softer version of itself, but again . . . unmistakable. He kept his head down as he drank coffee and messed around on his iPhone, but every few seconds he would glance up. Every time the door opened.

I forced my brain to slow down long enough to create an inventory. What did I want? In ten years, had he forgotten me? Would he have shown up *after* his meeting with Gus and Fiona if they hadn't hurried things along with Gus's need for caffeine and Fiona's need for romantic extravagance? Though Culver City celebrity sightings were pretty commonplace and the locals were mostly leaving him alone, it seemed, countless sets of eyes all around the room had zeroed in on him. Surely he didn't regularly sit on couches in the middle of coffeehouses all by himself in the middle of the day. Did he keep looking up when the door opened without even remembering why? Did it all feel like déjà vu, and he couldn't quite figure it out? He didn't have the benefit of magazine covers and movies to keep me fresh in his mind. Would he even recognize me when he saw me? Had he looked up when I walked in? While I was getting my bearings, had he looked straight at me and not recognized the forty-year-old version of a much younger blast from his past?

What if he'd always wished he had gotten my phone number? What if he had dated countless supermodels and actresses but always missed the girl who had told him he might have a career writing greeting cards? What if, against all odds, he wanted *me*? I'd be flattered, but would I be interested?

"We'll always have Sri Lanka."

I stopped breathing when I heard the words from just behind me. *Behind* me? And yet there was Hamish MacDougal, still in *front* of me, relaxed on the couch. I turned around slowly.

"Oh. Hello," I said with confusion when I saw the balding, slightly heavyset man before me. Something in his eyes was familiar, but nothing made sense. "Um . . . I'm sorry . . . What did you say?"

He took a deep breath, I think in relief, as a kind smile crept across his face. The smile was as evident in his eyes as it was on his mouth, and my brain began wrestling with itself, trying to figure out where I had seen him before. But it all came crashing down on me in the most spectacular, mind-blowing, humiliating way possible a moment later when he opened his mouth and spoke again, in a dialect that was unmistakably Irish, even to my uncultured ear.

"I said we'll always have Sri Lanka. It's good to see you, old friend. I wasn't sure you'd come. Honestly, I wasn't sure I'd recognize you, but you haven't changed a bit. I'd know you anywhere."

The room began spinning as I sought understanding. How was that possible? How had I so masterfully deceived myself for so long? I glanced behind me to make sure I hadn't hallucinated Hamish. Nope. He was there. What in the world was happening?

The man behind me kept talking, his voice so familiar. "Um . . . Well, I guess I've changed a bit, haven't I? I'm so glad you showed up." I turned back to him, my mouth and eyes wide open. "Oh yeah, that's Hamish MacDougal over there on our couch. Don't worry. We can ask him to move."

It was a good thing he wasn't responsible for deciphering *my* dialect right then. I'm pretty sure my stammers came out as some sort of cross between English and sea otter.

My friend began to look concerned. "So, um . . . I guess maybe we should exchange names after all this time, huh? I can't even tell you . . . I felt like a perfect fool for not asking your name ten years ago. But maybe this is the way it needed to be. I'm Guthrie Walsh."

"Livi! You came!" I heard Fiona's voice as she came running over. She wrapped her arms around me. "Did you see him?" she whispered in my ear. "He's over there on the couch."

She stopped short, and I allowed myself only a brief peek at her face as she examined the man I was speaking with. I didn't know how I would explain it to her. After all, I hadn't yet figured out how to explain it to myself.

"Um, Fi—"

"Oh, did you meet Gus?"

I didn't know if I could handle any further layers of confusion.

"You two know each other?" the man and I asked at the exact same time.

And then it started to click—at least a little bit—and I began looking around for a Rita Hayworth poster to cover the *Shawshank Redemption*–sized tunnel I was preparing to dig in order to escape the situation. "You're Gus?" I asked. "Fiona's boss? *That* Gus?"

I started to feel a little better, now that the two of them were looking as confused as I was.

"Yes. And how do you know Fiona?"

Fi jumped in first, thankfully. "Gus, this is my best friend, Olivia Ross."

Gus slapped his mostly bald head. "No!" He looked at Fi. "The screenwriter?"

Fi winked at me. "The screenwriter."

It was Gus's turn to stammer, and even his stammering sounded Irish. "I—I—well, what do you know! We were just throwing around ideas in the car on the way over here, and Fiona was telling me the plot of your Jack Mackinnon movie, and I think it sounds fantastic. I had just told her to see if the rights were still available. And that's yours?"

Confusion and joy bubbled up from my toes. "Well, no, actually. It's *yours*. It's . . ." Tears rolled out of my eyes. "It's the one . . . It's the one I was writing . . ."

"Oh, sweet girl!" He pulled me into his arms for a tender embrace. "Let's go sit," he said as he pulled away. "Fiona, do you mind carrying on with Hamish for a few minutes? I'd love to get caught up with Olivia."

Fi hesitated. "Sure," she finally replied with a very con-fused glance at me before she joined Hamish on the couch.

"I meant what I said, Olivia," Gus said to me as we sat. "I was interested in your script even before I had any idea Fiona's friend was you. Can you send it to me?"

I wiped my eyes and snapped back to reality as I heard the kindness in his voice. The same kindness that had made such an impact on me a decade earlier. I don't know how I had confused things so spectacularly, but there was no doubt I was sitting with the same stranger with whom I had had the most meaningful first conversation of my life. And in ten years, he had not forgotten me. He had honored the commitment that I had fully intended to blow off.

"Of course I can send it to you." I smiled, finally ready to be present. "Want me to e-mail it? I didn't bring a paper copy, but—"

"That's okay. I didn't bring my actual Academy Award either. And no, before you ask, I don't have the armful I said I would have, but I'm hoping the one will count toward my fulfillment of our bargain."

He winked, and I collapsed into a fit of giggles. "This is crazy!"

"I know. Funny how things work out, isn't it?"

"You have no idea! Look . . ." I chewed on my lip and looked over to the couch. Yep, Hamish MacDougal was still there. Hamish, whom I had never met before. Hamish, who had alternated between being the muse and the nemesis in my mind for a decade. Hamish, who was totally into Fiona and whatever she was saying, from the look of it. "The truth is I thought you were Hamish MacDougal. I mean, not when I met you. I didn't know who Hamish was when I met you. But a couple years later I saw him on something, and—"

"Hamish is Scottish. I'm Irish."

"I know! And I told everyone you were Irish. I called you Sexy Irish Guy for the first two years—" *Oh, kill me now.* If only I had followed Deborah Kerr's example and gotten hit by a taxi on the way in. "I never intended to tell you that."

Gus laughed as he pulled out his phone. "Don't be so hard on yourself. I was pretty sexy back then." He winked again and my nervousness melted away. I knew this guy. I *liked* this guy. "Ah, here we go," he said as he scrolled. "My old agent from the acting days found this in some files and sent it to me a few weeks ago. My headshot." He turned the phone toward me as he said, "From about ten years ago."

I covered my mouth and felt vindication wash over me. "Are you sure that's not Hamish's headshot?"

"Oh, I'm sure. Shortly after this headshot was taken, I got my last acting role."

"Which was?"

"Well, I had a small role in a little film you may have heard of called *The Princess Diaries 2: Royal Engagement*, thank you very much."

"And that's where you met Shonda Rhimes!"

He chuckled. "That's right. And it was right around then I decided I was tired of auditions and all that. I wanted to work behind the camera. So I went to film school and began transforming into the fine physical specimen you see before you today." He smiled genuinely. "The benefits of producing."

"And now here we are, with Hamish MacDougal, whom I spent the last eight years thinking you were. And you're my best friend's boss. I mean, this really is crazy." I shook my head, still in disbelief. "But hang on . . . Did you plan on coming here today? Fi had been texting me that you guys were meeting with Hamish, and she'd been trying to convince me to be here today—to meet him, not you. But were you not planning on coming?"

He laced his fingers over the top of his head and leaned back in his chair. "I wasn't sure, to be honest. But then Hamish called and asked if we could pick him up in Culver City instead of Malibu, and I thought, 'Why not?' I told them we should grab some coffee, and Fiona suggested this place before I had a chance to. And here we are."

I noticed the wedding ring on his finger and asked, "Do you have kids?"

"Three." He smiled and once again pulled out his phone to show me pictures. "You?"

"Nope." I shook my head. "No kids. Never married. Never . . . anything."

"Well, I wouldn't say 'never anything.' I'm not sure if you've read about it in the trades yet, but I think you're about to sell a screenplay in a major deal with the production company that brought you last year's Best Picture winner. But I should warn you." He leaned in closer and I followed suit. "I'm not sure who you see as Jack Mackinnon, but based on the conversation in the car, I think Hamish MacDougal is pretty interested in the role." He lowered his eyebrows and his voice. "Between you and me, I'm not sure he's right for it."

"But I don't understand!" I was saying thirty minutes later as the four of us sat laughing at a corner table, the unrecognizable commoners facing out so Hamish's jarringly beautiful famous mug could face the corner. "Why did you bid on me?"

"Are you kidding me, lass?" Hamish asked in his thick Scottish accent. Yep. I could tell the difference. He turned to Gus and Fi. "She was wearing this killer dress. Knocked my socks off."

Fiona nudged me and said, "I know! I told her she was the most gorgeous woman in the room that night."

"Hang on," Hamish said. "You were there too?"

"She was in charge of the whole thing!" I boasted. "Top to bottom, her event."

"And remember?" Fiona turned to me. "We ran all over the place looking for him."

"For me?"

I nodded to Hamish and confirmed. "Like I said, I was sure you remembered me."

He reached across the table, grabbed my hand, and lifted it to his lips to kiss it. "I'll remember you now, Olivia Ross." He turned to face Fiona as he stood from his chair. "And you. You remember that you're having dinner with me on Friday, don't you?"

She smiled as she and Gus both stood as well. "Who are you again?" Fi winked at Hamish, and the expression on his face was one I had seen on the faces of many men through the years. Men who were completely defenseless against Fiona's charms.

"Are you sure we can't give you a ride back to your hotel?" Gus asked him.

"Nah, I'll take a cab. Thanks, chum. Talk to you next week." They shook hands.

"I'll walk you out," Fi said to Hamish.

"See you later?" I asked her.

"Yeah." She scrunched down and hugged me tightly. "Crazy day, huh?"

I squeezed her back. "Crazy decade."

"But it's turned out pretty okay, all in all."

"And now all that's left is for you to marry Hamish MacDougal and have lots of beautiful Scottish babies that we can dress in little baby kilts," I whispered into her ear.

She pulled away and grinned at me. "Sheesh, Livi . . . I just met the guy."

"That didn't stop you from saying that to me when I'd *never* met the guy."

"Good point," she responded with a laugh. "By the way," she continued softly, her eyebrow quirked as she slipped her purse strap up on her shoulder. "I'm glad to see you're finally ready to take some chances, but covering up Stella McCartney with a men's shirt isn't so much voguish as it is criminal. But don't worry. We'll work on it." Then she followed Hamish outside.

"Well, my friend," Gus said with a sigh as it was his turn to go. "We'll be talking soon."

I stood up and hugged him, and I suddenly felt sad. So much good was happening, and my relationship with Gus was just beginning, but I felt sad.

"You know, Fiona and I had this friend. And he once said something about saying everything you need to say to someone. I think sometimes you get the chance to do that, and sometimes you don't. But what I need to say to you, Guthrie Walsh, is that I'm who I am today at least in part because I met you ten years ago. For better or worse, you jumpstarted so many aspects of my life, and that was without even knowing your name. Thanks for that."

"Do you know what I treasure even more than our time in Sri Lanka?" His eyes twinkled as he grabbed my hands in his and clasped them to his chest. "This moment. Right now. We'll always have this, and I'm so very grateful." He leaned in and kissed me on the cheek and then followed after Hamish and Fiona.

I took a deep breath and swiped at my eyes. I started to grab my things to go, but then I had to collapse back into the nearest chair, where Hamish had been sitting. All of the emotions associated with ten years of February 4 pooled inside of me and threatened to break free. I breathed in and out. In and out. And then I lowered my head onto my folded arms on the table.

"I thought I might find you here."

The deep breathing and blocking out of my surroundings had created a calm that had just begun to permeate, but in an instant the peace was shattered. In its place, jackhammers began drilling and angels began singing and seismic shifts occurred—simultaneously. It all came together to form the familiar but nearly forgotten opus entitled "True Love and Slow-Burn Regret in E-Flat Minor."

I raised my head slowly from my arms and attempted to breathe in and fill my lungs, but it was as if I'd forgotten how. Sharp, shaky intakes would have to satisfy for the time being.

There was no confusion as to who the voice belonged to, and so much more than déjà vu swept over me at the sound of it. I braced myself one more time in anticipation of the agony and the euphoria, then turned as I stood. And then I was face-to-face with him for the first time since Boston. I was in that coffeehouse with him for the first time in nine years.

And I knew in an instant that I was as in love with him as I had ever been.

"Well, isn't this ironic?" I croaked out at the sight of him.

He stuffed his hands in the pockets of his jeans and took a tentative step toward me. "You know, I've spent a lot of time analyzing that song, and I have some issues. I've been thinking of preparing a class-action lawsuit against Alanis. She's responsible for an entire generation of people not actually understanding what irony is."

Despite the current out-of-body moment I was experiencing, I smiled and thought back on what Fiona had said. Liam had always been funny. "Is that right?"

"That's right. You see, *ironic* is defined as 'happening in the opposite way to what is expected, and typically causing wry amusement because of this.'"

I grabbed onto the chair to stabilize myself as he took another step.

"So some of what Alanis classified as ironic, okay." He shrugged and then pulled his hands out of his pockets and crossed his arms. "Finding the black fly in your glass of chardonnay? Sure. I guess. You don't expect that, and I suppose it could cause wry amusement, as long as it wasn't a rare year of wine or something. But some of the other things . . . I just don't know."

Another step. Another moment that I wasn't sure my knees would hold out.

"The old guy who won the lottery and then died? Who was amused in that situation? Was the guy who got pardoned from death row two minutes after he was executed wryly amused? I think Alanis needs to answer for that."

I nodded and swallowed down the lump in my throat as my eyes floated over his figure from head to toe and back again, not allowing myself to linger anywhere for long—although I did get tied up on his left hand for a while. I hadn't expected it to be bare.

"What are you doing here, Liam?"

The corner of his mouth slid up, and my eyes got tied up there for a while too. "I was in the neighborhood."

"Really?"

"No." He chewed on his lips. "The truth is . . . Well, I guess I needed to see how this whole thing played out. I was pretty invested, too, you know."

"You saw Hamish?"

"I did. I'm glad he showed up."

"Are you?"

"I don't know. Should I be?" He appeared uncomfortable for the first time as his feet shuffled. "He looked pretty cozy with Fiona."

I glanced at his hand again. "Are you married?"

Nice, Liv. Subtle.

"I'm not."

Breathe. "Were you?"

He shook his head. "Nope. I, um . . ." Another step. "She was great. She just wasn't . . ."

Say that she wasn't me. Say that she wasn't me. Say that she wasn't me.

"Well, she just wasn't very patient with me at baseball games. I think I irritated her. She liked to watch in silence."

I did a double take and then mentally chastised myself. *"Say she wasn't me."* Where had that even come from? I'd converted too much to the Heartlite Network school of thought already.

"Well, you can't have that." I fiddled with the buttons on Caleb's shirt and was overwhelmed with a desire to be wearing just about anything else right then. But I wouldn't have *been* anywhere else for anything. "It's an important part of the experience for you. To be able to talk through the plays and stuff, I mean."

He gesticulated between us with that beautifully ringless left hand. "Exactly. She just never seemed to understand that. And do you know what else? She's not a big fan of sunsets."

I gasped in genuine horror. "What do you mean?"

"Well, it's not like she hates them or anything . . ."

"How could anyone hate a sunset?"

He smiled at me. "Unfathomable."

With one more step he was close enough to touch me. Close enough that I could touch him. And if he came any closer, I knew I might not be able to stop myself.

"More than anything, she wasn't—she *isn't*—the person I see when I close my eyes and think about all of my favorite moments in my life. Not even the ones that haven't happened yet. In the end, Samantha and I both wanted better than that for each other. And for ourselves."

I swear my heart was in my throat, and if I hadn't had my tonsils out when I was eleven, I wouldn't have had room left in there to breathe at all.

"You're my favorite person, too, Liam."

He smirked. "No, I'm not."

"No, you're not. But I promise you you're a very close second."

I jumped into his arms, which instinctively opened for me. I felt his hands on my back, and then around my waist as he held me just as tightly as I held him. I told myself not to cry—not because I didn't want to appear weak or make my already puffy eyes puffier, but because I couldn't stand the thought of releasing any of the emotion I felt. It was all too good.

"I'm so in love with you," I whispered, my lips brushing against his ear. "I've *always* been in love with you."

He pulled back to look at me and said, "Well, *that* would have been nice to know."

And his lips were on mine before I could think. Not that there was anything to think about apart from the way everything about his kiss felt new and exciting, and yet safe and familiar, all at the same time. And I guess I thought a little bit about how if it were a movie, we wouldn't stop kissing until the credits rolled.

His hand gently traced its way from my forehead, where hair was brushed out of the way, down my jawline and neck, finally resting on my collarbone for just a moment before wrapping his arms around my shoulders. As our lips separated, I leaned my head back and looked into his eyes.

"You've gotten taller," he said as he planted kisses along my jawline.

"I'm wearing Fiona's shoes."

His hands grasped the open collar at my neck and pulled me closer to him. "And whose shirt is this?"

"Caleb's."

He pulled his head back and examined me. "Who's Caleb?"

I slid my hands up his chest and then threaded my fingers through his hair. "I don't want to talk about Caleb right now."

"Okay. What about Hamish? Do we need to talk about Hamish?"

"Who?"

"Good answer."

My breath caught in my throat again—a sensation I looked forward to never getting used to—as he lowered his lips toward mine but stopped just short of the target that had been ready and waiting for him.

"I love you," he whispered, and I felt myself melt. "At this point it's looking like that's never going to change. I tried. There's just nothing I can do about it."

Happiness equaled warmth, but it was more than happiness causing the heat I was feeling.

A thought suddenly occurred. "Do you live here now?"

He looked around the coffeehouse and I followed suit—and I only noticed one uptight-looking old lady who clearly had no love in her heart staring at us like maybe we shouldn't be making out in the middle of a busy coffeehouse midday on a Monday.

Where's your sense of romance, lady?

"You mean *here*?"

I laughed. "Still making jokes, I see. But I didn't mean Mugs & Shots specifically. I'd probably settle for anywhere in Los Angeles."

"I don't live here. But I will."

"You'd move back for me?"

"I moved *away* for you. Why wouldn't I move back?"

With that, he planted a quick, passionate kiss on my lips before pulling away and throwing his arm over my shoulder. I grabbed my stuff, and we walked out the door together into the bright California sun.

We'd walked for a couple of blocks before he asked, "So where's your car?"

I raised my hand to shield my eyes as I looked up Venice Boulevard one way and then turned and looked the other way.

"Do you even know where you parked?" When I didn't answer, he began to tease me. "West, east? Left, right? Just past the yellow pole? Anything?"

Oh, how I'd missed him teasing me. "Of course I know. I'm in the Heartlite parking garage."

He leaned against a streetlight and crossed his arms and smiled at me. "And where might that be?"

"I'm not even sure I want to tell you now." I began walking decidedly in one direction, not having any clue if it was the right one. I crossed my arms, fully aware that my attempt at huffiness would lose all credibility if he were able to detect the smile that had overtaken my face. The smile that I figured might never go away.

"Oh really?" I heard him say through his laughter, the sound of which was way too far away. "Is that how you're going to play this game?" My heart raced as the laughter got closer, accompanied by footsteps picking up the pace. "Hey, wait up!"

I turned around to face him just as he reached me, and he captured my lips with his once again. And there was absolutely nothing funny about it.

Sometimes the joy of life can't be

contained in a simple verse,

Or captured in a few brief lines.

Sometimes the greatest joy comes from the attempt.

Sometimes struggling to find the words

Makes the emotions all the sweeter.

But sometimes there's absolutely nothing that could

ever be written in a stupid greeting card that could

even begin to explain the way you're feeling.

So why bother?

The Olivia Ross Real Life Collection®, Number 1

ACKNOWLEDGMENTS

Just think of how cute it would be if I wrote all of my acknowledgments in the form of Heartlite-esque greeting cards! Goodness, that would be adorable. The truth is, I could never be a greeting card writer. I have too much to say, and when you give me an unedited space . . . yeah . . . I'm not going to keep it short and snappy. So, in some ways, these acknowledgments are probably lined out *exactly* like my greeting cards would be.

Usually I spend a year or two with a story. Approximately six to nine months writing it, another few months editing it, several months preparing for it to launch into the world, and then my world completely focuses on it for weeks or months after others in the world have been introduced to it. This story . . . well, this story is different. I've spent nearly a decade with Olivia Ross, Fiona Mitchell, Liam Howard, and Hamish MacDougal. A *decade*. Just *think* about how much has changed in the last ten years. But as I write these acknowledgments, it seems fitting to focus my gratitude on those things in life that remain unchanged.

I'm still married to the kindest, most supportive, funniest, most challenging (in the good way) man in the world, who believes in my ability to achieve my dreams so much more than I ever could.

I'm still the mother of two remarkable human beings, who have somehow morphed from boys to men (Let's all sing "Motownphilly" together, shall we?) right before my eyes, and who make me proud every single day.

I'm still the daughter of loving, supportive parents who taught me to love Jesus and taught me to love pop culture . . . and the combination of those two loves probably explains who I am more than any other explanation ever could.

I'm still the sister of the biggest cheerleader anyone could hope for, even if she inexplicably refuses to read any of my books. Some things will probably *never* change.

I still have the best friends in the world—people like Jacob, LeeAnn, David, Anne, and Zaida—not to mention Jenny and Secily, who met these characters a long time ago and who helped keep this story alive in my heart and mind even when it looked like it might never see the light of day.

And along the way I've gotten to meet new author friends who inspire me and encourage me, and whose successes feel like my successes, because they're doing great things and being great people and I'm so proud of them. People like Nicole Deese, Janine Rosche, Carol Moncado, Mikal Dawn, Susie Finkbeiner, Jessica Kate, Rachel McMillan, Sarah Monzon, Tracy Steel, Melissa Ferguson, Toni Shiloh, Katie Reid, and so many others . . . but I have to stop now because I'm seriously already breaking into a sweat because I'm sure I'm forgetting so many people. And then there are my dear, beloved reader friends! They have welcomed me into their lives and laughed along with me (and, more than once, *at* me) and become such vital members of my community. Chief among those readers I treasure are those who make up my reader group, The Book Club Closest to My House. Without them, none of this would be nearly as much fun.

I'm still part of a church family that I love so much—and I'm also blessed to get to spend my workdays on staff, serving that same church family alongside a team of cohorts (Amy, David, Jacob, Kaari, Kristen, Secily, Tonya, and Travis) I adore.

I'm still pinching myself that the journey brought me into contact with people like Kelsey Bowen, who helped begin to shape me into the writer I want to be by believing in me when I'm not sure there was much reason to (and I'll always be grateful that she became a dear friend in the process). And in the time that I worked with Jessica Kirkland, she was an unwavering advocate for this book and Olivia Ross . . . even as Sarah Hollenbeck, Cadie McCaffrey, and Hadley Beckett each took their respective turns at bat. And now I have the great privilege of working with a team that includes Jocelyn Bailey, who presented me with the most exquisite editorial letter that finally allowed me to see not only what this story was, but what it could be. After the amount of time I had spent with these characters, it was no easy feat to make them seem fresh and intriguing in my heart and mind, but she did it. Then Leslie Peterson helped make sense of my new enthusiasm—and she understood even my sloppiest of jokes. (Another difficult feat.) The entire team at Thomas Nelson/HCCP . . . we're still on our first date, but I'm having a great time so far, and sure like where it's heading. They're all amazing, and I'm totally crushing on them now.

I'm still one of the biggest pop culture nerds on the planet, and I don't see that changing anytime soon. For this particular book, I owe a big "Thanks for the inspiration!" to Alanis Morissette, George Clooney, Ralph Fiennes (who I actually really liked in *Maid in Manhattan*), Tom & Meg & Nora Ephron (always), Vera Wang, Shonda Rhimes, Eva Longoria, Tom Hulce, and so many others. And I owe the biggest, humblest, most bowing-and-scraping apology to *While You Were Sleeping.* I love you and I didn't mean those awful things I said about you.

Most importantly, I am still a follower of a God who cares about the details. A Savior who *loves*—even when we forget that that's what we're supposed to do too. I'm so incredibly grateful to know that he loves us enough to never stop fighting for us. Now, forever, and always.

The Bethany Turner Keeping It Real (But Not Short and Snappy) Collection®, Plot Twist Edition

DISCUSSION QUESTIONS

1. Olivia believes that in life there are leading characters and supporting characters. Even she eventually has to acknowledge that it's not really as simple as that, but do you think there's any truth to her worldview? Do you think some people are naturally better suited than others for a life in the spotlight?

2. Along those lines, Olivia has an epiphany while she's standing in the spotlight at the Lakeside Society auction. She observes that when the spotlight is on someone, they can't see the people all around them in the darkness—literally and metaphorically. Do you think her theory helps explain any instances of celebrity behavior? In the story, does it help explain the personalities or actions of any of the characters?

3. Which of Fiona's many glamorous jobs sounds most appealing to you? Why?

4. Do you believe in fate? Destiny? Is there an example from your own life of difficult-to-explain, seemingly coincidental circumstances?

5. After their initial time as a couple, Olivia and Liam discover they have a deep foundation of friendship between them. Have you or someone you're close to ever become good friends with an ex? As a rule, how

likely is a successful friendship between two people who used to be romantically involved?

6. Liam warns Olivia she shouldn't ask questions unless she's sure she wants to know the answers. Have you ever been eager for answers or explanations, only to eventually feel as if you were better off not knowing?

7. Olivia allows herself to "get caught up in the romance rather than the checkboxes" in her relationship with Malcolm, and then feels as if that backfires on her. How might her journey have been different if she had adopted that philosophy in her initial romance with Liam instead? Conversely, how might things have turned out if she had followed the more tried and true Olivia Ross relationship rules while dating Malcolm?

8. Have you ever had a friendship as close as the one Olivia and Fiona share? They bonded as young children and then stayed together into adulthood. Who is your oldest friend? How did you meet?

9. Once Caleb convinced Olivia to go to the coffeehouse in 2013, who or what did you think would be waiting there for her? Did you see the plot twist coming?

10. We spent every February 4 with Olivia, from 2003 to 2013. What do you think her life looked like on February 4, 2014?

ABOUT THE AUTHOR

Photo by Emilie Haney of EAH Creative

Bethany Turner has been writing since the second grade, when she won her first writing award for explaining why, if she could have lunch with any person throughout history, she would choose John Stamos. She stands by this decision. Bethany now writes pop culture–infused rom-coms for a new generation of readers who crave fiction that tackles the thorny issues of life with humor and insight. She lives in Southwest Colorado with her husband, whom she met in the nineties in a chat room called Disco Inferno. As sketchy as it sounds, it worked out pretty well in this case, and they are now the proud parents of two teen-agers. Connect with Bethany at seebethanywrite.com or across social media @seebethanywrite, where she clings to the eternal dream that John Stamos will someday send her a friend request. You can also text her at +1 (970) 387-7811.

seebethanywrite.com
Instagram: @seebethanywrite
Twitter: @seebethanywrite
Facebook: @seebethanywrite